PRAISE FOR PAUL DI FILIPPO

"Di Filippo is like gourmet potato chips to me.
I can never eat just one of his stories."
—Harlan Ellison

"Di Filippo is the spin doctor of SF—and it is a powerful medicine he brews."
—Brian Aldiss

" Paul Di Filippo does dazzling new tricks with English.
And then he puts the wonderful language and
the wild science together...."
—Rudy Rucker on *Ribofunk*

"An author who genuinely comes close to defying all
attempts at description. A true original."
—*Infinity Plus*

"In terms of composition, narrative description and voice,
Di Filippo is well nigh masterful."
—*Sf Site* on *A Year in the Linear City*

"An often genuinely funny mixture of Raymond Carver,
Harry Harrison, and Douglas Adams."
—*Booklist* on *Fractal Paisleys*

"Out of a rich impasto of language, a story that is sensual,
sexual, and hot takes shape around one of the most engaging
heroines since Southern and Hoffenberg's Candy."
—Samuel Delany on *A Mouthful of Tongues*

"Paul Di Filippo's *The Steampunk Trilogy* is the literary
equivalent of Max Ernst's collages of 19th-century steel-
engravings, spooky, haunting, hilarious."
—William Gibson

T0064805

Also by Paul Di Filippo

THE SUMMER THIEVES

A NOVEL OF THE QUINARY

THE SUMMER THIEVES

A NOVEL OF THE QUINARY

HUGO AWARD-NOMINATED AUTHOR
PAUL DI FILIPPO

Night Shade Books
NEW YORK

Copyright © 2021 by Paul Di Filippo

All Rights Reserved. No part of this book may be reproduced in any manner without the express written consent of the publisher, except in the case of brief excerpts in critical reviews or articles. All inquiries should be addressed to Night Shade Books, 307 West 36th Street, 11th Floor, New York, NY 10018.

Night Shade books may be purchased in bulk at special discounts for sales promotion, corporate gifts, fund-raising, or educational purposes. Special editions can also be created to specifications. For details, contact the Special Sales Department, Night Shade Books, 307 West 36th Street, 11th Floor, New York, NY 10018 or info@skyhorsepublishing.com.

Night Shade Books™ is a trademark of Skyhorse Publishing, Inc. ®, a Delaware corporation.

Visit our website at www.nightshadebooks.com.

10 9 8 7 6 5 4 3 2 1

Library of Congress Cataloging-in-Publication Data is available on file.

ISBN: 978-1-949102-51-2

Cover illustration by Fred Gambino
Cover design by Daniel Brount and Kai Texel

Printed in the United States of America

For Deborah, who makes summer last forever

"And good-bye, wanderer! Good luck to you," she said to Casher O'Neill. *"You will remain miserable as long as you seek justice, but when you give up, righteousness will come to you and you will be happy. Don't worry. You're young and it won't hurt you to suffer a few more years. Youth is an extremely curable disease, isn't it?"*

—Cordwainer Smith, "On the Gem Planet"

THE
SUMMER
THIEVES

A NOVEL OF THE QUINARY

THE SUMMER THIEVES

A NOVEL OF THE QUINARY

CHAPTER 1

High atop the rocky Salazar Escarpment, Johrun Corvivios could see clear to the western horizon: a vista of undulating greensward pied with the slowly moving scattered forms of the giant herples that constituted the valuable cattle of Sweetmeats Pasturage. (The Corvivios family employed over five hundred transgenics, as domestics, herders, slaughterers, and packers, choosing not to rely on human workers or the simplex robot mechanisms that were the only type permitted them by the old Artilect Recension.) Massive as Gaian elephants, the sartorized creatures were dumb as a bag of pebbles, their only drive and function being the transformation of grass into succulent herple protein, a delicacy highly prized throughout the worlds of the Quinary.

The gustatory essence of the pale meat was deemed irreproducible even in this age of molecular fabricators that could build nearly anything to template from the atomic level on up. The term *âmago* was applied by philosophers and gourmets and regulators alike to any naturally raised organic product to denote its superior quintessence not found in the assembled version. Some critics and esthetes even went so far as to discern the *âmago* in

1

a sculpture or painting that came straight from the unmediated hands of the artist, and not out of a fab hopper. Johrun was not one of these latter hypersensitive souls—he thought such high-flown fancies a lot of hooey—but he could definitely attest to the unmatched virtues of grass-fed herple steak over the molecularly accreted competitor. And he was not biased simply from eating the delicacy all his relatively young life!

Twenty-five years old, Johrun was the son of Landon and Ilona Corvivios. His grandparents, Xul and Chirelle, still living, had been the first to come into possession of uninhabited Verano, along with partners Brayall and Fern Soldevere. Halfway around the world, the elder Soldeveres still ran Danger Acres, a hunting preserve, with the help of their lone offspring, Arne, and his wife, Fallon.

And from Arne and Fallon, in the same year as Johrun's birth, had sprung Minka Soldevere, to whom Johrun had been betrothed at their mutual infant christening—in honor of the demands of the Diminuendo Aleatorics, the sect in which the families had long been postulants.

A fey beauty of elfin physique and features, Minka was soon to return home from her education offplanet. And then she and Johrun would be wed, uniting the clans at last.

Anticipation of their wedding formed the undercurrent of Johrun's thoughts as he regarded from on high his family's slowly roving cattle—with undiminished appreciation, despite their familiarity. But now both Minka and Sweetmeats Pasturage faded into the background, for Johrun meant to fly.

Johrun flexed his powerskin wings and looked upwards. The pallid lavender sun of Verano—the star dubbed Wayward's Spinel in the M68 globular cluster—seemed pinned at midpoint to the wide dome of the sky. Soft warm breezes, scented with traces of vetiver, clawbush, and the effluvia of the towering lakecrab colonies, ruffled Johrun's chestnut hair, now longer than he really liked it, but neglected during the recent busy days of roundup, slaughter, packing, and shipping.

Despite all the brute work falling to the splices, the men of the Corvivios family—Grandpa Xul, his son Landon, and Johrun himself—still found themselves kept on the go in a supervisory and troubleshooting capacity. Nor were Grandma Chirelle or Johrun's mother, Ilona, left as idlers. Gran ran every financial aspect of the family business, dealing with customers and the necessary Quinary officials, while Ilona kept the physical plant afloat, making sure the strangelet furnaces supplied all the needed power, repairing machines, jockeying the transport braneships in and out upon landing and takeoff. Yes, the Corvivios family might own half a planet, with an annual income on the order of a hundred megachains, matched likewise by the Soldeveres, but they did not coast on their vast fortune like the wealthy of other worlds. No ceaseless round of parties and galas such as the swells enjoyed on Patenaude, no lazing around the ranch with a Dandler's Punch in hand, nor the preening costume displays and fevered gambling of the habitués of the continent-long racetracks of Mokshan.

So this was the first moment in many weeks that Johrun had had free. And no other use of his leisure time appealed to him more than flying. So up to the top of the high shaley bluff he had hiked, a pleasant walk of an hour or so from the ranch. He had arrived mildly sweaty and appreciative of a brief rest before the exercise ahead. He contemplated the beloved panorama while sipping boost water from a small hip flask. But now he was ready for flight.

The smart rig he wore featured fifth-force impellors and lifters carefully calibrated to diminish the wearer's weight without negating it entirely. The point was not to float and cruise like some bulky utilitarian liftsled, but to emulate a graceful avian, insofar as human muscles and skills could comply. Achievement in the face of preset challenges, not a free ride. Thus constrained by the art, as in unmediated hang-gliding, one needed to launch from on high. Takeoff from the ground was not feasible, even given the technological reduction in the mass-to-muscle ratio of the flier.

With typical caution and mindfulness, Johrun ran one last set of diagnostics on his gear. He tapped at the soft textured vambrace on his forearm and saw it display the reassuring icons. As part of its background operations, the vambrace registered with muted pings the irregular but nearly continuous updates to the Indranet that occurred every time a branedrone popped out into the Wayward's Spinel system and disseminated its updates in a burst of information. Given that interstellar travel and communications would always be less than instantaneous, the galactically scattered nodes of the Indranet could never be totally in sync. But as the branedrones shuttled continuously from star to star, satisfying some best solution to a travelling salesman's algorithm, spreading and receiving the freshest reports from each system, the vast and vastly separated apparatus of the Indranet attained a surprising level of intersystem uniformity.

Johrun stretched a transparent protective jelly band across his eyes, where it stuck tight around the edges of his sockets. Information lurked at the corners of his vision. Flexing his knees, he launched himself from the scarp's rim. Arms and tethered wings outspread, he fell, the wind combing his hair, then caught a thermal and soared high, aimed away from the ranch.

As always, he felt instantly accepted and welcomed by his maternal planet, a part of the whole global mechanism. Almost more than the physical joys of soaring, this feeling of being embraced by his world constituted the true allure of flying. The atmosphere was like a warm bath, the sunlight his mother's gaze.

Verano was a Harvester-engineered world. Its entire improbable ecosystem, very close to a monoculture, and its climate of perpetual summer were the direct product of intervention by the unknown race of cosmic forerunners who had been seemingly long extinct by the time humanity arrived on the galactic scene. These enigmatic accomplished beings had sown myriad worlds with secret subterranean engines and distributed invisible agents, all beyond human unriddling, which worked to maintain the design of each planet—all for purposes unknown. Thus the endless desert world of Sandhill could function in an unlikely equilibrium, as could the snowball planet of Itaska and millions of other tailored planets.

And surely the Harvester nanomites of Verano had integrated themselves into Johrun's physiology, rendering him as much a part of the biome as the grasses or lakecrabs, and giving him that feeling of inseparable belonging.

But the Harvesters had not earned their name through this planetary manipulation alone. Rather, the indisputable record of their galaxy-wide cull of every sophont and sapient species that had preceded man—leaving many civilizational relics and vestiges as confirmation of their several truncated existences—had earned the super-race its designation. For whatever reason, in a very short and concentrated span some ten million years ago, the dominant overlords had reaped their clients' species without exception, then vanished from the galactic landscape, taking everyone to parts unknown. Perhaps a distant other galaxy, perhaps even another undiscovered brane.

Humanity now reigned as the only species of higher intelligence across the whole Milky Way and its satellites, as far as ships had explored, from Triangulum II to the Magellanic Clouds, from Fornax to the Sculptor, from Hercules to Barnard's.

Were the Harvesters still lurking behind the scenes, awaiting the proper moment to gather up the human species as it had the others? By inhabiting these pleasant engineered worlds, had the human race placed itself in the equivalent of a corral or feedlot? Neither big thinkers nor barstool philosophers provided any solid or satisfying answers, although debate was endless, and so mankind simply went about living as best it knew how, across all the niches previously occupied by other galactic races.

But such past and possible future apocalypses mattered not one whit to Johrun at this instant. Instinctively tilting his wings this way and that, he exulted in his easy movements, the flavor of the air, the warmth of the sun, his hair whipping in the wind. No matter what other wonderful planets existed in the universe, how could anyone desire to leave such a perfect place as Verano, except perhaps temporarily, as his father had, in search of a mate? But that quest did not apply to Johrun, for he had his preordained Minka.

Minka, who, despite her considerable charms and her identical upbringing, somewhat bafflingly did not feel the same as Johrun did about the all-sufficiency of Verano. Minka, who, at age twenty-one, on the very eve of their formal wedding, had expressed her sudden desire to attend the University of Saints Fontessa and Kuno on Loudermilk III. Minka, who had been generally absent from Johrun's life for four years, except for brief return visits at the holidays. Minka, who, though still offworld at this moment, was due home for good in just three days, her schooling finally finished, the day of their wedding now imminent!

Spiralling higher and further out, the placid herples below him like ruminant city busses, Johrun contemplated his feelings for Minka, and their likely future together.

Although their families were separated by half a planet, the children, starting at age three, had grown up for long stretches side-by-side, sharing their daily routines. This was accomplished by the simple expedient of each youth swapping families for a stretch. Johrun would spend several months at Danger Acres, with Aunt Fallon and Uncle Arne, Grandpa Brayall and Grandma Fern, learning the ins and outs of the Soldevere life. Then Minka would journey with Johrun back to his home and become integral to the daily routine at Sweetmeats Pasturage. Lutramella, the beloved splice who had midwifed Johrun into the world and served thereafter as his nursemaid and companion and mentor, had monitored both children—although Minka, for inexplicable reasons, had never really cottoned to the transgenic.

In truth, the two clans really functioned as one extended family anyway. But the elders were careful to also enforce periods of separation on the children—ameliorated only by regular contact from household to household across the local Indranet—so as to break any patterns that might make the pair feel like siblings. Although the goal was to yoke the two dynasties, they wanted to preserve some of the independent traditions and outlooks of each clan. And besides, a happy union would be unlikely if Johrun and Minka thought of each other as sister and brother. Cousins, perhaps, would be a tolerable status.

And the tactic had worked—at least in Johrun. Familiarity had blended with distance and otherness to produce an ardent fascination with his betrothed. The notion of pleasing his elders by fulfilling a destiny that spanned generations contributed to the power of her attraction. Johrun could barely conceive of joining his future to any other mate.

And yet, and yet—this pleasant fatedness did not blind Johrun to some of Minka's more jarring or less pleasing qualities.

She was in some sense flighty, her bright hummingbird mind flitting lightly from one topic to another, as though always dissatisfied or in search of some new thrill. Sometimes that search could manifest as a fascination with peril. On several safaris with Danger Acres clients, Johrun had witnessed Minka take incredible risks that had endangered not only her, but the customers in her care. Once when their party was stalking a willigorgon, Minka had deliberately broken cover and allowed the slavering monster to barrel at her, shouldering and firing her ceegee rifle only at the very last second. The tiny but powerful color-glass condensate charge killed the beast instantly, of course, exploding a giant gout of flesh from its back. But the willigorgon's momentum laid it out nearly at Minka's feet, causing her to hop coolly aside to avoid being crushed by its crashing bulk. Such forced dalliances with unnecessary extremes were alien to Johrun.

Almost equally foreign was Minka's reluctance to take important matters seriously. Johrun understood how a person might rank different matters of importance in alternate orders from himself. But simply to deny that something as vital as, say, the future of Verano itself carried any weight—incredible! And yet Minka had asserted just such a sentiment.

They were both nineteen years old. Minka was currently living with the Corvivios family. She and Johrun were supervising a team of splices as they sowed a new sector with little herple spratlings. The creatures were still small enough to rest on one's palm. They merely had to be spaced out on the prairie at regular grazing intervals. No predators would trouble them.

Johrun admitted the task could seem boring—unless one contemplated the end result, a profitable and impressive herd of mighty meat machines. Still, boredom did not justify Minka juggling the spratlings like toys, three at a time, as she skipped along with the splice workers behind the floating sled. She couldn't hurt the primitive creatures, but her actions were disrespectful and distracting. Johrun finally had to ask her to stop. She complied with a world-weary sigh, tossing the spratlings higgledy-piggledy onto the sled.

Johrun sought to jolly her up. "Minka, my scamp, can you believe that one day you and I will be making all the decisions about the running of our world? Such a responsibility—but such an affirmation and a joy."

Minka pressed her booted foot against the side of one of the helpless spratlings just planted on the grass and tipped it over. Unable to right itself due to the weight of its upper part, it gyrated its several basal foot-arms in frustration until Johrun set it aright.

To Johrun's disbelief, a scowling Minka promptly toppled it again. "Queen of all I survey—and what I survey is so very stimulating! A field full of insensate meat factories. On the other side of this perfect unchangeable world, a hunting lodge full of the unspeakable in pursuit of the uneatable. What an honor indeed, for Queen Minka the Mad!"

Johrun regarded his fiancée with wonder and alarm. Her beautiful golden hair, pinned up in a roll; her delicate sprite's features; her subtle curves—all at odds with her grimace and belligerent stance.

Seeing Johrun's dismay and puzzlement, and perhaps realizing she had overstepped some boundary, Minka softened her attitude and expression. Into her sparkling blue eyes even crept a tear or two.

"Oh, Joh, I'm so very sorry. It's just that the certainty of our future and its limits bring me down low sometimes. Why should we be in thrall to the dead hand of the past? I want—I want excitement, adventure, mystery! Haven't you ever felt those urges?"

Johrun looked around the well-known and well-loved landscape. A planet all their own? And one so congenial? Could there be more to life than that?

Before he could answer, Minka had tossed her arms around him and began pasting kisses on his handsome tanned face. He responded in kind, and they soon toppled to the fragrant cushiony grass. The sled and the splices worked dutifully on, moving further away from the engaged couple, by their training respectfully unheedful of any doings of the humans outside their realm of responsibility.

At the end of their coupling, one wayward spratling bumping up in stupid repetitiveness against Johrun's bare leg, their disagreement seemed retroactively erased.

Or just buried.

Life had gone on without such unease erupting again between them. Although perhaps Minka's desire, two years later, to be schooled offplanet before settling down to married life represented a more circumspect outlet for the same irritable feelings.

Without him realizing it, Johrun's soaring flight had taken him far away from the Salazar Escarpment. Flying with unconscious instincts, he had let his ruminations preoccupy his attention. His vambrace supplied his current coordinates which the largely landmark-empty pasturage did not readily reveal. Were he to land now, he'd have a three-hour hike back to the ranch. Not an entirely desirable prospect, despite the ever-clement Verano day. He started to bank, intending to fly at least partway home if the air currents allowed, and his eye caught an extraordinary sight.

A full-grown herple lying on its side, unmoving, seemingly damaged, possibly dead.

Pulling his wings in close to his torso, Johrun arrowed down, braking himself only at the last moment, landing with practiced finesse.

Standing beside the vast creature, Johrun could readily see it was now a corpse. And however it had been killed, it had been further mutilated. Most of its meat had been rudely gouged out of its soft protective carapace in a process utterly unlike the sophisticated methods of the Corvivios harvest. A marine stink emanated from the sun-heated carcass.

Completely a product of the sartorization alembics of the Pollys, the herple fused several Gaian oceanic genomes into one magnificent land creature. Its base derived from various echinoderms, part starfish, part sea cucumber. In effect, the foundational part of the herple resembled a giant rugose mattress with many agile and tough arms or legs. Next, the succulent innards of the Gaian scallop, protected by the lightweight borrowed parchment-like skin of a shrimp, formed the bulk of the drumlike body. A palette of flavor genes from many other species could be inserted. Lungs were installed. Distributed ganglia provided the herple's limited functionality. The herple would trundle slowly in a random walk, its ventral starfish mouth pressed to the nutritious grass, getting bigger and bigger and more delicious and meatier with every passing day, squirting out the occasional almost odorless pasture-replenishing liquid excrement, until finally harvested and slaughtered.

But not this specimen, cut down before its prime and wastefully ravaged.

Johrun opened a line of communication through his vambrace. Soon he had his father Landon displayed as a life-sized shaped-light eidolon beside him. At first, focused on Johrun, the older man showed no worry or concern. Only a few decades older than his son, his vigorous health supplemented by the best technics of the Smalls and Pollys that wealth could purchase, Landon Corvivios resembled a big brother more than a parent. His good looks did not entirely mirror Johrun's face, for the son had also inherited the high cheekbones of his mother Ilona and her strong jawline.

Wearing rumpled blue coveralls soiled with yellow splashes of spratling nutrient goo, Landon said, "What's afoot, son? We didn't expect to hear from you until dinnertime. Have your recreations palled already? Are you that eager to have me assign you some chores? You caught me wrestling with the feeder lines in the south nursery. I can always use another hand. And your irresponsible granddad is zipping up and down Lake Jinji in the dynafoil with your flibbertigibbet grandmother in tow on her waterskis. At their age! But it's the reward for founding this half-assed dynasty, I assume."

Johrun responded by angling his vambrace's cameras to take in the dead herple. "I wish it were something so innocent, Dad. Look at this."

Immediately Landon grew serious. "This can only be the work of poachers. Where are you?"

Johrun relayed his coordinates.

"Stay there. I'm coming out with splices and rifles. I'll be by your side in under ten minutes."

Landon severed the connection. Chafing at the wait, Johrun surveyed the scene for further clues. He had been too distraught to notice earlier the most obvious traces of the intruders. A playing-field's worth of grass flattened by the impression of some big ship, and the tramplings of many feet as the poachers had gone about their business.

Johrun had just finished doffing his flight rig and peeling his jelly visor off when Landon arrived, helming a capacious fifth-force barge, open to the air, that held ten splices seated on benches. Only two rifles constituted the promised armament. These ranch splices were no warriors, and served only as some kind of hopefully intimidating corps of supporters that might convince any unsavvy intruders that they were outnumbered.

Johrun accepted a weapon. Landon clapped him on the shoulder. "Here's where all those safari days might finally prove useful. Not that I anticipate any shooting. I'm going to bring the Quinary in. Their damn protection costs enough that we should get some use out of the policy. But first, let's find the rascals and make sure what's happening. I'd hate to bring down the Quinary on some morons who strayed from Danger Acres. I delayed the search until I reached you."

Landon employed his vambrace to run through the high-resolution imagery provided by the satellite surveillance system which the families had put in place around Verano. Tapping into the ubiquitous Harvester informational substrate would have been invaluable, but human technology had never broken those codes or modalities. And attempts to monkey with the larger planetary engines had often enough proved so disastrous as to discourage any and all future experiments. The whole population of the Quinary still talked about the fate of Atlantropa, a world literally split apart like a ripe melon from pole to pole by such tampering.

"Here we have them," said Landon. "Not misguided tourists, that's for sure."

His vambrace displayed in shaped-light diorama the suitably magnified scene as scoped from above. A hulking and battered pewter-colored braneship—perhaps a Rulan Class Cargomaster similar to the newer ones that officially serviced Verano—with its ramp down and activity around it, including the loading of stolen meat. Pulling back from the closeup revealed more slaughtered herples around the perimeter of the illicit doings.

"Let's go stop them," said Johrun eagerly.

"We're only two against so many. I only brought the weapons in case they attacked us first. And besides, I don't fancy killing anyone today, even such slimy bastards. Let me launch the emergency takedown request drone now that we've ascertained the situation."

Landon played commands on his vambrace. "Done! The Quinary response should be here promptly."

Johrun contemplated this extreme and expensive measure. Luckily the Veranonals could afford it. Other folks in such an extreme would have had to endure longer response times.

The key to galactic society, travel at faster-than-light speeds, was accomplished by passage through those alternate dimensions known as branes. Several continua adjacent to the brane that housed the human universe mapped onto the native realm in unique ways. Not featuring standard components such as planets or suns, galaxies or nebulae, instead merely a senses-defying patchwork morass and miasma, these alternate universes, once they had been laboriously charted, allowed navigation at varying "speeds" and "distances" which translated into skipping blithely across lightyears back home. Pop into the neighbor brane, spend a few hours or days in some kind of quasimotion, and then reemerge at your faroff destination.

Some branes offered speedier passage due to radical topologies, but were inimical to organic life, and could not be used by people. And, being further displaced across the higher dimensions of the "bulk"—the supersystem that held all branes—they demanded higher energy fees for entrance and exit.

The drones that carried the incessant Indranet updates used the conventional, slower, cheaper routes.

But for emergencies, drones could be dispatched across the high-energy branes, travelling many parsecs in minutes.

Landon had just launched one such, aimed at the nearest Quinary affiliate.

Landon mused, "I suppose we should keep an eye on them, even if we don't immediately engage. If they were to flee before the drone arrived, they'd get off scot-free."

"Let's go!" said Johrun.

Landon and Johrun hopped aboard the barge where the splices sat placidly. A mix of canine, llama and Calvino huntoon, along with the human portions that endowed them with sapience, they lived for herding, and their current acrid scent cloud indicated their unease with the situation.

The craft lifted and sped toward the coordinates of the poachers. Johrun exulted in the swift passage through the lilac-hued afternoon air. For once he could understand the pulse-lifting thrills of all things uncommon that allured Minka.

With no trees or hills to conceal its approach, the Corvivios barge was easily spotted from far away by even the naked eyes of the criminals, not to mention their sensors. Realizing this, Landon activated the ship's tannoy and broadcast a loud call.

"Avast, intruders! Cease all depredations!"

The command did not produce the desired result. The poachers immediately began to scramble to gather together their gear, close up their ship and depart. A brace of armed guards dropped to one knee and began to fire at the barge. Luckily they were not using expensive intelligent ammunition, and the range was extreme. Or perhaps, merely intending to intimidate and hold off the rightful owners without incurring a murder, they aimed astray. In either case, no shots impacted the Corvivios craft or its occupants.

Landon settled the barge to earth a safe distance away. Johrun slapped on his jelly goggles and dialed up the magnification.

The guards remained vigilant by the extended ramp, but the last pirate stragglers were already hustling safely inside.

Johrun felt anger and frustration. "They're going to get away!"

"Patience, patience, son. Ah—it's here!"

The Quinary takedown probe had brane-egressed just outside the atmosphere of Verano, then dived through the air at hypersonic speed, fetching to a dramatic halt just above the invaders. Onboard the spiky missile, the vizier-level artilect— one of the highest grades of machine proficiency still permitted to special users under the terms of the Artilect Recension— instantly evaluated the situation to confirm Landon's original message.

Satisfied, the representative of the Quinary began deplatforming the criminals in precise stages, keyed to the unique tags of their property.

The first suite of privileges to be shut down involved the Indranet. Johrun could tell this, because the outside guards fumbled at their dead vambraces, cut off from instructions. But, recovering, they decided independently to resume firing at the Corvivios party. Not acceptable.

The next pulse from the takedown drone deplatformed all the power equipment reliant on the technology supplied by the Motivators, effectively shutting down the propulsive and life-support systems. The ship went inert, and within minutes its crew raced out and down the gangway, knowing that the next deplatforming, by the Brickers, would close up the ship entirely. And indeed, the next few moments saw the Cargomaster seal itself tight and the guns of the poachers go dead.

Once the door closed, the hapless poachers congregated in a confused mass for a short time. Then many of the pirates split off and began to run away—a desperate yet useless maneuver. This flight triggered the Polly deplatforming: all the many implants, prosthetics, adjuncts, add-ons, boosters, cyber-codicils, wet-ware and cellular hacks were taken offline. In a few cases, where the individual was heavily enhanced, this tactic would result in death. And indeed, Johrun saw several poachers collapse.

This fourth-stage deplatforming utterly sapped the remaining resistance of the pirates, and they ceased all activity, hostile or defensive, congregating in a nervous clot. None of them cared to risk the fifth-stage Smalls-centric deplatforming, which involved the denaturing and repurposing of selected fabricated materials. No one wished their clothing turned into infectious compositional dust that would attack a specific individual based on genomic targeting.

Gauging the rout complete from their safe remove, Landon lifted the barge off the ground and flew low to where the rabble stood.

Johrun had never seen such a disreputable bunch before, all crawling skin-sigils, scars and feeble sneers revealing various designer teeth. He nervously kept his rifle trained on them. Landon seemed less concerned about any remnant dangers they might represent—especially with the Quinary agent still hovering over the scene. He ordered the splices off the barge and instructed them to trot back to the ranch. They gamboled off, happy to be out of the action. Landon shooed the pirates onto the empty benches. The comatose poachers were laid out on the floor.

Lifting easily, the craft spun about and zoomed ranchward through the midday eternal summer sky, where gold-tinged clouds like the living galleons of Pinula V cruised loftily and serenely.

Landon spoke to his son as he guided the barge. "We'll incarcerate this lot in one of the storage sheds until the Quinary comes for them. What with the bounty on their Cargomaster and any individual reward money, we might earn back the cost of the takedown drone launch—or even turn a profit."

"Don't forget the loss of the slaughtered herples though."

"Hmm, yes, of course. Well, if these butchers flash-froze the meat for transport, we might be able to recover it. Can't sell it of course—immature, not top grade, badly processed. But it could go into the larder for our splices. Let's see how it goes."

Landon immediately sent a request to the Quinary through regular Indranet channels. The outgoing mail sat in the Verano-system buffers until a drone happened to pop into their space. The drone disgorged its cargo of information, absorbed all the latest updates from the Verano Indranet, then departed. Several hours later, after the poachers had been incarcerated and Johrun and Landon had told their story over and over to the appreciative other family members, an affirmative reply came back.

Using the unlocking protocols supplied, the Corvivios family gained access to the sequestered Cargomaster. They found the stolen thawing meat just reaching ambient temperature, were able to stabilize it with a nano-preparation from the Smalls—not used generally, due to its effect on the meat's *âmago*—and bring it home to the family facilities. All this occupied a good number of hours until a late dinner, which was a happy but low-energy affair, given the day's exertions.

At the expansive table, laden with many imported foods other than herple, in the familiar yet always cherished presence of his grandparents and parents, an exhausted Johrun basked in a mellow and cheerful glow. The events of the day had marked some kind of graduation, he felt. By discovering the poachers and taking part in their capture, he had passed from being merely an adult child, an apprentice, and protégé on the ranch, to a fully fledged partner. And when he was married to Minka . . .

Thoughts of the imminent return of his betrothed, fantasies of their future, supplanted mental reruns of the poacher incident. One idyllic scene after another ran through his mind.

Johrun realized he had dropped out of the general conversation into a kind of pleasant fugue only when his mother Ilona said, "Son, shouldn't you be thinking of heading to your room? After all, you still need to log an hour or so of current events."

"Oh, sure, Mom. See you all tomorrow."

"Bright and early," Landon reminded. "Even victorious warriors can't coast on their conquests."

In his room, Johrun plopped down gratefully on his bed with its light green linen coverlet suitable for the unchanging clime. Arranging a comfortable pile of pillows, he summoned up with his vambrace the latest galactic news—at least the freshest headlines accessible on Verano, delivered throughout the day. Grandpa always said that a good citizen of the Quinary should stay current with the broad stream of politics and culture across the Milky Way and beyond, keep abreast of the big integrated economy and the separate planetary affairs. Just because the family owned their own world and were insulated by its wealth was no reason to feel disunited from the myriad other planets in the galaxy.

Ranked by algorithms that balanced Johrun's preferences with objective scales of importance, the headlines and the talk and the shaped-light video paraded across his drowsy attention. A conflict between the nations of Karst and Obdalia on Coombe over rights to a new strike of strangelets. The latest fashions from the famous designer Sugarbloom. (Johrun perked up significantly at the bare-bottomed models.) And the very creepy recrudescence of the phagoplasm plague on the otherwise lovely grotto world of Irion. The spread of these brain parasites was insidious, as the malign agents were both hard to detect, once embedded, and hard to separate from their human hosts without harming the latter.

There came a knock at Johrun's door just as he was approaching the saturation point of learning about all these distant people and doings that bore little real relevance to his own life. He welcomed the intrusion and called out, "Come in!"

The household member who entered was not whom he had expected.

But it was perhaps the being Johrun loved best—or at least loved in a perdurable and powerful manner which no other entity could ever share.

Lutramella exhibited in her appearance many of the qualities of her main Gaian ancestors: otter, weasel, ferret. Traces of the mauskopfs of Spunkwater and the mellivores of Geronimus were also discernible. Possessing an almost boneless, sinuous grace of movement, perhaps only a bit tempered by age, she was lightly furred in chocolate, ecru, fawn, and cinnamon, as could be seen on her limbs exposed by her modest grey tunic and shorts, as well as on her mobile, alert, intelligent face, whose hybrid physiognamy reflected her fusion of animal and human. Quivering whiskers and a wet black nose comported in surprising harmony with anthropic lips and eyes. Compact round ears clung close to her skull. She stood six inches shorter than the man.

Lutramella it was who had assisted at his birth. Lutramella it was who had nursed the infant Johrun, tended him hour to hour until the age of three, his constant caretaker and companion. Lutramella it was who had been ever ready in later years to nurse a bruise or listen to a wild story or fancy, to accompany the lone and sometimes lonely child in play.

Johrun jumped up off his bed and embraced his nursemaid. She hugged him back, her fur warm and pleasant. She smelled like old clothes in a cupboard, of youth and security and love.

Johrun stood back from the splice. He suddenly realized how she had come to be less in his thoughts over the past few years, as other matters grew to dominate. He saw her now with mature eyes that detected definite signs of aging. By intent, the lifespan of most splices was much less than that of humans, and they were seldom privileged to experience the anti-aging technics that could easily extend their lives.

"What brings you here, Lu?"

Lutramella's husky voice evoked burrows and marshes, dark moonless nights crouched for prey. "I was worried you might have been hurt today."

"Hurt! By those louts! Dad and I had them begging for mercy within minutes."

Lutramella allowed herself the shadow of a grin, revealing small sharp teeth. "Then the takedown drone was just there to observe, and played no part. What a waste of Corvivios chains."

Johrun waved off the sardonic observation, but then admitted, "Well, maybe we had a little help."

"Just so long as you escaped harm, it doesn't matter how, and I'm glad." She paused and looked down at her bare and slightly webbed feet with their long and capable hard-nailed toes. Raising her eyes, she said, "But there's another reason I came, Joh. It's to ask a large favor."

"Ask away!"

"Your wife-to-be returns soon, and your wedding will mark the end of our special relationship, I think."

"No, never, Lu!"

But even as he spoke, Johrun acknowledged the truth of this statement. He could not imagine Lutramella sharing a household with stringent and self-minded Minka.

"You know I am enrolled in the Quinary databases as your splice alone, not the family's. So I ask you this: could you manumit me, before you marry?"

"Set you free? But what would you do? Where would you go?"

"I have some plans—some dreams. And some savings. Gifts of a few-score links here and there that I've saved over the decades. But after two decades, it amounts to a couple of thousand chains."

Johrun did not hesitate, even though this whole concept and request was utterly unforeseeable. "Only a couple of thousand chains? Not enough! I will endow you with twenty times that amount, and set you free at once!"

And as good as his speech, Johrun carried out the necessary protocols via his vambrace. Money was transferred, and the formal notifications of Lutramella's freedom were broadcast—or at least buffered, till the next outsystem drone arrived—and ping!, the letter of freedom shot out across the stars.

"The galaxy knows you are your own mistress now, Lu."

The slim chimera was silent for some time, her expression unreadable. She said, "Remarkably, I feel much the same as I did a minute ago. I thought I would not. Could I ask one more thing? Might I sleep on my floor pallet here in your room tonight, one last time, as when you were a boy?"

CHAPTER 2

Striding at a brisk pace that Johrun had to stretch to match, Grandpa Xul led the way across the ranch grounds, past the splice stables—not crude communal bunkrooms or stalls as on other latifundia, but rather resembling the spartan dormitories of an underfunded state school—past the windowless abattoirs and automated meat-cutting facilities, past the refrigerated warehouses, and past the various storage sheds.

(Gone from one certain shed were the dismayed poachers, those bumbling ruffians, now wearing obedience collars, having been picked up a day ago by a security squad dispatched by the Motivators affiliate based out of Zarrinjub, a nearby planet sharing the star-packed M68 globular cluster with Verano. The impressively armed and stern-faced squad had loaded the prisoners aboard their sleek Mazurka Class ship the *Indomitable*. Then, before departing this brane for their base, they had bounced halfway around the world to pay a social call on Aunt Fallon, with whom the commander had once served, in her premarital days as leader of "Fallon Brujan's Brutes.")

The day, as ever on Verano, was exquisite: air like floral perfume after a dawn rain, the wan amethyst light from Wayward's Spinel lending even mundane objects a fairytale aura. Whatever else the Harvesters might have been—saviors, executioners, or something in between—they had definitely manifested a certain artistry in their planet-sculpting.

"Do you really think the fabricators will finish the new house by the time Minka arrives tomorrow?"

Xul smoothed his impressive white mustachios. His words attempted to prolong some suspense, but the truth of the matter could be read in his hearty anticipatory attitude. "Well, let's run the numbers. Always a useful exercise, to have the hard facts arrayed. We set the hephaestus units a-building seventy-two hours ago, and they can enclose ten cubic meters per hour, including laying down all the HVAC and circuitry. When they're done, you have to factor in the interior finishing and furniture genesis. Your plans describe a compound of some seven thousand cubic meters. So far, so good. But wait! I'm forgetting the exterior finishes! I must ponder further—"

Johrun threw a mock punch at his grandfather's shoulder, and the centenarian winced and pretended to be pained. Johrun knew full well that in reality Xul could have still deployed a large degree of the youthful strength he had retained, as well as the rough-and-tumble experience derived from his decades of adventuring, and taken his grandson to the woodshed. After all, had not Xul and his companion, Brayall Soldevere, Minka's grandfather, wrested the title to Verano from the infamous and redoubtable Honko Drowne, the Red Lion of the Spires, and lived to boast of it?

"Give, you old rascal! Don't keep me on tenterhooks!"

"Yes, yes, I'd say your new home should be finished just about the time Minka steps off the University ship from Loudermilk

III, or maybe thirty seconds after. Give or take an order or magnitude on that last figure. But wouldn't the best way to gauge the progress be to eyeball the place?"

Their walk had brought them up to the structure in question, and they stopped now to appreciate what the fabricators had rendered.

The plans for the residence where Minka and Johrun would soon live had been selected by Johrun himself. (Minka had been in charge of choosing the design of their separate home at Danger Acres. As yet, it remained her secret. As the yoked scions of both families, the couple would spend half the year at each holding.) Johrun had picked as his architectural model the Aestival Gazebo of Margravine Thais on Bueno Corso, fabbed in pastel marble and quartzite. A truly romantic conception, distinct from the other utilitarian ranch buildings, the light and airy structure, incorporating almost as many pavilions and loggias as boxed-in rooms, seemed perfectly suited to the Verano clime.

It would be strange to live as man and wife, apart from the family, but Johrun was eager, already picturing himself and Minka lounging at the breakfast table together before the day's chores began, bantering and exchanging passionate side-glances.

Xul's vambrace blarped an alarm, drawing him to a hephaestus machine that was stuttering: laying down the same patch of laterite patio tile over and over in a rapidly accumulating useless stack. He took it offline with commands from his vambrace and summoned its replacement, which began to decohere the excess material before completing the job properly.

"I still think we should have started the project sooner, and not taken a chance on it being unfinished tomorrow."

"You know the duties of the ranch came first, and how busy they kept us. We could have turned the builder modules loose to operate without regular checks while we were in the field. But you saw how this one just went astray. Would you have us running in from the far pastures every time a unit went glitchy? As for splice supervision with something so delicate—chancey at best."

"Sometimes I wish the Recension didn't limit what machines could do for us on their own."

Xul said sternly, "Never doubt that Bondi Rainstick and his Silicrobe Boys saved humanity from extinction when they stopped the Sly Artilect and its many nodes in their tracks and then imposed their universal strictures. No, limits on self-governing action and some degree of machine inefficiency are much more acceptable than cyber-perfection and human nonexistence."

"You're right of course, Grandpa, but still—"

"No equivocating! You've verified that your honeymoon cottage will be finished when Minka arrives. And she won't even see it till a week after that! So let's tend to our duties and get this ranch ready for our departure."

The formal University student shuttle ship from Loudermilk would be arriving not here, but at Danger Acres, naturally enough, bringing Minka back to her own hearth first. And although the Corvivios family would be present for the reunion, the elaborate marriage itself—more of Minka's meticulous arranging—would not take place until after several days of pre-nuptial revelry. And only after the happy conclusion of that ceremony would the newlyweds return to Sweetwater Pasturage for an extended stay.

Johrun and his grandfather and Landon spent the rest of the early day putting all systems into idle, and rehearsing the boss splices—Arbona, Tucker, and Pieface, three corvulpecans of superior wit and initiative—in the maintenance of the ranch infrastructure.

During his lunch break, sitting on the terrace outside the kitchen in a comfortably squelchy biomorph lounger, enjoying a sandwich of rocklamb and cress on marshwheat toast and a mug of beer, Johrun noticed Lutramella exiting softly from the kitchen. She carried a tray of food. Always permitted the full run of the family's residence—in fact she had her humble private quarters in a far wing of the manse, and not in the general stables—her presence was no surprise. Nonetheless, Johrun intuited something amiss.

The splice halted at Johrun's beckoning. She wore not her usual grey outfit but a more colorful gold-and-green striped blouse, a taupe waffled weskit that fell below her slim, almost non-existent hips, and black ophid-compressive tights that stopped mid-calf. (*Did she really need such circulatory aids?* Johrun wondered. True, she was nearly thirty-five, well past middle-age for a splice, but he always pictured her as eternally fit.) As always she went barefoot. But if her somewhat gayer clothes showed a spirit inclined to celebrate, her face conveyed the opposite sense.

"Lu, stop a minute. What's happening, where are you heading?"

"I have to take my meal in my room."

"But you always enjoy eating with the household staff— Boysie, Hanzl, Trinket, and the others."

Lutramella's dark eyes regarded Johrun with neither self-pity nor anger, just calm acceptance of reality. "They don't want my company since you freed me."

Sliding his plate onto a side table beside his beer, Johrun came quickly to his feet. "This indignity won't stand! I'll deal with them right now!"

Holding her tray one-handed, Lutramella put a warm paw on Johrun's arm to halt him. "Please, Joh, don't. Anything you could do would only make things worse. And in any case, I'll be gone from the estate soon."

Lu's departure—retrospectively obvious—shocked Johrun. Somehow, in the press of events—the end of the roundup, the poachers, the upcoming return of Minka, Lu's manumission— he had never contemplated that, once sovereign, she would want to leave. It only made sense, though: without official status, her presence among the Corvivios family would be anomalous. He knew she would not want to remain as a charity case of any sort—although Johrun would have sponsored her in his life forever.

"You'll be gone? But where? And when?"

"Not until after your marriage, of course. I wouldn't miss that for the world! I am invited, aren't I?"

"Invited? You head the guest list!"

"Oh, good, I'm so glad. When I see you and Minka wed, my duties will finally be over."

Johrun took the tray from Lutramella, set it down on his chair, and embraced her. The chimera's wiry form, familiar as his own reflection, conveyed tactilely all of Lutramella's usual strength and dignity. She hugged him back, and then they unclasped each other.

"As for where I intend to go," the splice continued, "I thought the money you so generously endowed me with might cover my passage to Vinca's Ebb, and my longterm sustenance there. From all I've heard, it's a nice quiet place."

"A world full of superannuated free splices, who spend all their time knitting, tending vegetable plots, and playing cat-an-cribbage? You're too vital still for that fate, Lu!"

She shrugged. "I suppose, in one sense. But in another, my life's mission is over now, and only peace and inactivity loom."

Johrun could not conceive of counterarguments at the moment. "Be that as it may, you're not to take your meals alone, whenever I'm free. Here, sit, and we'll finish our lunch together."

While they ate, Johrun allowed himself to conduct a rambling but enthusiastic monologue touching on Minka, her fine qualities, familiar anecdotes from their youth, her imminent return, and the future he anticipated for them. Lutramella listened closely, interjecting a mildly pertinent question here and there. When Johrun finally wound down, she said, "When did she last write to you, Joh?"

Johrun had to pause and cast his mind back. The answer he came up with startled him a bit.

"It must have been six months ago. But it was a very tender message. She blew me endless kisses at the close. I played it time and again."

"I would have hoped for more frequent contacts between two people destined for each other."

"But this was her senior year, and she had so much to do! Why, mastering the categorical logic of *Krokinole's Manual of Essential Niceties* alone required endless hours of memory work." Minka's self-directed degree was designed to encompass all the technics that would help her guide Danger Acres into the future, and a firm grasp of *Krokinole's*, which laid out all the cultural taboos and requirements, quirks, and kinks of the hundred thousand major starfaring cultures of the Quinary, was deemed essential. "And she knew how busy I myself was here—"

"Nonetheless. To stay silent for such an interval bespeaks—"

Johrun stood up abruptly. He was a little irked at Lutramella's insinuations and criticisms. "There's no need for you to pass judgment on matters about which you can know nothing. I realize you and Minka had never formed the closest of bonds. But I'll thank you to keep your wet black nose out of my love life."

Lutramella's flattish muzzle quivered. "As you wish, Joh."

Johrun stalked off then. As soon as he was out of Lutramella's sight, he felt guilty at his harsh rebuke. But ire and pride swiftly reasserted themselves, and he put aside any thoughts of the affront he had unjustly given his loyal companion.

Landon and Xul were finishing the mothballing of some machinery—mainly covering the vehicles and equipment with powerskin tarps against Verano's occasional tempests. The planet's eternal summer did not preclude some humdinger blows, and warm rains and winds could be as powerful as cold. And although weather satellites revealed no impending fronts, one could never be sure what the unknowable Harvester planetary programming intended.

Declining his help, his father said, to Johrun's chagrin, "No, sir, you can take off the rest of the day until our departure this evening. The lusty groom needs some idle time to anticipate the marital rigors ahead. Human partners are more demanding than chimeric ones, after all."

Grandpa Xul chuckled at the risque jab, and Johrun was perforce made to ponder his father's admitted dalliances with the more nubile of the splice work force, assignations that had continued intermittently from Landon's adolescence down to the present day, with Ilona's tacit consent. Johrun himself had never adopted the habit of using the splices that way. Except for one lone instance, when he had lost his virginity to a young pantherine girl named Hylana who worked as a domestic, he had steered clear of their musky charms. Of course, he and Minka had been enjoying sex with each other since they were both thirteen, a release that Landon, raised alone or in tandem with his rough-and-tumble "cousin" Arne, had not benefited from.

Johrun wasn't quite sure why he hadn't exercised any of his very adequate libido on the splices. Perhaps the familiarity of having a splice—Lutramella—as his wetnurse and nanny (again, a status not shared with his father, since Grandma Chirelle had been much more hands-on motherly with her boy than had Ilona with hers) had disinclined Johrun from such practices. But in any case, since that onetime bout with Hylana, Landon had simply assumed that his son Johrun was carrying out the family tradition, and the older man would josh about it now and then.

Grandpa Xul seconded the dismissal. "Go and finish your packing, boy. If you absolutely want more work, you can ask your mother and grandmother if they need any help closing down the house."

By vambrace, Johrun tracked down Grandma Chirelle in her greenhouse, a large attachment on the south wing of the ranch. In truth, the ambiance inside the glass room hardly differed from the clime outside. But here Chirelle safely raised those exotic plants she did not wish to become invasive species on Verano.

Grandma Chirelle looked up from feeding a wriggling medusa shrub. Her milk-chocolate centenarian's skin betrayed hardly any wrinkles, giving her a countenance beyond even the youthfulness one normally associated with a top-notch anti-aging regimen. Her wide mouth registered a big welcoming grin.

"Johy dear! Give me a hug!" Extending her arms wide made batwings of the drapery of her oversized aquamarine spidersilk gown.

Only Grandma Chirelle called him "Johy." From anyone else, the nickname would have grated, but from her it conveyed boundless love.

"Is there anything I can do for you before we leave, Grandma?"

She put finger to lip. "Let me think . . . Yes, one thing. Move this heavy pot of butter roses out from under the shade of the taliesin tree."

Grandma Chirelle had Johrun shift the rose pot's new vantage a half-dozen times—each spot no different from the others, to his eyes—until he was sweating profusely. Then, finally satisfied, she signalled she needed him no more.

Ilona Corvivios lurked in her office. Although all her multifarious business for the family was conducted via vambrace and the Indranet, and could be accomplished anywhere, retreat to her office signalled the need for no disturbances—an incontravenable signal, even by her husband.

Johrun got permission to enter this familiar room via vambrace.

An extravagantly enormous chamber that featured a life-sized fabbed model of a herple, but colored in a rainbow of non-realistic shades, the big room also displayed in one corner a lab bench at which Johrun's mother continued the kind of subatomic researches she had been trained in by the Smalls. Emergency suppression and containment mechanisms ringed the island of activity to quash any rogue constructs eager to chew their way through person, house, and planet.

Ilona slid off a stool at her workbench and crossed the room to greet him. Raising her face shield, she offered one cool cheek for a kiss. Still an inch taller than her son, the woman wore a yellow duster, belted and buckled tight, fashioned of some sort of glistening silicrobe-resistant active material. A transparent smart shield like a welder's mask had protected her face. The faintly apprehensible smile on her handsome, sharply planed face, delivered upon Johrun's appearance, was equivalent, he knew, to Grandma Chirelle's hearty embrace; the maximal response from differing personalities.

When Johrun had first taken notice of his mother's somewhat distant nature toward him—mainly by contrast with the warmth exuded by Uncle Arne and Aunt Fallon toward their girl Minka—he had felt confused and sad. Confiding tearfully one day to Lutramella that he felt unwanted by Ilona, he had been heartened by the splice's simple response.

"Your mother loves you to the fullness of her own special heart, and no one could love or be loved more than that measure."

Accepting his nanny's analysis, Johrun found that with the supplement of Lutramella's unstinting warmth and constant attention and encouragement, he and his mother could have a quite fond relationship.

"Do you want to see my latest trick with the lakecrabs, Johrun?"

"Yes, of course."

Ilona conducted him to her workbench. In a sizable terrarium a half-dozen of the native golden ten-limbed crustaceans were secreting not the foundation of one of their normal towers, but rather some kind of broadcasting antenna.

"I've figured out how to turn each colony into a computational engine. The nodes will communicate via their antennae. It should be possible to employ their distributed machine power to hack the futures market for herple meat. Theoretically, we could increase our revenue stream by five percent."

Johrun regarded the laboring crabs. Somehow, despite having no features that could convey emotions, they looked morose.

"But, mother—is this strictly necessary? Aren't we wealthy enough already? And these crabs, a natural part of the ecosystem— Shouldn't they be left alone?"

Ilona regarded her son soberly, as if he too might benefit from nano-manipulation of his cellular functioning. "The dynamical heuristics of the Quinary are ever-shifting, Johrun, and what suffices today might not serve tomorrow. We always have to keep our edge."

Johrun knew better than to argue this point. "I suppose." He paused, then said, "Is there a last-minute task other than subverting the planet's baseline species that I could help you with? Any customer complaints that need the personal touch perhaps?"

Schooled in all aspects of the family business, Johrun enjoyed some chores more than others, and he liked dealing with the faraway customers who bought the produce of the ranch. He would imagine their exotic, faroff planets, the kind of lives they led, so different from his own. Often, after business was settled, Johrun would attempt to engage the clients in idle, transmissions-lagged talk about their worlds—really just quotidian stuff that yet seemed alluringly strange. The contemplation of such non-Veranonal lives gave him a whispery sense of the vastness and range of the Quinary.

Of course, such knowledge could be easily gleaned from the Indranet, which featured countless encyclopedia entries on the half-million settled worlds of the Quinary, as well as colorful documentaries and virtual tours. But in Johrun's estimation, there was nothing that compared with actual interaction with these far-flung fellow citizens, even at a remove.

And yet he had declined the offer of a University education or a Grand Tour such as Landon and Arne had once undertaken in search of their mates. Both options had been proposed to him when Minka had upset the applecart of their marriage with her decision to study offworld. But when it finally seemed possible for him to actually set out into the galaxy, he had felt disinclined. His bonds with Verano were too strong. Thoughts of spending even a night or a week away from this bosom of this perfectly welcoming world to which he was spiritually attuned filled him with instant homesickness. He guessed he was by nature, and would always remain, an armchair traveler, eager to dream of foreign lands, but happiest by the hearthside.

Ilona seemed affronted by his last question. "Complaints about the legendary Corvivios herple meat? Not since we discovered the trouble with that bloom at Lake Squill. I never experienced a parasite with such a long latency period before. It even survived passage thru the herple gut. And for it to persist through all the post-slaughter safety protocols! But in the end, I learned a lot from dealing with that plague and the recall. No, all the accounts are up to the minute, all our bills are paid and our receivables indrawn, and our customer relations are fine. You can go get ready for our leavetaking without a worry about any of that."

In his room—a palimpsest of the transient concerns of all his ages, from a youthful mineral collection through handmade models of famous braneships to a collaged poster of Pondicherry dream queens, including the pillowy Pinki Luxmeade—Johrun finished the task of packing that had been ongoing for several days. He paid particular care to his wedding garments: jacket and trousers of supple swamp-bamboo fabric from Venex, in seaberry blue, with much silver braid and frogging; white, high-necked shirt of Gilike gauze; and low boots of quagga leather.

By the time he finished, he was feeling hungry. That simple scant sandwich many hours ago had done its job and retired. Memory of lunch brought back his blaggardly treatment of Lutramella, and he flushed afresh. He would show her solicitous deference during the next week, whenever he should have time from being with Minka.

Dinner would be waiting for them at Danger Acres tonight. So after sending his luggage to the ship with a lagomorphic house splice named Dowpook, Johrun grabbed only a snack, before joining his assembled family members outdoors at the ship.

The main family branecraft owned by the Corvivios clan was a lush and sprightly Devilbuster ketch named *Against the Whelm*. With comfy cabins for a dozen, as well as cubbies for splices and a capacious hold, it easily served all their needs. Little runabouts, such as the *Golden Branch* that had ferried Landon and Arne in search of mates, constituted other options.

The sun was dropping faster, painting long mauve shadows across the landscape, and everyone eventually hustled aboard in the usual dithering of leavetaking. Chirelle had forgotten some jewelry, Xul needed to give one last instruction to Arbona, Ilona stood stockstill reading via her vambrace the latest updated figures from the central bourse on Halting State.

On the ship, Johrun caught up with Lutramella as she turned away from the portion of the ketch devoted to human use and toward the splice cubbies. Those compartments were empty this trip, since the human employees at Danger Acres would attend to the needs of the visitors, and no Sweetmeats retainers were needed.

Johrun took his old governess by the elbow. "You ride up front this time, Lu. Not only is the trip only four hours, but I want you by my side."

Her chimerical face, which Johrun had long thought he knew how to read, betokened neither delight nor injury. "That will be a pleasure, Joh."

The festively decorated lounge sported equipment that drove a high-resolution shaped-light diorama. When the normal cabin lights were extinguished, the effect was as if the hull of the ship had gone transparent. At the moment, the wraparound display showed only pretty wallpaper, stock footage from various Quinary worlds. Johrun shivered as a pink ice whale smashed its way through the slushy crust of an ocean on Rana III.

Claiming seats and drinks, the family finally registered their unanimous appearance. No one made mention of Lu's presence, as she and Johrun had always been inseparable. Casting his approving eye over his clan, Grandpa Xul commanded their takeoff via vambrace.

The ship would be following an exo-atmospheric ballistic trajectory, mostly suborbital, under simple fifth-force power.

Exiting and entering the brane made no sense for such a short journey. In fact, mappings between the branes of less than ten Gaian AU or so were very tricky and almost impossible, not to mention dangerous. The old human dream of short-hop teleportation remained just that.

The lounge display shifted to a realtime view. Johrun felt as if he were floating in the middle of the air.

As the ship climbed, the sky darkened beyond accountability by the sun's mere setting, and soon the stars of the globular cluster leaped into magnificence. This stratospheric view of the cluster far outshone even the spectacular night sky of Verano as seen from the ground. Capricious lanes of russet dust limned the Simurgh Nebula. Densely packed in a chaotic array, the orange, blue, white, green, yellow, and purple suns of a dozen sizes and color gradations seemed, synesthetically, to emit an actual roar like a conflagration big as the galaxy. Crowding prominence to prominence almost, they beckoned the humans with their unimaginable riches and variety, as if to say, *Among us you will find every desire of your hearts.*

Johrun heard a sob and sniffle and turned to see Lutramella in tears that snailed her fur. He realized with a start that this was her first time in even suborbital space.

"You like it, Lu?"

"I feel—I feel that I could die now in peace—but that I have so much to live for!"

Johrun grinned. He patted her paw and fetched her one of the mango-kiwi lhassis she favored.

The hours necessary to traverse half the planet sped by quickly, and *Against the Whelm* put down at Danger Acres during that timezone's late afternoon. While luggage was trucked by the lodge's human bellhops (jobs at Danger Acres were filled by offworld recruitment, and were considered highly desirable), the two clans that owned Verano—Soldevere and Corvivios—exchanged hearty greetings.

Uncle Arne and Aunt Fallon, his soon-to-be father- and mother-in-law, a matched pair solid as beer kegs, practically squeezed the breath out of Johrun. Grandpa Brayall and Grandma Fern, somehow seeming as if they were calmly fording a rushing river under pursuit of a herd of angry bellhorns, even while standing still, delivered a more dignified welcome.

Brayall took Xul one side for a private conference, and Johrun was struck, not for the first time, by the air of oldtime roguery that somehow sprang up instantly between them. Their shared history prior to taking possession of Verano was stuffed with wild deeds and bold assaults on destiny. A legacy not always obvious when each man was sedately catering to whimsical tourists or herding giant snails.

The immediate reunion over, the families repaired to a private dining room in the grand lodge, whose halls and lobbies and gamerooms thronged with guests. The feast was extravagant, featuring such rarities as roast Drummeran cuckoos and pâté of tundraworm, and Johrun hoped he would not wither under a steady assault of such rich collations during the upcoming week.

Finally, on the way to retiring for the night, Johrun tracked down Lutramella. Although the splices did not wear vambraces —the Indranet was not open to them, although, Johrun realized, Lu could now legally participate—they were chipped with locators.

He discovered her in her assigned room, more attic than penthouse.

"Lu, come sleep in my suite. I'm sure there's suitable accommodations."

She accompanied him without assent or demurral.

In the room, though, she spoke.

"I am very sorry I hurt your feelings earlier today, Joh."

"And me as well. But all that's easily forgotten between two old friends, no?"

"That's what I had hoped. You do know, Joh, how much I want you to be happy."

More than a little drunk and weary, Johrun wanted to bring the conversation to a close. "Of course, of course. Now let's get our rest."

In the morning, after a breakfast buffet of two-score dishes, the two families haunted the landing field where Minka's ride would soon set down. The University ran a very dependable homegoing service for its students.

The ship broached the atmosphere with a boom and grew quickly larger. But at some point it became apparent that this was not the regular shuttle from the establishment of Saints Fontessa and Kuno. It was a private pinnace of the Utopian Turtletop class, painted in eye-boggling polychrome fractals.

Johrun pinged the craft's transponder and it identified itself as the *Bastard of Bungo*, the name of the protagonist of a popular picaresque adventure.

Down onto the invulnerable glascrete pad the gaudy craft settled. Door open, ramp down—

Minka appeared. Dressed in a revealing blouse and skirt ensemble of black wispaway fabric that left her midriff bare, she looked flushed, hectic, and disheveled. She traipsed lightly down the ramp as if her entrance were utterly condign, and close behind her lollygagged five other young men and women, wearing foolish hats and hefting half-empty bottles, from which they continued to swig.

CHAPTER 3

Attempting to conceal his lingering peeved perplexity, Johrun contemplated his bride-to-be as she sat across from him at the long dinner table, a green cloth river on which the best silver-rimmed red china and palladium flatware that Danger Acres provided seemed to float like pleasure boats. She was chatting gaily with the man on her right, the High Serendip Eustace Tybalt, ranking member of the Diminuendo Aleatorics and the fellow who was to marry them a week from now. Tonight's banquet was not limited to the family, and in fact included those of the invited wedding guests from across the Quinary who could manage to attend the whole seven days of festivities. (Many others would arrive on the wedding eve.) On Minka's other side sat Strategos Raymour Honeycombe from Banoff's World, longstanding patron of Danger Acres, and the sole hunter ever to bag a Crandall's Gorgon with only his soliton pistol after his ceegee rifle malfunctioned.

Under the shaped-light cressets that illuminated the hall, tuned to mimic colored flames, Minka looked both alluring and demure, her blonde hair assembled into delicate whorls, her subtly painted lips inviting as an oasis in the desert. Catching Johrun's fixed inspection of her, she half-turned towards him for a second without interrupting her conversation with the Serendip and flashed Johrun a short wink. Johrun experienced a disconcerting mix of desire and wariness.

Most of a day had passed since Minka's disturbing arrival, and whatever agitations she had undergone on the voyage home that had rendered her so slatternly had been remedied. With the aid of the lodge's superb spa facilities, including a long cleansing purge in the sauna, followed by massage, pedicure, manicure, and all the other technics of the beauticians and nutraceutical wielders, she had reemerged as the radiant and self-possessed young woman who, four years ago, had set out for Loudermilk III.

Looking back on Minka's infrequent visits home during her University tenure, Johrun had to wonder if there had been a gradual progression toward her disarrayed state of this morning. Had he been so eager to see her during such reunions on Verano that he had overlooked any changes in her manner and comportment and attitude? He found he could not answer the question retrospectively with any degree of certitude.

Whatever the case, she managed now to convey all the polished elegance, powerful aspirations, and strong-willed brilliance of intellect that had marked Minka during the years in which they had matured side by side. Perhaps only a subliminal fever gleam in her sapphire eyes betrayed her previous state of mind.

And yet—there was no denying that such precision and nonchalance had been far away when Minka and her inexplicable companions moseyed down the ramp of the *Bastard of Bungo* a double handful of hours ago.

Leading the parade, Minka had stumbled at the juncture of ramp and glascrete pad. She recovered sloppily and then, catching sight of her parents, had hurled herself into their puzzled embrace with a loud squeal. Taking the measure of the other family members as they stood in mute witness, Johrun saw that all were equally startled at Minka's condition. They hardly knew how to react when, in turn, Minka plastered their cheeks with sloppy kisses and inflicted too-tight squeezes.

When it came Johrun's turn to accept her overly enthusiastic greetings, Johrun took the opportunity to whisper into her ear, "What's the matter with you, Minka?"

She made no reply, but instead bit his underlip hard enough almost to draw blood and definitely hard enough to elicit a yelp.

Only Lutramella escaped these rough affections, with Minka actually recoiling from the silent dignity of the splice.

When the prodigal had finished her greetings and stepped back, she finally thought to address the circumstances of her return, in an overloud slurred voice. But she directed her speech first not to the Veranonals, her kith and kin, but to her companions from the ship.

"Well, pals, here they are. The family. Just like I described, right? And, and—there's the lucky guy I'm gonna marry. And his folks. Say hello, y'all. C'mon, get acquainted!"

The quintet of strangers did not have the good manners to appear uneasy. Nor did they introduce themselves. A couple merely raised their bottles in mocking half-salute.

Minka grew exasperated. "Oh, hell, I gotta do everything! Alright, here goes. Pay attention now!" She rattled off the names in rapid-fire sequence. "Anders, Trina, Viana, Braheem, and Ox. And my folks are the Shoal—the Shoal—the Soldeveres! There!"

Feeling somehow semi-responsible for Minka's callous behavior, Johrun undertook more formal introductions. He stepped forward and extended his hand to the nearest fellow, a well-wrought athletic type with close-cropped black hair specked with crawling artificial silver mites which respected his pate's exact perimeter. He wore loose billowy trousers in a harlequin pattern and a sleeveless umber shirt of form-hugging synthetic material that delineated an impressive musculature.

"My name is Johrun Corvivios. My parents; Landon and Ilona. And my grandparents, Xul and Chirelle."

Of an age with Johrun, the young man addressed seemed to realize at last the awkward and even insulting deficiency of their entrance into what was supposed to have been a touching family reunion. He took Johrun's hand firmly and said, "I'm Anders Braulio. We're all classmates of Minka's, fellow graduates of good old Saint Squared U. Our post-diploma celebrations, I fear, foolishly protracted themselves past the departure of the University shuttle, and so I offered to bring people home, since I had my ship handy. First stop was Verano. Minka did say she was very eager to return."

This last bit seemed blatant placation. Johrun looked to Minka to see if she would confirm the statement. But she had sat down unceremoniously, cross-legged on the grass, and was moaning softly and holding her head while her parents fussed over her.

Anders continued, "Let me present my friends." Johrun shook the hand of each in turn.

Wearing a short polka-dotted frock, her auburn hair in rolls, Trina Mirid resembled one of Johrun's adolescent dream queens, lush, vivacious, and eternally beckoning.

Viana Salp affected a plainness of dress and style which did not completely conceal a gamin's attractions, including probing brown eyes.

His skin a splendid mahogany, sporting the distinctive facial hair patterns associated with the Obligates of Cofferkey, Braheem Porter seemed impish, barely restraining immoderate deviltries.

Clearly Ox Nixon's genome—whether baseline or sartorized —placed him far from the median of human genotypes. Nearly

seven feet tall and correspondingly bulky, he boasted a low brow
ridge, teeth like a horse's, and blunt-fingered hands big as cake
plates. His outfit seemed to have been patched together from het-
erogenous animal skins. The pressure of his grip, though obviously
restrained, felt to Johrun like getting caught in a hydraulic press.

The other family members came to the fore now and greeted
Minka's school chums. Patriarch Brayall Soldevere said to
Anders, "Are you of the Braulios on Puddingstone?"

"None other."

"One of your uncles was here just last year. Zerb Braulio."

"And a splendid time Uncle Zerb had, never ceasing to regale
us with his daring exploits afield under your guidance. I think he
bagged at least two cryptosyntrips."

"No, four!"

"When Uncle Zerb discovered I was friends with Minka, he
asked if I could get him a discount on his next stay."

"Tell your uncle his room and food are comped when next
he visits!"

After his rude start, Anders had become the soul of charming bonhomie. Johrun disliked him immensely.

However, Johrun was glad to see tensions diminishing. But
his relief was derailed at the sounds of Minka, on hands and
knees, copiously vomiting. He hurried to her side, but Arne
and Fallon already had the situation under control. They gently
hustled Minka away for her restorative treatments—first stop,
one of the resort's doctors—while Brayall Soldevere dealt with
these unexpected new guests, who, after expressing no desire
to hurry off, were invited to participate in the full seven days of
celebrations.

And now here they all sat at the same long table. Although,
thankfully, the graduates had been assigned places down at the
far end—where, Johrun noticed with some slight guilt at her

placement, also sat a quietly observant Lutramella, the only one of her kind present. The wedding crashers seemed to be having a good time, regaling their more staid seatmates with stories and commentary that must have been droll and humorous, judging from the laughter that flowed. At one point Ox Nixon awed the crowd by chewing and swallowing the perdurable shells left from a serving of green oysters from the Hoatzin Littorals. His rumbling voice carried all the way to Johrun. "Ox need more calcium for strong bones!" Johrun assumed he was acting the savage. If not, the University of Saints Fontessa and Kuno had let their matriculation standards slide abysmally.

The whole dinner, once anticipated keenly as the kickoff to a splendid week, had swiftly become an almost unendurable trial for Johrun. He had dreamed of the moment when Minka would be by his side once more, when they could converse privately and sweetly, taking up all their old ways, before assuming their public roles for a week as two scions heading for the altar, the culmination of three generations of striving for the perfect union of families. And certainly fate would favor them with a free hour or so each day where they could renew the lovely carnality they had enjoyed as teens. In Johrun's dreams, the week was to have been a pre-honeymoon honeymoon.

But instead, if tonight were any gauge, the next several days would find Minka acting strangely un-Minka-like, with the presence of her school buddies casting a spanner in the works. Johrun vowed to fight the disruptions of schedule and atmosphere with all his might.

Finally the sit-down portion of the meal ended, with all the diners adjourning to an adjacent salon, the Red Claw Room, for cordials and sweets.

Johrun knew this room intimately, as he did the entire extensive Danger Acres holdings. Spending half of each year with the

Soldeveres, he had roamed all through the rambling lodge, from big public lobby to stockrooms and kitchens, laundry, and quarters for the help. First, as a child, playing with Minka; then, as a teen, helping out with various assignments from the Soldevere elders, until he knew the operation of Danger Acres almost as well as he did the requirements of running Sweetmeats Pasturage.

Not that he was as thrilled with the resort's demanding clientele as he was with the brainless herples.

This room, like the entire resort, expressed a carefully cultivated sense of wildness and primitiveness that concealed sophisticated luxury: the combination of roughing it and being coddled that the patrons most desired. The architecture of the lodge featured seemingly untempered natural surfaces of wood, stone, glass in rustic lines, with seemingly handmade furnishings. But all was cunningly fabbed, and the chairs, couches, stools, baths, and beds featured pampering ergo-squirm tech, and individual climate-control could modulate even the perfect Verano temperatures for those who might desire their private quarters to conform to their home worlds.

The walls of the Red Claw Room hosted numerous trophies representing a fraction of the prey that was hunted at Danger Acres, from the nano-taxidermied heads of bog wolves to elaborate mosaics formed from the fangs of the flying anomalocaris. Leather-covered banquettes and small pedestal tables completed the scene. The dinner guests soon arrayed themselves into small conversational groups as wait-staff in the lodge's colors of orange zest and basalt grey circulated with the drinks and tidbits.

On a small platform at one end of the salon, a band began to play: brass, woodwinds, and electric bağlama. The signature sound of Loftin's Invigorators. A few frisky partners and triads began to dance in the clear center of the room.

Johrun tried to cut Minka out from her crowd, but she ignored his tactics and plonked herself down practically on the lap of Anders Braulio, who reacted in an entirely too-intimate handsy fashion.

"What a wild week!" she exclaimed. "One day we're skylarking on Irion, despite that horrid phagoplasm plague, and the next we're crossing the maddening mystical marches of the interbranes. And finally, I'm home." She grew sober, deflated, a light departing from her eyes. "Home," she repeated dully, as if the word represented an entirely alien concept.

"Minka," urged Johrun, not attempting to conceal his actions from her cohort, "step away with me, please, just for a moment. I have so much to say just to you."

"Oh, later, Joh dear, later. Once I'm settled. I haven't been back more than a few hours, and my brain's still all awhirl from the transition."

"What you need," offered Anders, "is something a little more potent than these wan aperitifs." Anders unpocketed from the jacket of his newly fabbed mint-green formal wear a slim flask. "Try this. It's vision-cactus rakia from my homeworld. Guaranteed to relink a synapse or three."

Minka eagerly downed a slug, and then the other students— Raheem, Ox, Trina, and Viana—staged a mock scrum for possession of the flask.

Disgusted, Johrun stepped away. Surely Minka's somewhat pardonable irritability would soon subside, and a good night's sleep would restore her to wholesome affability. And she had called him "dear" after all.

Through the open windows and doors wafted the scent of the Verano night on the continent of Karst Notturno: spices, florals, animal pheromones. Johrun meandered through the chattering crowd, receiving with as much grace as he could muster all the congratulations of the guests. These were the friends of his parents and grandparents, and Johrun knew most of them only by swotting up on their Indranet profiles. He really had no pals of his own age, and had contributed no names to the list of attendees.

Johrun came upon Lutramella almost by accident. He had been thinking that she might need some companionship, as the only splice in the welter of humans. But instead he found her at the center of a raptly attentive group of four or five folks of impressive mien. Though still barefoot, the splice wore a suit of rich brocade, all lime green and scarlet threads depicting the imaginary children's book landscape of the Slumbering Realm. Despite being well into her chimeric middle-age, she exhibited an admirable posture. Her alert expression reminded Johrun of all the times she had winkled out some small misdeed he had been seeking to conceal.

One fellow—an academic by manner and looks, a lofty stigma which he shared with his peers—was speaking. "But how can you reconcile the Chimera Revolt on Trosper X with their ostensible adherence to the ethical precepts promulgated by Thomas Equinas?"

"Very easily. You are interpreting those texts from a human perspective. When you read them in light of trans-genic code-shifting, they invert, and their support for rebellion becomes obvious."

Lutramella's human audience began passionately debating her remarks, allowing Johrun to signal her to accompany him.

"Excuse me, esteemables, but I am called away."

Reaching Johrun's side, Lutramella took his arm in hers, just as when he was a child, then smiled, keen incisors prominent. They exited the Red Claw Room and followed a gravel path among cinnamon-scented shrubs and plashing fountains.

No one else was about. Overhead the wealth of the cluster's stars paraded their rainbowed glories, cumulatively casting almost as much radiance as a moon. Under their light, Lutramella's fur resembled flocked velvet.

"I am enjoying the start of your wedding week, Joh."

"So I noticed."

"I wish you were too."

"What makes you think I'm not?"

Lutramella said nothing, forcing an eventual admission from her ex-charge. "All right, I confess. I'm having an awful time. Who wouldn't feel dismayed when his blushing bride returned home spiked to the gills and with a gaggle of boorish friends in tow? What am I to do, Lu?"

"I suspected her focus on the good things she left behind during those four years away might be wavering, Joh. That's why I asked how often she had written. But don't despair. Now that Minka is back, I'm certain the old rituals and sights and sounds and feelings will bring her around to her former self."

"I hope you're right."

A gentle bending of the path reoriented the walkers to face the resort again. The extensive building, with its many wings and rotundas, all alight, seemed a ship at sea. Johrun suddenly felt weary and adrift. Moreover, his condition seemed to have lasted forever, and have no end in sight. The last time he could recall feeling normal and happy was when he had launched himself from the Salazar Escarpment a few days ago. Everything since had been confusing and dire.

Trying to shake his black mood, Johrun asked, "Where did you learn to converse in that fashion? You awed those stuffed shirts. They were hanging on your every word."

Lutramella looked down at the ground, then back up. "I am a free splice now, am I not? Thanks to your infinite kindness."

"Yes, of course. And don't mention that trivial deed of mine again."

"And the laws state that any infractions I incurred as chattel are thereby excused by my new status, so long as the violations involved only those special prohibitions specific to unfree splices, and no generalized criminal offenses?"

"You have summarized everything very accurately."

"In that case, I feel I can tell you the truth. Ever since you got your first vambrace—you were three years old, I think—I have been using it as well. At night, with me beside you when you slept—oh, so soundly my tired little Johrun slept and dreamed!—I would employ your open window on the universe. Your continuing biometrics kept it forever logged on. I muted the sound, dimmed the display, and turned on captions. How to read, of course, all splices are taught, to make us better able to navigate the human world. In this manner I have educated myself. At no small cost. Since many mornings after too little sleep I had to drive myself to my duties. But I never gave less than good service, did I, Joh? And the prize was worth the price. Although for the past several years—when you matured, when we did not share our quarters—I have been bereft of such learning. This has been an excruciation. So much goes on every day in the Quinary, and there is so much to know!"

Johrun felt disconcerted by this revelation. Not precisely peeved, but again unmoored. "Is that why you asked to share my room the other night? To use my vambrace again"

Lutramella halted and turned to catch Johrun's gaze with her own. Her dark hybrid eyes captured flinders of the stellar panorama above.

"I never thought of such a deed, nor touched your vambrace that night. I only wanted to feel that the bond which we had always shared before was still alive."

Johrun said nothing. But in response he sent his fingers to play a short passage on his vambrace. Lutramella shifted from foot to foot, but otherwise showed no unease at what might be the initiation of severe penalties against her for her illicit education, despite any disposable legalities arguing otherwise.

Johrun's vambrace split apart along its organic underseam. He peeled off the wide Indranet cuff.

"Hold out your arm, Lu."

She did as he asked. Johrun fastened the device on her, and it snugged itself to her dimensions.

"It's registered to you now. I just prepaid ten years' Indranet access. I'll get a new one for myself when we go back inside."

Johrun was not prepared for Lutramella's collapse. She crumpled to a furry pile on the grass at his feet. Alarmed, he hoisted her up—she weighed so little compared to a human—and walked her around until she had recovered.

Back on the porch of the lodge, in the light spilling from inside, Lutramella could not tear her eyes away from her new possession. But finally she cast a beaming look at Johrun, hugged him, kissed the tip of his chin, and ran inside.

Johrun followed slowly, reflecting that at least if his own life were a mess, he could still improve someone else's. That he had positively affected the future of one he held so dear made the realization all the sweeter.

In the Red Claw Room he hoped to find Minka sober and willing to humor him with her company, alone together, as lovers should be. But instead he encountered the five graduates deep in their cups and bellowing out their alma mater's song, "To Saints Fontessa and Kuno We Pledge Our Shining Troth Eternal," having suborned the paid musicians of Loftin's Invigorators to supply the tune.

Shaking his head, feeling utterly enervated, Johrun decided to head to his room for sleep.

On the way, he stopped first at the offices of the lodge, intending to quickly fab another vambrace, for he felt somewhat helpless and naked without the device. He empathized all the more with Lutramella's long deprivation.

To his surprise, he found his Grandfather Xul and his future Grandfather-in-law Brayall closeted there, having absented themselves from the party. He was obviously interrupting a deep conversation. Both men looked concerned.

"Is there anything wrong?"

Xul clapped a hand on Johrun's shoulder and grinned with an effort. "Nothing really, boy. Just a small query from the Brickers that needed our attention. You know how heedless of local time they are. Back on their world, it's just noon and some functionary feels he has to perform at least one task before lunch, to justify his pay. In fact, it's all handled now. So you can rest easy about your future."

That seemed an odd thing to say. But Johrun had no energy left to pursue the matter. He hugged the two old men and said, "I'll see you at breakfast then." They nodded as if eager to see him leave, so they might resume their discussion.

After securing his new vambrace, Johrun wended his way to his room. There, thinking of how he had counted on spending this night with Minka, he fell quickly asleep before he could brood overlong.

CHAPTER 4

Anyone encountering for the first time the breakfast buffet at Danger Acres would have instantly understood why the wildlife resort enjoyed a sterling reputation among the majority of discerning worlds in the Quinary as a place that catered most ingeniously to both the creature comforts of its patrons, and their quest for entertainment. Similar hunting preserves, such as Fannerl Groves on Wembley and Pendury Lagoon on Wezn 6, might offer luxury, but only of the staid, conventional type found in any urban hotel. The genius of Danger Acres was that the place combined hearty frontier cuisine and ambiance with sophisticated embellishments, enjoyed in a festive atmosphere of make-believe, all conducing toward a gay abandonment of cares.

This inspired refinement had been initiated not by the rather stolid Brayall Soldevere but by his wife, Grandma Fern, whose own upbringing on the world of Zatcho, known for its nearly seamless run of holiday entertainments, had contoured her tastes and imagination.

The long floating table that hosted the breakfast choices— other meals at the lodge were more formal affairs—featured nearly

a hundred homeostatic serving pots, racks, platters, and dispens-
ers, holding everything from simple porridges and fruit compotes
to entire succulent legs of marsh venison exuding fragrant steam
and rich juices. Several cooking stations, staffed by agreeable chefs,
offered customized plates at the order of the diner, such as griddle
cakes with a choice of sweet or savory stuffings. Ferrying beverages
and removing empty plates, the many indulgent servitors—whereas
Sweetmeats Pasturage got by with five hundred or so transgenics,
Danger Acres employed over a thousand humans—wore the costumes of a score of primitive tribes from across the many cubic
lightyears of the Quinary. The waitpeople dressed in the bodypaint
and wisp-frond skirts of the Korbanese had been chosen for their
admirable physiques, and elicited smiles, sighs, and salacious sug-
gestions from men and women alike.

Johrun entered the big high-ceilinged room feeling refreshed
and more optimistic than he had been last night. A solid sleep
plus the eternally cajoling and revivifying airs of Verano, slipping sweetly in now through open bays of the Prandial Prowl,
had wrought their usual effect. For the millionth time he
acknowledged the good fortune that had bequeathed to him
such a planet, from birth to the present moment. At this early
juncture of a fresh new day it seemed entirely possible that all
of yesterday had been a mere bad and uncomfortable dream,
and that when Minka appeared this morning she would be the
smiling, open-faced girl of old, eager to hurl herself enthusias-
tically at him, as she had done when they were twelve-year-olds
and Johrun called to her from the strider-speckled waters below
the ledge where she teetered, daring the girl to dive off and into
Lake Yusaima.

The Prowl was already half-filled with lively chattering
customers, for the business of Danger Acres was to continue
unabated during the wedding week. Tours and hunts alike had

to be conducted as usual. (The Soldeveres did not exclude any visitors interested just in viewing—at a safe remove, of course—the exotic beasts which the other clients were intent on bagging.) There had been some debate about shutting the enterprise down for the duration, and making the week an entirely private affair. But the wedding party, even though it numbered over two hundred, certainly did not need the entire facility, and in fact would have rattled lonesomely around the big lodge like a cup of dried peas in a hogshead. And so the wedding guests were mixed in with the regular clientele in a scintillating blend.

Johrun looked about for familiar faces, saw none, and, with a sigh, arranged a solo seat at a small table near one of the windows. He would have liked to dine with his parents, and Minka's, so as to get their candid reactions to Minka's wayward displays—last night in public, everyone had been very formal and noncommittal—but that could wait. (Memory of Xul and Brayall's strange late-hours tete-a-tete cropped up, but led nowhere.)

After getting a carafe of accra tea and a chilled glass of plum juice from a very vivacious young blonde woman whose rump was painted in teal and lemon stripes and whose shaped-light nametag read CANDELA, Johrun found his appetite suddenly stoked, and he strolled over to the food concourse. There he heaped his plate with flaky cream-leaf, dashed eggs, meaty choucroute, and sweet-potato strings. Back at the table he ate with gusto while consulting his replacement vambrace. (He wondered if Lutramella had gotten any sleep at all last night, or if she had stayed awake until her lust for knowledge was temporarily sated.)

The bride and groom's official schedule for the week ahead consisted of an elaborate audiovisual presentation laying out all the arranged activities that would culminate in the wedding of Minka Soldevere and Johrun Corvivios just six days from now. Johrun had played no part in scripting or filming this show, and was surprised to find a digital avatar of himself performing, reciting lines he had never said. He resolved to counsel Minka against such license after they were wed. No point in making a fuss about it now, though, given that it was a done deal.

In any case, the major activities outlined for today, aside from endless eating and drinking (Johrun tried to estimate exactly how many tuns of imported Smokestone prosecco this crowd could consume) were to consist of an extensive pool party, followed by a formal ball that evening. Tomorrow's main exercise was to be an actual safari. Guest who wished to shoot had been asked to register in advance and provide some Quinary-certified credentials attesting to their competence. Johrun was not surprised to learn that some fifty individuals would be going out armed, in five separate squads. After all, many of these folks were friends of the Soldeveres, and had probably been active patrons here before.

Johrun found that he had been pre-registered as a hunter, and so had Minka. He and Minka would be under the guidance of *Bona* Jebb Tipstaff, the head safari master, who oversaw the other twelve *bonas*. Normally Tipstaff did not conduct hunts himself, and his participation in this one was obviously a tribute to the romantic couple. Johrun knew him well, and liked the man's modest expertise. He could not object to that aspect of the plan.

But although long experienced in the sport, Johrun was not a true enthusiast, and in fact sometimes felt that recreational killing held not a few distasteful aspects. Especially since some of the hybrid prey animals had been designed with higher levels of intelligence, so as to provide more challenging sport. Much better to raise dumb food beasts such as the herples, even if the stock animals all ended up just as dead for the pleasure of humans as those trophy beasts. However, as the cynosure of the celebration, and also as the future co-owner of Danger Acres, Johrun could hardly be expected to deny his participation.

After mopping up the last of his eggs, Johrun placed a call to Arbona, the chimera they had left in charge of their ranch, and learned that all was well there. He contemplated another run at the buffet, but had to acknowledge he was well stuffed. So he got up to search out someone, anyone, who could further his various desires, whether that be Minka, his parents, or even Lutramella. Johrun was curious to learn if possession of her own vambrace had perhaps changed the splice's plans to leave Verano and retire offplanet. Maybe a solid connection to the Quinary at large would satisfy her desire for a change of scene, and she could be persuaded to finish out her days at Sweetmeats Pasturage. Surely if his quiet old nursemaid stayed out from underfoot, Minka would not object to her presence . . .

At the busy entrance to the Prowl where newcomers and departees were in flux, Johrun was nearly bowled over by an enormous figure trotting backwards through the crowd so as to address those following him. Ox Nixon, one of the illustrious alumni of Saints Fontessa and Kuno, was outlining his planned assault on the buffet.

"And after I wipe bare the platter heaped high with chive fritters, I will make my move on the unsuspecting bison haunch, followed by three or four game pies and enough cups of hot mocambo to float a battleship!"

The women, Trina Mirid and Viana Salp, laughed heartily at Ox's declaration, urging him on with cries of "Tell us more!" and "What next?" The elegant Braheem Porter declared, "Ox, you were ever the best trencherman at Saint Squared U. I recall when you drove the refectory prefect to quit his post and join the Order of the Huddleston Martyrs."

Johrun deftly sidestepped the blind steamroller approach of the giant and saw Minka, striding abreast of Anders Braulio. She looked more self-composed, less manic—although her gaze still exhibited an unnatural restlessness, a kind of darting apprehensiveness.

Coming alongside his future bride, Johrun clasped her upper arm, pausing her while he leaned in for a kiss. Minka allowed his lips to graze her cheek. Then, apparently reconsidering her demure stance, or motivated by some imp of the perverse, she grabbed Johrun by the ears and glued her lips to his in a demonstration of unbounded lust.

When Johrun broke free he found the five students grinning at his obvious discomfiture. Minka herself seemed unconcerned with her overweening display. Johrun glared back hotfaced at the others until Anders broke the standoff. The handsome fellow, dressed in supple golden leather trousers and a cream-colored kameez, looked well recovered from any overindulgences of the night before.

"Journeys end in lovers meeting! The wisdom of the ancients is borne out yet again! I think we are all just settling into ourselves after yesterday's confusing arrivals and social plunges. Let us all just wrap ourselves around some breakfast, and we'll be solid, sensible citizens again."

Anders draped an arm in comradely fashion over Johrun's shoulder and Johrun was perforce made to accompany the gaggle of graduates.

At their chosen table, Ox quickly began to make good on his boasts. He seemed more food-processing machine than man. Braheem, Trina, and Viana attempted to sample at least a tiny bite of everything, leaving much wasted food behind on their plates before multiple returns to the buffet. Anders and Minka ate more conventionally. Johrun had no stomach for more food, but did drink too much of the stimulating hot mocambo, leaving him jittery, while he listened to Minka explain her post-graduation travels to him.

"I did so want to see the fabled Glass Grottos on Irion. And Irion is much closer to Loudermilk III than it is to us here. Merely two days' crossbrane travel. And I knew it might be my last chance for a while to make such a visit, since I had to return home to my duties."

Johrun wanted to object to this arid classification of their wedding and married life, but bit his tongue.

"And with Anders having his ship handy, it seemed destined. Despite all the nervous nesters warning us that the phagoplasm outbreak would make such a visit impossible. But we persisted, and luck was with us. The day of our arrival marked the first time the area around the Glass Grotto was deemed free of the pests."

Anders interjected, "Well, we did skirt the clearance by a few hours, knowing we had to be back here by a certain day"

"Oh, but it was so worth it! The shimmers, the refractions. the reflections, the facets—it was like being enclosed alive in some diamond worn by a goddess!"

Johrun's cautious nature returned to the matter of the health risks on Irion and the interdiction. "The phagoplasm plague— what's the exact nature of that? I'm sure the authorities must have had good reason for forbidding any trespassing."

Anders waved away Johrun's concerns. "Paltry and exiguous! The infestation consisted merely of a kind of semi-sentient stealthy mycocelium that is wont to inveigle its animal victims into a kind of involuntary syzygy. Completely macroscopic, not like some kind of invisible germ, and hence easy to avoid. The Blue Doyens of Irion were utterly overreacting. Why, they lost millions of chains in stymied tourist trade! And of course I was there, ever vigilant, for the whole excursion, to make sure no harm came to your bride."

Johrun resented the proprietary note in Anders's voice, but again chose not to rebuke the man. After all, these annoying school chums of Minka's would be gone in a few days, and he and Minka would have the rest of their life together to share. He could be magnanimous and tolerate the gaffes and crudity of the gang.

"Well, I thank you, Anders." Seeking to change the subject, Johrun said, "I expect to see all of you at the swim today and the dance tonight."

"We wouldn't miss it! But what I'm really keen on is the hunt tomorrow."

"Do you shoot?"

"Yes, of course. My uncle Zerb—that esteemed patron of this establishment whom Minka's grandpop knows—taught me from youth. I registered early this morning. And while it took some doing—Minka had to intervene—I'm to form part of your party, under that Tipstaff fellow. Just me, though. Ox, Braheem, Viana, Trina—they all would rather climb a prickle-pod tree bare-arsed than go on safari."

Johrun could feel his ire rising, but tamped it down. "That's fine. We hunt gryffoths tomorrow, you know. Big game. Have you ever gone up against such?"

"No, but I don't anticipate any difficulties. Does it really matter what kind of beast stands on the wrong end of a ceegee rifle?"

"No," said Johrun. "It only matters what kind of hunter stands on the working end of the gun."

And realizing he would never deliver a more satisfying riposte or engineer a better departure line, Johrun stood to leave.

"Minka, I'll call for you at noon."

The young woman seemed more subdued than eager. "I'll be ready."

Out in the main lobby, Johrun brought up the locator tags on his extended family. Somewhat to his surprise, he found all eight of them clustered in the same room. Could there still be any planning left to do for the wedding that would bring them all into such late council? Johrun resolved to find out what was happening.

The boardroom of Danger Acres was reached down a long offlimits corridor behind the main registration desk. Broadcasting his private identity to all wards and baffles, Johrun's vambrace secured him admission past several locked doors. Through the last one, he encountered all his beloved family—both those linked by blood and those linked by spirit— seated around a big circular table of scented silver marne wood. Inexplicably, they regarded his entrance not with joy, but with varying degrees of muted chagrin, solicitous affection, and peeved upset. Johrun was taken aback by their less-than-enthusiastic reception, but tried to make light of the situation.

"Do I intrude on the secret plans for my bachelor party perhaps? Were you arguing over how many naked temptresses can fit in a cake? If so, I'll leave . . ."

Landon, his father, stood up and attempted a half-hearted smile. "You officious young dolt! Come here. If I thought you really wanted a bachelor party, I'd have already arranged for the importation of a bevy of beauties from the Sarzanan casinos! No, this is strictly a business meeting, concerning an unexpected matter that lands with unfortunate timing. But since you've tracked us down here, you might as well get in on it. Although after you learn all, you need not really trouble yourself with the annoying affair, since there's nothing you can add to its solution."

Landon conducted Johrun to an empty seat next to his, and the young man dropped down, awaiting the offered explanation. Brayall and Xul, the elders, looked significantly at each other, and then Johrun's own grandfather, Xul, spoke.

"You are aware, I am sure, of how the Soldeveres and the Corvivioses came into possession of Verano."

"Of course. It's a living legend. You and Grandpa Brayall, before even you knew Grandma Chirelle and Grandma Fern, won our world in a game of chance from its original discoverer, Honko Drowne. He grudgingly made over the title to you both, the Brickers affirmed the transfer in their registry, and that was that."

"Yes, this is the essence of our history. Or so we always affirmed. But yesterday we received an official communication from the Brickers on Bodenshire stating that they have recently uncovered something amiss with the original transfer and registration, upon application for investigation by a third party. It appears that Verano might not be properly endorsed in our names."

Johrun shot to his feet. "This is ridiculous! The planet not ours? How could any such huge discrepancy have gone undetected for generations? We have to straighten this out at once!"

Landon gripped his son's arm and tugged him back into his seat, saying, "Yes, yes, of course. What do you think we're doing? We've sent all the relevant digital documents and testimonies by drone, and are just awaiting a response. But you should be warned that all of us might have to travel to Bodenshire in person to resolve this vital matter—that is, if our transmitted credentials are deemed insufficient or flawed."

Johrun's excitement dissipated and he grew sober. "It's a question of your *âmago* then, I take it."

"Yes, that's precisely it," said his mother.

That same ineffable quality, *âmago,* that distinguished real herple meat from fabbed herple meat applied to humans as well. In a time when one could produce fakes and forgeries, living and inanimate, that were indistinguishable on most levels from the originals, there still resided a numinous quality in the originals that could be discerned on certain quantum levels and validated by complex interrogations. Thus the live, in-person testimony of a human or chimera, backed up by brain transcriptions and other subtle biometric data, would take precedence over any secondary documents or information, however authentic seeming. So by appearing on Bodenshire and subjecting themselves to deep vetting, the family could potentially put an end to all doubt about the validity of their claim, by notarizing the data with their authentic experiences.

Johrun asked, "Why must you all go to testify? Wouldn't just Grandpa Xul and Grandpa Brayall, as the founders, be enough?"

Grandma Chirelle explained with her knowledge and authority as keeper of forms and accounts. "It's the fact that all eight of us constitute the current ownership of Verano. The Brickers need to interrogate us all, to make sure that we are not, say, seven dupes and one malefactor. But you and Minka are exempt, since we have not yet officially enrolled you as co-owners. That new status, not inherent at your birth, was to be one of our wedding presents to you."

"And when would this journey have to take place?"

"That's what we can't say, until we hear back from Bodenshire. Maybe it won't have to happen at all. Our documents might be deemed sufficient. But if the Brickers do summon us, we'd have to go at once. We cannot let a potentially mortal wound like this fester."

"And so the wedding might have to be postponed?"

"That's the worst possible outcome, yes."

Johrun stood up, feeling suddenly weary and hopeless. His incipient marriage to Minka seemed cursed and doomed. But he tried to put a game face on. "If so, I will certainly need to take advantage of that offer of a warm armful of chorines from the Sarzanan casinos."

Landon stood also and clapped his son's shoulder. "That's the spirit, lad. Buck up and don't worry about a thing. It's just a bump in the road, after all. Don't sweat it, enjoy this time off from the cares of the ranch. I can't imagine many of our guests would object to staying a few extra days in the lap of free luxury here, while we make a quick jaunt offworld and back. If we have to subsidize their losses back home, we will. What better use of our vast riches, eh?"

Johrun walked toward the door, still confused and despairing. Minka's father, Arne, called out.

"No need to burden Minka with this affair, Joh. We were trying to spare both of you. But I think you'll agree that since there's nothing she can do, it would just be an extra worry for her."

"I agree. I won't say a word." Johrun did not add that he doubted if Minka, in her current condition, would even care.

Leaving, Johrun noted that no one else in the conference room got up to go. Plainly there were yet more aspects of the trouble to discuss which they saw fit not to encumber him with.

Out in the public areas of the lodge, amidst the unconcerned and happy clients of an enterprise they did not realize was built on quicksand, Johrun ambled about aimlessly, his thoughts in an awful muddle. Some of the wedding guests attempted to engage him in conversation, often with offers of sharing a drink or a snack or a quick game of bag toss in the games loggia. But Johrun fobbed off all the potential distractions with as much grace and charm as he could muster, still aware of the necessity of maintaining a facade of happiness and ease. He did not encounter Minka and her crowd, nor Lutramella, and was disinclined to actively seek them out. Perhaps talking with Lutramella about this blow might have softened it, or given him confidence in a good outcome. He did want to confide in the trusted splice, as he had so often done in the past. But although he had not been specifically enjoined to secrecy, he felt that the matter was not his to share with anyone outside the immediate family circle.

Eventually, whether by semiconscious intention or mere chance, he found himself following a flagstone path away from the main buildings. After a few minutes' walk across the verdant sward dotted with tiny low primula flowers, the path terminated at a monument. In the center of a flagstone circle rose a tall plinth, atop which was the model of an old-fashioned braneship, a beat-up replica familiar to Johrun since birth: the Jangalo one-person explorer named *Bumming Around*. The plinth bore this inscription:

DROWNE'S LANDING
HERE HONKO DROWNE FIRST
TOUCHED THE LOVING SOIL OF
VERANO AND CLAIMED IT FOR HIS OWN—
ALTHOUGH HE WAS NOT TO HOLD IT FOR LONG
THANKS TO THE GOOD FORTUNE OF
THE SOLDEVERE AND CORVIVIOS CLANS

In the light of what he had just learned, the words that had always seemed slightly mocking of Honko Drowne now seemed to direct their gibes in a much more intimate direction.

CHAPTER 5

The luxurious outdoor pool at Danger Acres, situated just a little ways off from the main lodge, remained open to the skies year round, taking advantage of the perfect clime of Verano. Surrounded by rambling patios and terraces at several levels, both sunken and elevated, the area also hosted many tables and upright chairs, along with comfortable ergo-squirm loungers, all of the seating capable of being sheltered under large umbrellas checkered in the orange and grey of the establishment, should clients wish shade or should a sudden short rain shower manifest. Bars overflowing with drinks stimulating and soothing, carefully tended fire pits where a dozen delicious dishes roasted (the distinctive smell of barbequed herple prominent), changing cabanas with soft towels—all features were predicated on a deft indulgence of the customers.

The main in-ground pool was proportioned for a stadium, with long sloping shallow end and a much deeper back half. Side pools, some heated, some chilled, some turbulent with jets, offered more sedate bathing than the active pool where both children and adults roughhoused and frivoled, away from the designated lanes for swimmers clocking their laps.

Had this been the totality of the facilities, no one would have felt unfulfilled. But the Soldeveres had aimed for an even more dramatic and enticing attraction.

Above the in-ground pool floated a noncontinuous ziggurat of unboxed water.

The lowest floating slab of water, whose undersurface hovered about four meters above the pool, conformed to the length and width of the water below it, and was itself some four meters deep. The slab above that was spaced at an equal interval, but was about half the linear dimensions, and centered. There was a third and finally a fourth watery mesa as well, in similar ratios and alignments.

A floating fifth-force projector at all eight corners of each water brick kept the liquid mass aloft. In event of catastrophic failure, a most ingenious system was in place to prevent the people on the ground from being crushed by tons of liquid. The entire falling bulk of water would be instantly flashed away into an adjacent brane by concealed dimensional engines. The normal imperfections and hazards attendant on such teleportation from a planet's surface did not apply, since the water cared not for any unachievable destination; it was a one-way trip.

Theoretically, any swimmers unfortunate enough to be present in the floating slabs at the time of such an unlikely catastrophe would be excluded from the expulsion by a type of Maxwell's Demon filter that recognized their vambraces and shielded them from the forced transit. The hapless individuals would then of course fall from a maximum height of thirty-two meters, if in the top tier, sustaining commensurate injuries. But given the state of medical intervention provided by the Pollys, their fate would be trivial, compared to being banished to another inhospitable universe.

The upper pools were accessed by a mechanism elegant and easy to use.

At the edge of the whole pool complex closest to the lodge, a series of partially railing'd floater plates circulated slowly through the air like the seats of an otherwise invisible Ferris wheel. When a plate reached the nadir of the circuit, ground-level, a person stepped on and was lofted upward. Each slab of water featured an adjacent floating platform onto which the rider could step from the moving plate. From there, diving into each floating slab was trivial.

One final feature added to the fun. The suspension mechanism also recognized the presence of a vambrace, and would allow a swimmer to force themselves out the bottom skin of each water brick and plummet to the next one.

This aspect allowed for massive games of tag across all four floating levels and into the ground-based pool, with players exiting and entering the levels and employing the floater discs in a wild rumpus which sometimes got so out of hand that intervention by the lifeguards was mandated.

Such a scene was underway when Johrun emerged from the lodge with Minka by his side.

Amazingly, he had found his fiancée waiting in her room at noon as he had stipulated. Her noxious chums were nowhere about.

Johrun had arrived still anxious about the bad news conveyed by his family council, and worried about making a slip and disclosing the troubles to Minka. But when the door to her room opened and he saw her in an absurdly tiny swimsuit fashioned of scaly yellow lizard skin mottled with iridescent crimson blotches, he forgot everything except his desire for this woman, and their long separation.

Johrun plunged into the room, swept Minka into his arms and sent the door slamming shut with a rearward kick. He snatched her up and hurtled toward the bed. Minka seemed nowise averse to this impetuous siege, and in fact had wrapped her legs around Johrun's hips and her arms around his neck. Her signature bottled scent of sea pine and orris filled his nostrils. He toppled with her onto the unmade bed. Dressed in a fluffy white belted robe, swim trunks, and biopoly scuffs, Johrun was soon bare. Having less clothing to remove, Minka outpaced him, and without any foreplay they were instantly engaged in sex.

At one point Johrun had both hands around Minka's waist, thumbs pressing her supple belly, and he thought to feel something anomalous beneath her skin, a lump or submerged sac or organ suddenly adrift. But amidst the sensory deluge flooding in from elsewhere he could not be sure he had felt anything, and a moment later the impression had dissipated.

Minka's lovemaking matched Johrun's in intensity, and in fact she exhibited rather more facility and innovation than the last time they had connected—about six months ago. Johrun tried not to think about what such educational developments betokened.

When they had finished, and after Johrun had recovered some portion of his senses, he anticipated an interval of tenderness and cuddling. But upon reaching out to stroke Minka's face, he found her staring at the ceiling, her cheeks wet. He levered himself up on one elbow.

"Minka, darling—what is it? What's wrong?"

Her voice was stony, almost possessed, as if emerging from the end of a long tunnel. "Nothing is as it seems. We can't know anything. And nothing lasts."

"Yes, of course, of course. Philosophy 101. If that's all you learned at Fontessa and Kuno, Uncle Arne should ask for a refund. I mean, come on, we all acknowledge those harsh truths. Life's meaning is hidden, and our span all too short, a mere two centuries or so. But these stern realities are not for this moment,

Minka. Not while we are young, and on the eve of our marriage. Right now they can still be ignored or postponed or even mocked. And we should do so."

Minka got up with a sudden and almost violent spastic movement, before assuming her normal graceful stance. She reclaimed her suit and then added her own robe and scuffs. Perplexed, Johrun was bound to follow her lead. When both of them were dressed she turned to him. Inexplicably, her face showed nothing but the same slightly daft and reckless glee she had flashed on and off since her calamitous arrival. It was as if her intense despair of just a minute ago had been wiped clean from her memory.

"I'm so eager for a swim, Joh! Let's go! It won't be as private as Lake Yusaima, but it'll be much more fun!"

Biting back all his incoherent confusion, Johrun accompanied Minka out of her room.

In the corridor, he asked, "Where's your gang of reprobates?"

"Oh, Anders and the others couldn't wait to get in the water, and I was still enjoying a croissant and mocambo I brought back to the room. He's such a big child sometimes. So I told them just to go ahead. I hate to be rushed, you should know that."

"Of course. And I'm very glad you stayed behind."

Minka did not see fit to return Johrun's enthusiasm.

Exiting the lodge with Minka, Johrun quickly observed that her estimation of her fellows' eagerness to play had not been overstated.

The five graduates were dominating the various pools with a boisterous game of multilevel tag. They jostled others boorishly and hogged the water, but the lifeguards did not intervene, perhaps in deference to their status as favored wedding guests of the owners. Their ruckus was replete with much shouting and many catcalls, gibes, and challenges issued whenever their heads emerged from the water.

"You're slower than Tullian loris!"

"You couldn't catch your grandmother if she were wearing a glitchy mechasuit!"

Johrun spotted a familiar figure reclining on a lounger: Lutramella. The freed splice wore a modest one-piece swimsuit in blue and white that revealed her gracile limbs and short pelt with its subtle gradations of several colors. She did not boast a waist per se, nor hips nor bust, but seemed all of a solid, flexible roundness. Two empty chairs to one side of the splice beckoned. Johrun ambled over, Minka following.

"Lu, you look the most relaxed I've ever seen you."

The splice smiled. "Tensions I hardly knew I was harboring have vanished with this." She held up her arm with its vambrace.

Minka frowned. "What is that creature doing with an instrument so far above its station?"

Johrun realized that he had not had a moment to tell Minka about Lutramella's manumission, so he explained.

Minka sniffed. "If she takes her illusory new freedom to Vinca's Ebb to be with her own kind, I won't mind. But otherwise ..."

Johrun sighed inside. So much for his dream of a future household on Verano that would offer his old nursemaid a pleasant end to her days. But he couldn't worry overmuch about that, with other crises on his mind.

Johrun took the chair beside Lutramella, and Minka occupied the one furthest from the splice. She clapped her hands and exclaimed, "Oh, Anders, don't take that! Get him!"

Anders Braulio appeared to have just been nominated "it," and the game apparently called for anyone he tagged to retire from the field.

Currently at ground level, he heaved himself from the water and rushed to the circulating aerial discs. He hopped on one, but did not wait for its slow ascent. He leaped upward to the

next disc, catching its rim and hauling himself onboard. In a
succession of such risky leaps he caught up with Ox Nixon hes-
itating on the third-level platform. The giant man's reaction
time seemed to match his bone-headed namesake, and he was
instantly tagged. From there Anders dived into the penultimate
water brick and caught up with a frantically flailing Trina Mirid,
quickly disposing of her. Anders slipped from the underskin
of that level and flashed through the intervening air like a bird
of prey and into the second layer with barely a splash. Here he
had more of a contest with the slippery and wily Viana Salp, but
in the end she too was nabbed. This left only Braheem Porter,
who proved the most elusive. The two men conducted a wild
wet chase that eventually involved all four floating levels before
Braheem was ultimately retired.

As the contestants were eliminated and returned to pool-
side, they spotted Minka and came to cluster around the bride
and groom, standing and heedlessly dripping over everyone
while they chatted. Johrun had his first chance to observe
Minka's friends in near-nude condition. Ox's body featured
heavy dorsal and ventral plates like those on a pangolin, riding
atop incredible musculature. The voluptuous Trina seemed a
confection of whipped cream and spongecake. Viana's figure,
although boyish, hinted at reservoirs of sensuality. To match
his giveaway symbolical facial hair, Braheem's dark skin
crawled with the golden glyphs associated with the Obligates of
Cofferkey.

Just moments after the last-named arrived, they were
quickly joined by the victor, Anders Braulio. Buff and potent at
the high end of the baseline human spectrum, without obvious
sartorizations, Anders seemed not even winded by his exertions.

"Ho, girl, did you catch all that chase?"

Minka said, "You were marvelous!"

"I could do it all over again. But I think I'll sit for a while. Ox, fetch me one of those delicious bloodmelon shandies from the nearest barista."

Anders turned to Lutramella. "Up, khyme, and let a weary human have your seat."

A red scrim dropped in front of Johrun's vision. He was about to speak out boldly when Lutramella, with a meaningful glance, forestalled him. Rising neatly, she said, "I was just about to take a swim. The chair is yours." She began to walk away.

Anders flopped into the seat. "Go and paddle about then. But beware of the deep end. Many a swamp rat has met a nasty fate when venturing over their head."

Lutramella stopped. "I can take care of myself, thank you. I enjoy the water."

"Yes, just like a musk vole in a dirty ditch."

Minka and the rest of the gang laughed. Johrun found himself standing, fists balled. But Lutramella's calm poise deterred him.

"*Vir* Braulio, would you care for a contest between us?"

"Why not? What did you have in mind?"

"Another game of tag. I'll be it, and you may have as long as you like to position yourself before the chase begins."

"Are there terms to victory?"

"Yes. If you elude me and get back to this chair, I will be your personal servant so long as you are on Verano. And if I tag you, you must surrender this chair and fetch me one drink."

"The wager is taken!"

Anders heaved himself to his feet, flexed his muscles in deliberately hyperbolic fashion, then trotted to the fifth-force ascenseur. In just a bit over half a minute, he stood atop the highest diving platform.

Sensing some interesting contest underway, the other users of the pool had mostly halted their own activities to watch.

"Ready!" he shouted down.

The man's obvious strategy, thought Johrun, was to place as much distance between himself and Lutramella as possible. Then, before she could ever reach him, he would be back on the ground, one way or another. So he imagined. But Johrun knew better. He smiled now at Lutramella, who held up one paw as if in salute and flexed her fingers to reveal the dark skin webs between.

"Good luck."

"Thank you, *Vir* Corvivios."

She sauntered over to the edge of the deep end, with Anders from high above keeping a keen eye on her the whole while. He certainly must have expected her to use the aerial discs to reach him, allowing him to dive away from her. But much to everyone's surprise, she plunged into the ground-level pool.

No sign of the splice for an interminable ten seconds . . .

And then a furred missile rocketed out of the pool, cleared the four meters interval of open air as if winged, and pierced the first floating layer, safe in the suspended water.

Now the spectators could see Lutramella's preparations for her next launch, as she built up speed by swimming underwater in a tight circle like some kind of madly animated flywheel.

Anders Braulio could see too. He moved as if to dive into the uppermost level. Then, thinking better of such a strategy, he stopped and stepped onto a descending disc. It was not as easy a shortcut maneuver to hop to a lower disc as it had been to jump to a higher one, and in his haste, the man almost missed his landing. He wisely ceased trying to outpace the mechanism.

Another explosive arrowing, and Lutramella was in the second floating pool. Anders had stepped off onto the platform at the third height. Lutramella surfaced her head and shoulders, treading in place effortlessly. The competitors contemplated each other. Anders obviously knew that if he entered the water he was doomed. But Lutramella could also just wait to tag him at the second level platform if he continued down on the discs. And to return to the fourth level would be mere prolongment.

"Why not join me, *Vir* Braulio! The water is splendid!"

Anders let out a muttered curse not totally comprehensible to those on the ground. Johrun was grinning so wide it almost hurt.

Finally deciding that he might stand some slim chance in the water, Anders plunged into the pool above Lutramella's. There he swam about in taunting fashion. "Come and get me!"

Lutramella began her circling. Anders waited for the best moment to exit his pool and pass her by in mid-flight.

Spray fountained upward as Lutramella blew through the top of her pool.

Anders pushed through the bottom of his level and began to fall past the splice.

Lutramella entered the upper body of water, turned on the head of a pin, and accelerated back out into the air before Anders had fallen more than halfway.

She caught him just before he hit the water, grabbing him in a bear hug. They struck the pool together, and she released him.

The two rivals descended separately the rest of the way via the water ladder.

A concussive round of applause greeted Lutramella when she emerged from the bottom pool. She smiled broadly. In a moment she had returned to reclaim her chair. Anders Braulio trailed glumly behind.

"*Vir* Braulio, if you still wish a bloodmelon shandy, you might get one for me while you're up."

Anders grumped off to carry out his penalty. His four friends had the good manners to congratulate Lutramella with what seemed like genuine admiration. Only Minka refrained from offering a kind word.

When Lutramella had her drink in hand and the others had wandered off to folic in the water, she beckoned Johrun to bend down for a whispered word.

"Please get me the strongest analgesics and myosinic tropes you can find, Joh. I've torn every muscle in my old body!"

The theme of the formal wedding ball for that evening had been conceived by Grandma Chirelle, always something of fanciful dreamer. Seeking to imply the possession of a superior history and lineage not actually enjoyed by the Corvivios and Soldevere clans—for, after all, they had been impecunious upstarts just two generations ago, not the rich and respectable planet-owners of today—she had chosen the theme of "Our Illustrious Pre-Quinary Ancestors."

The millennia before the establishment of the Quinary in its present form had been garish, rude, and outrageous centuries. Many new technologies had blossomed without any restrictions or oversight, and been employed in misbegotten ways. Devastating inter- and intrasystem wars had been waged. Outlaws and eccentrics, nonpareils and criminals of a thousand, thousand types had flourished, establishing colonies and secret redoubts across the galaxy, some of which had subsequently become lost and passed into extravagant legend. Belief systems and ideologies in mind-numbing profusion had been drafted, implemented, and forgotten. Myriad splices without the least utility had been sartorized into melancholy or extravagant existences.

And the baseline human form had been tinkered with to nearly unimaginable degrees. Almost as if humanity were unconsciously trying to fill all the old physiological niches of all the extinct sentient species that the Harvesters had reaped, the basic human template was warped across every possible parameter—limbs, brains, senses, desires, sizes, and functionalities—producing gods and demons, monsters and angels, improbable shapes and talents never before conceptualized. Many worlds at the present time still harbored remnants or even sizable populations of these outré creations, all breeding true of course, barring subsequent genomic interventions. But after these excesses, contemporary tastes, ethics, and fashions had dictated a return to the ancient bodily templates, leaving the majority of Quinary citizens looking—at least on the surface—just like their long-vanished Gaian ancestors. A figure like Ox was an anomaly.

But it was still amusing to masquerade now and then as some of the less horrifying individuals from this frontier era, reclaiming these figures as inspirations and sources of primitive courage, boldness, and fey whimsies. Such temporary impersonations of misguided and deluded ancestors also conferred the twin illusions of progress and superiority on the masquerader.

Thus the Danger Acres fabricators had been put to maximal usage all day, spinning out gaudy costumes whose historical patterns were drawn from the Indranet. But more vitally, the several beauty parlors on the premises had run chockablock and at full gallop, modifying the appearances of the guests as they dictated. Much of each makeover was the product of conventional non-invasive technics—smart paints and intelligent prosthetics. But a certain portion of the crowd indulged in temporary bodily modifications—organic barbels, tails, even extra arms or novel sensory organs. The Polly-trained staff were completely competent to fashion and embed such add-ons, all of which could be just as easily removed the next day. Unless, of course, the owner found that they enjoyed, say, having a pair of small wings at each heel, or a beard of living rasper beetles.

Johrun, after consulting and coordinating with Minka, in order to achieve some unity of appearance desirable for the bride and groom whom this whole affair was honoring, had settled on appearing as two members of the Logothetes. This philosopher clade from Bogoslof had been known for their outsized craniums and long, five-knuckled fingers with which they could form an intricate set of semiotic mudras. The look could be achieved with simple inorganic prosthetics, and the outfits associated with the Logothetes were plain floor-length gowns in muted pastels.

At first, Minka had objected to the choice. "Must we really pretend to be dusty, bloodless savants, especially on this festive occasion? I fear a presage of our life together! Why can't we go as the Fiendish Corsair of Maybeck and his child bride? I'd look adorable in torn bloomers and chemise."

"Totally inappropriate! My idea is a dignified and honorable impersonation."

Minka caved in with surprising alacrity. "Very well. Consider me a thing of chalk and equations from now on."

Arriving at Minka's room that evening, Johrun anticipated some hidden rebellion. But she presented herself with the requisite lack of adornments and oversized head and digits.

"I would kiss you," she said, "but the Fifth Postulate of Wetnoodle mandates otherwise."

"I'm glad to see you showing a sense of humor about this. Let's go down now and try to enjoy ourselves."

The Red Claw Room of last night's gathering had been deemed too small and unimpressive for tonight's celebration, and so the Behemoth Ballroom had been prepped. Likewise, the little assemblage of Loftin's Invigorators had been replaced by a full orchestra, the People's Harmonious Assemblage, under the famous direction of Maestro Chen Shortsleeves.

The orchestra was playing to a nearly full room as Johrun and Minka entered. Johrun felt the massed attention of the revelers like a physical blow. He saw his smiling parents and grandparents across the room, standing next to Minka's family. All eight of them were costumed like the famed platoon of Garibaldian Mazoi who had held out for days against incredible odds at the Battle of Blasted Heath. Johrun took comfort in their obvious approbation.

As he stepped arm-in-arm with Minka into the room, a small wave of murmurs and laughter began to build, until it reached a swift crescendo. Johrun saw no cause till he looked at his fiancée.

At some unseen signal, her gown had gone utterly transparent. And beneath it Minka was not only nude, but her pubic bush had been prinked out with flickering cold blue flames, and her breasts had been plumped up to unnatural size and equipped with prehensile nipples.

With a quick movement Minka shed her prosthetics—obviously gimmicked for quick release—and her useless gown as well. Her modified hair sprang out in abundant thick tendrils possessed of their own volition.

"Behold! The Sheelanagig of Far Embrazza!"

The laughter turned to wild hoots and applause. Minka pirouetted, accepting the crowd's salacious adoration.

In the front row of the ranks nearest Johrun, High Serendip Eustace Tybalt, he who was to officiate at their marriage, staggered visibly and had to be supported by his companions.

Without a word, Johrun stalked off, hardly cognizant of where he was going, heedless of entreaties from his family.

When he had calmed down, he found himself outside, some meters away from the lodge, at a small pavilion in the barely lanterned darkness. Overhead the uncountable polychrome tangles of stars regarded human follies unblinkingly and without sympathy. Floral scents drifted past on a mild current of ever-warm air.

Johrun took a seat and held his oversized head in his hands, unable even to form a coherent train of thought.

After some time came a dulcet cooing and a whispering from either side of him.

"Sister, what's this I see?"

"It's a bereaved young lad, susceptible to our tender wiles, Sister."

"Shall we comfort and beguile him in the manner of our sly kind?"

"Why not? It's the sad and natural way of all those with broken hearts, or with none."

Out of the thick shadows stepped two fabulous apparitions: female sprites, one lush, one svelte. Each wore enormous insect wings, and sported twitching fronded antennae blooming from their foreheads. Their human eyes were encircled by colorful paint, right out to cheeks and brow. Their clothing consisted of tiny stiff waxed-linen skirts and vinyl corsets and high-laced sandals.

For a moment Johrun felt truly transported back to some antique fairyland. And then he recognized Trina Mirid and Viana Salp.

"You two!"

The women sat down on either side of him. The bench was small and they had to press close.

"Yes," said plump Trina, "it is we, the Moon Moths of Selva Immortalis, here to reap your dying breath with our tender lips!"

Johrun replied wearily. "You're welcome to it."

Slim Viana laid a warm hand on his. "That girl of yours, she's such an attention hog. You should have seen her at campus parties. Never happy without being the center of all eyes."

"I begin to comprehend that the Minka I once knew is radically changed. But I am still hers, if she'll have me. It's our destiny."

"All well and good for the future," said Trina. "But what of this evening, while she flaunts herself?"

Viana's hand shifted to Johrun's crotch. "All may be allowed and forgiven on a night of disguises."

Johrun felt himself responding, willy nilly, to this unsolicited caress. He reached out tentatively to cup Trina's generous breast, and she pressed it into his palm. She did so resemble Pinki Luxmeade, the dream girl of his adolescence. He sighed and abandoned all scruples.

"I am not sure," he said, "how an actual Logothete would respond to your wantonness, but I can research the topic in the morning."

CHAPTER 6

The day of the wedding party's exclusive hunt did not fail to recapitulate an eternity of other perfect Verano mornings. Subtle lilac light like a downfall of candied flower petals accompanied the balmy breezes. The ambiance of the favored planet was a tonic in itself. People awoke from their indulgences at the Grand Ball of the night before with clear heads, easeful limbs and hearty appetites.

At least, most of the guests enjoyed that pleasant condition, especially if they had availed themselves of various unfailing Polly remedies and counteragents before falling asleep. However, Johrun had not been in any condition to do so. Back in his room with Trina and Viana and four snagged bottles of piquant nebbiolo champagne from the vineyards of far Durango, he had, like the scholarly Logothete whose rapidly shed costume he had flaunted, become too busy investigating all the topological combinatorics inherent in their three bodies. When he and the women had exhausted themselves in proving a large number of theorems, he had fallen into a coma-like sleep.

Some five hours later, around nine AM, a call on his vambrace shattered his deep and dreamless somnolence. Arising from subterranean caverns of unconsciousness, Johrun took a dull-brained moment to realize what he was hearing. When he registered that he was receiving a call, he knew that the caller had to be on his priority whitelist to get past his silencing of strangers and the trivial botherations of the rancher's life. And indeed, when he accepted the call, the shaped-light display revealed the image of that all-important figure in his world, Lutramella.

Her furry face turned partially away from the lens and evincing a small candid snarl, the splice was making a low growling noise that resolved into words. "Hate, hate, hate these dryboned menus! *Rowr!* I'd like to get the programmer's guts in my paws—Oh, Jo, you're there!"

Johrun levered himself around and scooted his butt back towards the bed's headboard and pillows, so he could sit upright. He was vastly relieved to discover that neither one of his fellow naked topologists was still present, although the musk of their exertions remained, as did a pair of crumpled Moon Moth wings, the glimmering disguise drab by daylight.

"Yes, Lu, I'm here—barely. What is it?"

"Many of the safari members are at the breakfast buffet already, and you are scheduled to leave in only ninety minutes."

"Thank you for the timely reminder. I had expected perhaps that Minka would call for me with time to spare."

Lutramella sniffed disapprovingly. "She's busy showing her friends how to mix a 'Danger Acres Powderkeg Shandy,' and shows no signs of missing you."

Johrun sighed. "I don't know what I'd do without you, Lu. Are you still set on retirement to that backwater planet?"

"It seems best for everyone."

"Will you come on the safari today?"

"No. I don't like witnessing all the killing."

"I understand. Very well, then, I'll see you later at some point, I hope." Johrun made to end the call, then halted. "How are your aches and pains from yesterday?"

"All better, thanks to the nostrums you fetched me."

"Well, I just wanted to say thank you for showing up that lout Braulio. It did my heart good."

"Any time, Jo. But with luck, he'll soon be gone, and we need never think of him again."

Once in the shower, letting the pulsed microjets of smart water pummel his abused flesh at their highest setting, and having downed some Polly restoratives provided by room service, Johrun felt himself almost fully rehabilitated. He assumed a look which he hoped conveyed dispassionate, generalized hospitality and vivaciousness with which to meet all the guests and his relatives and especially, in a public setting, the two sharers of his bed. He could only pray that the women had not already disclosed everything that had transpired last night.

His guilty conscience twinged. Really, how could he have been so self-pitying and self-indulgent? These past few days, from the incursion of the herple raiders through Minka's obstreperous arrival and the forced socialization with her undesirable pals, had rendered his behaviors abnormal. Johrun looked forward to an end to all this ceremony and a return to routine. The new routines of married life.

By the time Johrun reached the buffet, there was no sign of Minka and her squad. But Johrun did encounter his father, Landon. The man looked worried.

"More trouble, Dad?"

Landon gripped his son's elbow and steered him to a quiet corner. "It's this damnable mess with the Brickers. Overnight it's blown up. Right now it looks pretty certain that the eight of us will have to leave for Bodenshire imminently, to settle this dispute. Failure to do so could result in some really dire consequences."

"Would that be today?"

"No, tomorrow morning."

"And so the wedding would be postponed until your return?"

"Naturally. You wouldn't wish it otherwise, would you? To plunge ahead without us?"

To his chagrin, Johrun could not fully empathize with the carking bureaucratic demands placed on his elders, nor even with the real danger to their joint familial possession of Verano. All he could contemplate with dismay was the new necessity of entertaining everyone for extra days, of being on display, of dealing with Minka's outlandish whims. But none of this could he reveal, without sounding like an absolute whiner.

"Of course not! I need all of you here when our two families are finally united. The Corvivios and Soldevere clans as one! It will be the culmination of all our dreams."

Landon clapped his son on the shoulder. "That's the stuff! No need to fret. It's just a pit on the trail. Go and enjoy yourself on the hunt. There's still a slim chance we might be able to resolve it all remotely. If push comes to shove, I'll announce the delay at tonight's banquet. Make it into an excuse to extend the partying. No one will object, I'm certain."

Landon left with the air of a man juggling too many mental hatchets one-handedly.

Suddenly realizing he was starving, Johrun descended on the buffet and piled a plate high with various easy-to-eat wraps: sweet adzuki bean paste with dates; fish and potato frittata; peanut butter with slices of half-sour pickled melon rind. He munched as he walked, nodding to faces familiar and novel, as he looked for Minka. Finally finished with his breakfast, he gave up his fruitless visual search and just pinged her. His vambrace revealed her location—just a short distance away from the main lodge—and he hustled there.

Approaching the site, he abruptly realized where he was heading.

This was the lot assigned for the new home that would house Johrun and Minka whenever they were resident at Danger Acres, the mate to the fairy-like palace, the Aestival Gazebo of Margravine Thais, which Johrun had selected as their domicile when at Sweetmeats Pasturage. In all the hurly-burly of the past few days, he had neglected to inquire of Minka what kind of home she had chosen to be built for them here. He must make amends for that oversight!

Minka and her school chums, along with a few other curious bystanders, had congregated at the edge of the fenced lot. Minka was playing commands into her vambrace while her cohort laughed and pointed. To his astonishment Johrun observed that a flock of hephaestus machines were busy at work on the structure, even though it appeared already finished.

The building was—or had been—a large but still modest and tasteful chalet, all half-timbers and stucco and expansive windows, plainly influenced by the architecture of the alpine villages on Mittelgebirge—a planet, Johrun recalled, where Minka had once spent some memorable school holidays. Johrun could have imagined being very happy in such a place. But not as it was currently being deformed.

The hephaestus machines under Minka's controls were adding ridiculous candy-colored turrets and useless buttresses, dangerously cantilevered porches, and bulbous oriel windows, all without any regard for esthetics or gracefulness. The plain wooden roof shingles were being dissolved and replaced by round bullseyes of duralloy. The bridal cottage was rapidly being altered to a nightmare.

Johrun came up to Minka as she was exclaiming, "A circus, a carnival, the tents of a flaming rave! That's what's needed here, to house the union of two such ridiculous families!"

Impulsively, an angry Johrun spun Minka around by her shoulder. When she saw him, her manic expression of devilish anarchic delight writhed and morphed into a look of sheer panic.

"Oh, Johrun, where—"

With these words her eyes rolled back into their orbits and she dropped bonelessly to the turf.

Instantly remorseful, Johrun acted decisively, summoning the resort's doctor. During the short wait, he cradled Minka's head and shoulders where she lay.

Anders Braulio approached and looked down with no great worry. "I wouldn't be too concerned, Jay Cee. I've seen her like this before. She exhibited such a response during the pressure of senior exams. A kind of defensive and proactive quasi-dystonic neurasthenia, I believe. Completely harmless. She always recovers swiftly and is right as rain."

Johrun glowered at Braulio. "She never showed such behavior before, in all the span of our growing up together."

"To be fair, Jay Cee, you haven't known her on a day-to-day basis for four years now, as I have."

"Quit calling me 'Jay Cee!' And I refuse to believe such a dramatic collapse is normal, or anything close."

Doctor Fraisine Zahkuala, head of the Danger Acres medical staff, bustled up, a floating stretcher intelligently following her. A petite dark-skinned woman, more striking than pretty, with elaborately braided platinum hair piled high, she was attended by a flock of micro-effectuators and probes.

Minka stirred in Johrun's arms just as the doctor bent down for a look, the swarm of sensors and tools echoing the doctor's movements. Zahkuala's voice was deep yet lilting, the accent of her native metropolis of Grenfell on the world of Averett prominent. "I thought we fixed up this naughty girl when she came to me the other day with the galloping heaves. But look-sees like we need to do a major workup. Let's get her onto the floater."

Minka now jolted fully awake and, registering the doctor, assumed a look in which Johrun detected fear, slyness, and ill-concealed disdain. Pushing off from Johrun, Minka stood with easy alacrity.

"What's all this foolishness? I'm totally fine. Just a small spell. Surely you've heard of planet-lag before? So much interbrane travel over the past week. My system is still adjusting from all the jumps. I don't need any pesky Polly poking."

Braulio said, "I tried to tell them all this, Minka, but they wouldn't listen."

Johrun's scowl cut short Braulio's intervention. "Minka, dearest, don't you think you should let Doctor Zahkuala just perform a few simple tests? You don't want your condition to worsen, whatever it is."

"Ridiculous! I'm fit as a Gilike goat! And I'll prove it in just a short while by bagging the biggest gryffoth of the day! We've got a hunt ahead of us, remember?"

The doctor exchanged a quizzical and resigned look with Johrun. "No way I can jimmy open the boss's daughter's cells without her consent. I don't like it, but such it be."

"Very wise of you, Doctor. Now, let's be off!"

Johrun waved toward the bridal cottage, where the hephaestus machines were busy constructing a new wing along the lines of King Bismuth's legendary Undersea Folly. "What about this mess?"

Minka swiftly brought up the original plans for the chalet and sent them to the builderbots, who instantly began their restoration.

"Can't you enjoy a little jest, Joh? It's all in fun. You need to lighten up! Otherwise you'll be a most intolerable husband!"

Johrun bit his tongue to stop from replying that, contrariwise and more importantly, Minka needed to sober up, or she would be a most intolerable wife. "It's almost time to set out on the safari. Let's go to the stables."

Braulio turned to his four compatriots: Ox, Braheem, Trina, and Viana. Johrun was relieved to see that the two women were not making overfamiliar cow eyes at him nor leering nor giggling. He returned their neutral glances with relief.

"I'll see you four later today," said Braulio. "And I expect to be carried off on your shoulders as the champion hunter, when you see my conquest."

Johrun said, "Have you ever hunted gryffoths before?"

"Never! And I'm not even sure what they are. But my marksman's prowess extends to all prey."

"We'll see."

Johrun watched Minka carefully as they all walked toward the Danger Acres stables. She seemed alert, focused, physically unimpaired, making the kind of negligible conversation anyone might make under similar circumstances. Was it possible that the rigors of her University studies—along with perhaps some compensatory recreations that tended towards the hedonistic, as well as the aforementioned planet-lag—could have indeed weakened her nervous fibers? Johrun resolved to insist on a full checkup once all the pressures of the wedding were behind them.

The other forty-seven hunters were already massed at the stables, making Braulio, Johrun, and Minka the final arrivals. *Bona* Jebb Tipstaff and the four other *bonas* under his command stood ready to assume the guidance of their groups of ten. The stables presented a simple granite facade, fronted by a fenced paddock featuring a neat supergrass turf.

With the completion of the party, the rangy Tipstaff, attired with utilitarian simplicity, began his introductory lecture, leaning one arm on the fence with infinite insouciance. A gaily cocked battered bushman's hat, some proudly preserved facial scars and a sardonic mien conveyed that his words issued from a place of deep experience and uncompromising wisdom concerning all things artemisian.

"Welcome, bold and noble hunters, to Danger Acres, the finest such resort and preserve in all the Quinary. Our goal today is to provide you with the most exciting and rewarding kind of primeval experience, an ancient type of reality seldom encountered in today's effete and cosseted daily round. Human wit and courage, abetted by the finest weaponry, against the wiles and savagery of the most exotic and devious beasts to ever emerge from nature's forge, from Harvester legacy, or from Polly sartorization. Additionally, we hope to return most of you to the lodge still basically alive and sound of mind and body. For any in-field ministering, we will rely on the services of Doctor Odisho Sloat, a man who has seen more than his share of spilled innards."

Tipstaff nodded towards Sloat, a dour, troll-like figure.

"But to avoid any such mishaps from the get-go, it is imperative that you listen closely to the commands of myself and my four subalterns, obeying our instructions to the letter, without fleering contradictions or dilatory obtuseness, real or feigned. This is the practice that will ensure your safety! And of course, all of you have signed liability waivers, should you nonetheless decide to embark on some dangerous caprice.

"I will now turn this stultifying yet essential monologue over to our Weaponeer, Oshry Gaddam."

Gaddam, a potbellied, balding fellow, guided a tall floating arms locker front and center. He opened it to reveal three-score identical rifles precisely racked, elegant and matte black.

"This is your standard Isher Brothers Mark Topaz color-glass condensate long gun. Its ammunition consists of glasma particles which leave the barrel at almost relativistic speed. You may have heard the effect likened to 'hitting the target before you pull the trigger.' In any case, the particles carry great force, and usually one strike anywhere on the body is lethal to most quarries. If you were to fire one round per second for the next month, you could not exhaust the magazine's capacity. Deliberately, there is no smart targeting. You must aim your best with the attached scope. However, there is some trivial artilect programming in the scope that prevents shooting another human, by accident or intention. Of course, all this is familiar to you from the qualifying simulations, which I am happy to report you all aced. Now, if you will step forward in an orderly fashion, we will dispense the rifles."

Johrun, Minka, and Braulio received their weapons. The amateur hunters among the group hefted their guns with pride, awe, and flamboyance. The more experienced shooters quietly inspected the few moving parts of the rifles knowledgably, and employed their sights on the weathervane of the stables and other distant targets to assess if any calibrations were needed. The amazingly lightweight rifle felt familiar in Johrun's grip. He noted that Braulio handled his own gun with some familiarity, perhaps borrowed from that famous Uncle Zerb who had patronized Danger Acres before.

Tipstaff had returned to the forefront of his audience. "Next, the matter of transportation. While we could of course proceed easily in floaters to the district of our hunt, the Caramel Patches, we will instead be travelling via animal mounts. We here at Danger Acres feel that the leisurely ride heightens the anticipation delightfully, as well as conveying some small sense of the rigors that our distant ancestors faced when abroad for game.

Also, the slow progress allows anyone having second thoughts about participating to reconsider and return home on their own. Our mode of transportation frees up any employees from having to divert their efforts from the main safari in such cases. Your mounts, you see, are quite intelligent enough to guide you home. But here is Kellia Brancusi to make that plain!"

The large double doors of the stable opened and a woman appeared. From the waist up she conformed to Gaian norms, with long blonde hair and a winsome face. But her lower half represented the shaggy unclothed flanks of a satyr, from stubby little tail to hooves. A few spilled drops of moisture gleamed in her fur. As she trotted out into the paddock, she was followed by a line of simiak-entauroi, centaurs amalgamated from zebra-like equines and great apes. The velvety black, brown, and auburn pelts of the assorted apes segued subtly into the striped hides of the horse parts.

Brancusi paraded her charges once around the ring for the admiration of the oohing and aahing patrons. She halted at the closed gate and said, "*Mirs* and *Virs,* may I suggest that you acquaint yourselves with my gentle herd? They understand all simple commands, endearments, and mild chastisements. Once you select a steed, they will all reenter the stable to help each other don their saddles, then return unfailingly to your side."

Minka and Johrun made a beeline toward mounts whom they had found congenial in the past. Johrun's was a female named Tinkerbelle, while Minka held her reunion with a large male dubbed Plunger. Tinkerbelle's broad black wide-nostriled nose snuffled Johrun's scent appreciatively, while she groomed his hair gently with blunt fingers. A pleasant odor of ape and horse tickled Johrun's nose.

After patrons and steeds had paired off and the mounts departed to fetch their own tack, the hunters returned their attention to Tipstaff.

"And at last, but not without full import, let us become familiar with our quarry, the gryffoth, or *airavata volante*. Their natural recalcitrance and feistiness prohibit having a live specimen on show for you, but here is a vivid recording."

Tipstaff's vambrace threw forth a colorful shaped-light display showing a single gryffoth, initially standing boldly on the ground.

The creature, plainly a sartorization, consisted of the front half of a woolly mammoth mated to leonine hindquarters, the conjoined bulk sporting enormous wings suggestive of some commensurately massive owl. An informative graphic indicated the gryffoth stood some four meters tall at the shoulders.

While the hunters watched, the gryffoth used its enormous tusks to gouge the soil, coming up with some type of suitcase-sized pillbug that it immediately gulped down, despite the bug's desperate struggles. A second gryffoth approached, and the first expressed its resentment of the newcomer by rearing up on its lion legs, pawing the air with its barrel-like forelegs, and trumpeting as loud as a tornado-warning siren. The rivals smashed their heads against each other and clashed their tusks until the interloper gave up and stumbled away. The victorious gryffoth then began to canter, and when it had got up to speed it took to the air, zooming away until it was just a dot in the distance.

The patrons all manifested a stunned silence. Tipstaff blanked out the display, drily commenting, "The flight of such a monstrosity of course smashes all mere physics. But knowing that the sartors cunningly implanted fifth-force components, under the instinctive mental command of the brutes, explains all. A gryffoth can charge on land at speeds approaching fifty kilometers per hour. Their aerial attacks are four times as fast, and they jink and curvet in the air like a human with a fireworm up his arse. They are not naturally aggressive, but resent humans coming closer than one hundred meters. Did Weaponeer Gaddam forget to mention that each glasma bullet from your rifle decays into harmless muon neutrinos after fifty meters? So be it! There is no art without the challenge of the medium! I suggest you consider all this information intelligently, while we get ready to depart. We have extensive refreshments for the length of our three-hour ride, both coming and going. If all goes well, you will be back to the lodge in plenty of time to compose yourselves for dinner. And should any of you succeed in bagging a gryffoth, the lodge kitchens would gratefully accept the donation of the meat. Otherwise, the standard nano-taxidermy job comes cost-free—although transportation of your trophy off-planet must be arranged on your own nick."

Tipstaff turned away to consult quietly with his four lieutenants, leaving the patrons to murmur among themselves.

Braulio had lost none of his swagger in the light of this formidable presentation. "Does anyone care to wager a few chains on who will be first to bring down one of these pitiful dumbos? I of course will bet heavily on myself."

Johrun regarded Braulio with disbelief. "If you structure the wager so as to nominate which entity will draw first blood, gryffoth or overconfident human, I will be happy to put my bet on the animal."

CHAPTER 7

Several of the simiakentauroi carried the provisions, as well as camp stools and even a compact pavilion that hobermanned open to a colorful mesh-sided canopy offering welcome shade. Verano's equable clime did not preclude sweating. At the half-way mark of the lazy outbound excursion, having just passed through the small forest known as the Kentish Groves, an airy expanse of fronded blue tamarind trees, the party welcomed a stop. Although the simiakentauroi exhibited an easy gait, and although the saddles provided ergo-squirm comfort, many of the riders felt muscularly challenged past the point of ease. So a chance to stand and socialize, with a mug of non-inebriating Nimrod's Punch in one hand and a goat-meat kebab in the other, became more of a festive occasion than it would have seemed in other circumstances—even with Tipstaff and his lieutenants patrolling to make sure no one added liquor from a hip flask to the drinks, in deference to the wise motto that guns and drunkenness were akin to matter and antimatter, the conjunction of which was dangerous to all.

All the hunters on this exclusive outing were wedding guests, and so naturally Johrun and Minka had to function almost as host and hostess, accepting an endless stream of good wishes, the eternal jokes about the imminence of future offspring, and sometimes probing questions about their plans for Verano, once the planet slipped into their hands. Johrun bore up with a patient good will which morphed gradually to actual pleasure the longer Minka behaved herself. Her conniptions of the morning seemed extinct, and she was more like his girl of old, standing hip to hip and arm in arm with him, smiling and making amiable conversation. Anders Braulio, thankfully, had fixed his attentions on Grassella Hatherly, a slinky brunette old enough to be his grandmother, but of course preserved in virginal shape by the highest-grade Polly juvenescence technics that her gigachain fortune deriving from her family's strangelet mines could provide.

The *bonas* began signalling that it was time to mount up again. The simiakentauroi packed everything away. Tipstaff approached Johrun as he slung a leg over Tinkerbelle's girth.

"I hope I did not lay on talk of dangers too thick, *Vir* Johrun. But I always prefer to err on the side of scaring these reckless ninnies into caution, rather than risk losing anyone."

"No, Jebb, you did well." Johrun thought for a moment about asking Tipstaff to keep a special eye on Braulio. But, pleased by Minka's return to normality, and feeling that singling out the fellow would be grossly unfair and might reveal an unworthy prejudice on his part, he said nothing.

In due time the expedition reached the edge of the Caramel Patches, a zone so named because of the lazy butterscotch-colored streams that divided up the land into expansive turfy islets supporting only intermittent scrub brush. The gravel-bedded waters were shallow and almost without current, and the simiakentauroi forded them without even wetting the shoe tips of their riders.

Immediately, everyone came alert, scanning the skies and horizon for gryffoths. But none showed themselves immediately.

Braulio had come to ride alongside Johrun and Minka. "How is it that the lodge itself is not infested with these flying creatures? Surely they could range so far."

"They are geofenced to this locale. Trespassing beyond the borders causes them to feel very painful internal prods."

"A useful technique. It might even be applied to humans. By the way, I understand you've never left this planet."

Before Johrun could formulate an adequate reply, Braulio darted away, laughing. Johrun was left fuming. He looked to Minka to see her reaction, but she seemed intent on leaning forward and whispering foolish nonsense into the large leathery ear of her mount.

Tipstaff cantered up. "Form on me, Tipstaff's Warriors! Satellite coverage reveals the whereabouts of our prey!"

The four other groups had already diverged under their leaders to aim for different points of the compass, and other knots of quarry. The quick dispersal meant that soon Tipstaff and his ten were out of sight of the rest.

Without the full boisterous crowd, narrowed down to only eleven, Johrun instantly felt more isolated, more aware of the small human presence on Verano, just as when he flew alone on his wings through the far precincts of Sweetmeats Pasturage. But for some reason, his wonted contentment with this status, a verity since his earliest youth, had changed to a kind of skittish timorousness, as if his bonds to the planet of his birth had been tainted somehow.

Shrugging off the unnatural feeling as best he could, Johrun concentrated his attention on searching out the gryffoths. And his focus was rewarded in a short time by sight of a flock, a half-dozen soaring specks several kilometers distant. As the humans drew closer, the specks began to resolve into the aerial chimeras: hirsute, trunk-dangling mashups spiralling and acrobatting like elephantine hummingbirds. And the gryffoths took notice of the intruders, as evidenced by some assertive bellowing that carried easily across the narrowing gap.

Suddenly one of the flock peeled away, arrowing at great speed in a descent aimed at the hunters. The creature, a large male, presented the appearance of a hairy meteor arriving at cosmic speeds. The inexperienced hunters froze in place. Johrun managed to pull his rifle out of its saddle holster. But before he could take aim, the gryffoth had soared over their heads, arced back up and around the way it had come.

At the instant of its lowest approach, the hurtling behemoth discharged a substantial bolus of ripe and potent manure which splattered to the ground right at the foot of Braulio's steed, a very near miss. Scents of methane-rich fermenting hay and decomposed pillbug rose up, not completely unpleasant for someone raised around herple dung.

Braulio scowled and shook his fist at the retreating beast. "You flying compost heap! I'll wear your guts for a necklace!"

Urging his simiakentauros to a gallop, Braulio was quickly off toward the herd.

Tipstaff shouted, "After that rascal, if you will, *Vir* Johrun! I can't leave these others unprotected."

Johrun sent Tinkerbelle after Braulio at top speed, uttering some choice curses all the while. The ape half of his steed drew in great snuffling breaths to fuel its run.

He caught up with the ex-student only when Braulio had come to a voluntary stop himself. Tipstaff and the rest of the party were a good kilometer or two behind them now.

The herd had come down to the ground about two hundred meters distant. Females and immature gryffoths were placidly browsing while the males formed a restive defensive perimeter between their families and the humans.

Johrun laid a hand on Braulio's arm to stop him from moving closer. The burly fellow shook him off.

"Don't try to restrain me! I'm determined to get my revenge."

"Revenge? For what? The beast was just making a natural defense. After all, we're here to take its life."

"Call it what you will, I won't stand for it."

"You're just being foolish and pig-headed now. Let's go back to the others. Tipstaff will set up a more favorable ambush for us."

As Johrun tried to reason with Braulio, three of the male gryffoths began to move slowly toward the humans. They started to accelerate, their strapping leonine hindquarters working in uncanny concert with the massive front legs. And even while the chimeras were afoot, their wings seemed to come into play to add propulsion.

Johrun took instant stock of the situation. "We can't outrun them. We must separate, so that we make two targets, not one. Quick, you go that way! If we can each nail one, then maybe the third will relent!"

The two men galloped off in opposite directions.

Johrun halted. His scheme had worked. But not to his advantage.

One gryffoth chased Braulio. Two gryffoths bore down on Johrun.

Johrun brought his rifle up to his shoulder. Trained to this task, Tinkerbelle remained calm and steady. Cold sweat pimpled Johrun's brow and saturated his armpits. Fifty meters for lethality! This was stacking the deck in favor of the animals in a all-too-generous way! He put his eye to the scope, tracking the one beast that was the marginally closer opponent, and his vambrace automatically synced to the gun and began to recite the distance remaining.

"Six-forty meters, six-twenty meters, five-ninety meters . . ."

Johrun heard the signature ionic sizzle of another rifle being discharged. He took his eye away from the scope for a second, and noted with relief that Braulio had bagged his beast, which lay on the turf with an enormous gobbet gouged out of its middle.

"Three-thirteen meters, two-seventy-five meters . . ."

Johrun estimated that if he hit the lead gryffoth, he would have about ten seconds left to target the other and fire. Just doable. With luck and a calm nerve.

"Ninety meters, fifty meters!"

A curious placidity had descended on him. Johrun snapped off the shot as if aiming at a clay pigeon. The lead gryffoth catapulted to the grass head-first, flipping its hindquarters forward over its wooly mammoth portion that had plowed the ground.

Johrun swivelled toward the second behemoth. But before he could fire again, the air-warping clap of his first shot suddenly seemed to have an echo!

At the next moment, Tinkerbelle exploded beneath Johrun, sending the man hurtling through the air to impact the cushioning soil.

Johrun leapt to his feet. Every muscle ached. His rifle was nowhere to be seen. The second racing gryffoth seemed close enough to smell. Could he dive away to one side? No, this was goodbye to everything—

Suddenly the gryffoth was just not there. Instead, an atomized mist of blood, flesh, and bones in an expanding nebula enveloped Johrun, blinding him and knocking him down again.

He clambered erect, wiping gore from his face.

Two riders were approaching, the nearer at a relaxed canter, the farther figure at full gallop. The nearer was Braulio, and coming up fast was Tipstaff.

Braulio dismounted nonchalantly. "You're fine, I take it, despite my lousy aim. I was trying to help you with the second one, but got your mount instead. Awfully sorry."

Johrun confirmed Braulio's supposed bad aim with a glance. Poor Tinkerbelle had been riven by the glasma burst at a point just behind the saddle, resulting in almost instant death from shock and blood loss. Apparently the anti-murder artilect in the scope had not considered this animal target prohibited, despite human proximity.

Tipstaff careened up and leaped off. He quickly assessed Johrun's safety and integrity, then said, "Three prizes so soon! Though one is essentially irrecoverable without a wet-dry vac. I'm willing to call that a day!"

"You saved me. But how?"

Tipstaff hoisted his rifle. "Are you dim enough to imagine that my gun has the same limitations as yours? Your prior training was most egregiously lackluster! I could probably take down a suborbital craft with this. Automatic fire is a nice feature as well. How many glasma particles can dance on the tusks of a gryffoth? I think we achieved an estimate today!"

The rest of Tipstaff's Warriors, amateur division, were arriving now, looking pale and concerned and relieved. Johrun readied a warning for Minka not to rush to embrace him in his filthy state. But the injunction proved unnecessary. She sidled her mount next to Braulio. But instead of proclaiming her relief and thanks, she said, "Anders, that was very bold shooting from you. And Joh, you as well. I'm glad everything worked out okay."

Tipstaff took a towel from one of the pack animals. He handed it to Johrun while rolling his eyes at Minka's bland words.

"Here, go plunge in that closest rivulet and try to get somewhat clean. If you're going to ride double with me, you can't resemble the Inside-Out Wretch of Rackstraw Hollow."

The Indranet vitagraph on Anders Braulio, extensively compiled through deep data-mining by the personalized ferret partials leased from the Indrans themselves, held no surprises: no hidden predispositions, connections, motivations or antisocial behaviors that might have explained what seemed, in a certain suspicious light, to be an attempt on the life of his host. Johrun could piece no plausible causes together from the hard facts.

The Braulio family, long established on the Bricker-predominant world of Maradyth, was solidly well-off, although only in the upper-middle-class sense, not possessing anything like the planetary-level wealth of the Corvivios or Soldevere families. Like many of his relatives across several generations, Braulio had majored in engineering at the University of Saints Fontessa and Kuno on Loudermilk III: specifically, strangelet engineering, a discipline devoted to the many applications of that universal power source. While an undergraduate he had excelled at several sports, including marathon swimming and kine-roistering. Somewhat anomalously for such a physical extrovert and outdoorsy type, he had also been a key member of the University's Choir of Empyrean Throats, supplying a mellow tenor. And in fact membership in that sodality had been responsible for introducing him to Minka, who also sang in the group. An innocent and serendipitous connection if ever there was one. Fair-to-middling grades had not prevented Braulio from crossing the graduation stage, and he already had a nice journeyman's job lined up back home. He had not paraded on the Indranet any outrageous assertions or violent opinions, no blue japes or any greater number of visual testimonials to the joys of inebriation than his peers. The latest set of photos to be found under his Indranet digichop chronicled the post-graduation interplanetary tour he had undertaken with Ox, Braheem, Trina, Viana, and Minka. The visuals represented common and harmless tourist activity: riding the Rainbow Flumeway on Mingming Fan; eating a platter of burglar crabs on the beach at Apfelt Bay; visiting the famous Badway Oasis nightclub on Leschly II. The only slightly off-kilter photo depicted the six graduates foolishly skylarking at the Glass Grotto on Irion, despite a prominent shaped-light sign warning visitors of the recent phagoplasm incursion and declaring usage of the site to be undertaken on an at-risk basis only.

Sitting in a hot whirlpool tub in his room several hours after the safari's return, allowing the bath to soothe his aches while the Polly repair patches worked on his contusions, Johrun commissioned a lesser workup on the other four students. The swift report revealed similarly innocuous and harmless lives.

Faced with such an absence of malevolence, no grudges or greed to serve as reasons simple or complex, overt or covert, Johrun finally decided to accept Braulio's explanation: a sincere desire to help take down the raging bull gryffoth, and bad marksmanship abetted by nerves and the strain of having just faced down his own charging behemoth. No other scenario possessed any likelihood.

Just as he was stepping out of the tub, his vambrace brought a call from Landon Corvivios. Obeying tailored privacy protocols, the device of course excluded transmission of Johrun's nude condition. Johrun's father said, "Son, I need you and Minka to meet the rest of us in the boardroom as soon as possible. This obnoxious delay in your ceremonies has become an unavoidable reality, and we can't keep the circumstances from your bride-to-be any longer. It's not really fair. Although we thought to spare both of you, once you discovered the situation we should also have told her. Now we'll remedy that inequality."

"I'll be there in a moment."

After hastily dressing, Johrun scurried to Minka's room. He found her sitting in an almost trance-like condition at her dressing table, although she was already fully attired for the night's banquet. However, a gentle nudging of her shoulder roused her to a lively condition, and Johrun chalked up her deep abstraction to a host of obvious and excusable preoccupations.

"Oh, Joh, it's you. How are you feeling after that horrid hunt? I've never been on such an ill-fated expedition before."

Johrun took pleasure in Minka's concern. Her entrancing face and charms, at once familiar yet foreign, suddenly leaped into his eye and heart. He felt a sudden access of desire for her, a wish that they could be alone together on some deserted paradisiacal island. He knew he could not act on such a fantasy—at least not at the moment—but at a minimum he wanted to convey the enduring depth of his love for her. Maybe he hadn't been demonstrative enough since her return.

"I'm completely fine, dear. But I would have gladly sacrificed myself if your safety were at stake in the slightest way. I couldn't bear to see you harmed. You mean the world to me."

Minka responded as if Johrun's declaration were a trifling sentiment granted a stranger, such as "I hope you enjoy the show."

"That's very nice. Of course, I feel just the same."

Forced to content himself with this tepid reply, and not daring to ask for more, Johrun switched topics. "You heard the summons from my father just now?"

"Yes, of course. Do you know what it's all about?"

"I do. But better to let him explain."

In the boardroom, two generations of two families stood in a loose aggregation, seemingly arrayed so as to convey a sense of informality and inconsequentiality, as if the possibility of any real crisis were laughable.

Here were the eternal patriarchs and matriarchs, rugged and unique: Xul and Chirelle Corvivios; Brayall and Fern Soldevere. The men and women who had won a world and established its vital role in the Quinary, garnering a fortune along the way. Then their not inconsiderable offspring and their mates, more youthful yet still formidable—Landon and Ilona, Arne and Fallon—who had upheld all the earlier virtues and sophisticated the familial enterprises with new ideas and energy. Johrun felt an upwelling of pride and respect, affection, and awe, as if the eight practically radiated a life-giving light. He vowed always to be worthy of the legacy they represented, and to bring their beloved world of Verano to new heights of excellence.

Without unnecessary ado and in a concise and direct manner, Minka's grandfather Brayall explained the whole situation to her: a formal suit, mediated by the Brickers, asserting that the transmission of their title to Verano was improper, murky somehow, or even null and void.

For the first time in the past couple of days, Johrun thought to ask, "Who is making this ridiculous claim?"

Bryall said, "It's some kind of blind holding firm dubbed the Redhook Combine. Despite our best efforts, we have been unable to secure any information on the principals behind that moniker. And their past dealings are nonexistent. They seemed to have been expressly formed just to pitch in against us."

Minka appeared to be taking in these unsettling revelations with stolid acceptance, a kind of overly phlegmatic affect. "And do you feel you can defeat this charge?"

Minka's mother exhibited her soldier's gung-ho nature. "Absolutely! Our *âmago* is unbreachable. Once we are put under the inquestorial meshes, we will emerge fully vindicated. No one will ever consider stealing our summer world again!"

Minka mulled over this confident boast for a few seconds. "Your beliefs seem indisputable."

Johrun's grandsire Xul hugged the young woman. "The true Soldevere sangfroid! I'm very pleased to see you so stable and philosophical, Minka. Now, let's go entertain our guests!"

When the family members exited the lodge *en masse*, Verano's whispering dusk was half entrenched, unfolding a minute-by-minute evolving sky canvas of the more brilliant constellations. The Sand Whaler's Trident seemed particularly sharp-edged tonight. The pleasant stridulations of the various kinds of leafhoppers carried across the lawns.

The pre-wedding extravaganza scheduled for this evening consisted of an outdoor barbecue-cum-luau-cum-clambake under the benign skies. Vast colorfully brocaded rugs scattered with plump cushions and small low chabudai tables held the two-hundred-plus wedding company in relaxed postures conducive to leisurely drinking and eating and gay conversations. The cooking pits and carving stations and steam tables stood off a little ways, but not so far as to hinder the wafting of delicious odors. Diligent serving staff maintained a steady flow of drinks and platters. An informal style of eating with fingers and thin funnel breads added to the sense of careless abandon. The whole scene was lighted with just enough romantic flickering radiance from scattered torches burning aromatic oils with a rainbow of flame colors.

As if these indulgences were not enough to create a memorable occasion, entertainment from a large company of sylphs, the Troupe of Curious Portents, added to the ambiance. The sylphs hailed from the world known as Ferngully. Each tall, attenuated individual displayed a beguiling androgyny, partially childlike, partially lamia-like. Clad in skintight suits of various harlequin patterns, they performed their intricate weaving dances either singly or in groups to the accompaniment of only tabla drums and piercing flutes. As they meandered sinuously in the midst of the diners, treading with impossible precision among dishes and extended limbs, they maintained utter silence and a supreme impassivity of their expressions that contrasted piquantly with their suggestive motions.

Johrun and Minka were established in the center of the carpeted area, surrounded by their family and the more important of the guests, including High Serendip Eustace Tybalt, the future officiant of their vows, who seemed to have recovered from witnessing Minka's scandalous costume at the masquerade. Although, truth be told, he did cast a skittish glance her way now and then. In fact, the status of each attendee could be precisely mapped to the seating arrangement, with the periphery hosting the least important visitors. And while Johrun was pleased to find Lutramella granted seating within the familial circle, he was less gratified to find Anders Braulio and Minka's other classmates emplaced not much further away.

The evening wore on in a pleasant stream of food and chatter, drink and appreciation of the exotic sylphs. Johrun began to relax and feel at ease. Even the delay necessary to firm up their title to Verano seemed surmountable.

After several hours, Johrun felt a natural need to visit the loo. A battalion of luxurious portable units that flashed away all waste through a small brane-rifter had been established just beyond the seating area, to preclude long walks back to the lodge.

Crossing the carpet, Johrun stopped beside Lutramella and squatted to bring his face level with hers. They had not spoken since she had made her wake-up call that morning, a seeming eon ago, by the gauge of life-threatening activities and mind-whirling conjectures.

The splice raised a soft paw and placed it against Johrun's cheek. Her dark liquid eyes seemed ready to overspill. "I nearly lost you today. And I wasn't there when you needed my help."

"Never believe it, dear Lu! I lead a charmed life."

"Splices are hardened to recognize no such immunity to fate, Joh. It's not wise to claim that privilege."

Johrun took her paw away from his face and kissed it. "You're ever the darling old worrywart, Lu. But this time your trepidations are baseless."

"I sincerely hope so."

Johrun straightened up and moved on.

The row of toilets resembled not a tasteless utilitarian facility but rather a flock of beach cabanas, each separated from the rugs and from its neighbors by a modesty-preserving distance essential when so many cultures mixed. Each single-occupant unit was large enough to feature a small lounge chair and ablution area as well as the functional apparatus.

Johrun pinged the nearest unit and found it vacant. With torchlight at his back, he swung wide the door and strode across the threshold before he realized he was stepping into utter darkness. The cabin's lights were out—

A large hand gripped his throat and a fist slammed against his head.

He regained consciousness with a sourceless but unquestioned sense that only a second or two had passed.

Two hands clutched one of his arms, and he felt his own hand in contact with the metal slope of the toilet bowl.

His assailant was trying to push Johrun's hand into the throat of the disposal mechanism. Teleportation of some important portion of his flesh to an empty multiverse awaited.

Johrun swung his free hand up in an awkward arc, and clouted his attacker. He began to thrash about. He tried to yell, but found he could produce only a croak from his crimped throat.

The thumping noises produced by Johrun's frantic struggles must have unnerved the assailant, or convinced him that the possibility of an easy secret assault was gone. The fellow suddenly shoved Johrun away into a corner and dashed out the door. Johrun was in no position to see his attacker's silhouette against the exterior illumination.

Sore but unharmed, Johrun climbed to his feet. He used his vambrace in flashlight mode, and saw that the mechanical safety interlock on the expulsion mechanism had indeed been vaporized, as by a gun. Johrun knew that the brane rifter also featured software prohibitions against treating living human tissue in the same manner as waste, but suspected that such code, like all software, could be subverted as well.

Johrun adjusted his appearance as well as he could, and splashed some water on his face to help regain his wits. A blast of the cabana's antiseptic gargle, dialed up to maximum strength, soothed his throat somewhat. He used his vambrace and his Danger Acres managerial priorities to mark the unit as DISABLED and to lock the door after he exited.

Once abreast of Lutramella, he crouched down again.

"Did you notice if Braulio was up from his seat in the past few minutes?"

Lutramella looked curious when she registered his low and harshened voice, but did not inquire. "I have had my eye on him, on general principles. But he hasn't moved."

"What of Ox or Braheem?"

Lutramella showed dismay. "It did not occur to me to keep tabs on those two."

"And of course there they sit now, innocent as butterflies."

In the constrained rasp that fortuitously kept his words from being overheard by Lu's neighbors, Johrun explained what had transpired. Lutramella reflected on the matter, then said, "There are easier ways you could have been killed, and ways that would have even made your death look like an accident. This strikes me as vindictiveness of the most bitter sort."

"My thoughts as well. Who to suspect among two hundred strangers? I shall just have to pee in the bushes from now on."

Johrun rejoined Minka, who seemed genuinely pleased to have him back, granting him a kiss once he dropped down to the cushions.

Just as he claimed from one of the waitstaff a new drink specifically formulated to further soothe his throat, the constant music ceased, the sylphs retreated to the fringes of the celebration like dawn-frightened spirits, and all the members of the Corvivios and Soldevere clans stood up. Johrun's father motioned for Johrun and Minka to do the same. A treetop spotlight lit them up, and naturally the entire attention of the crowd was instantly focused on the group.

Grandpa Xul spoke in his commanding and confident voice.

"Kindly friends, both new and old! I cannot tell you how thrilled and pleased I and the rest of my family are that you have all honored us with your attendance at these celebrations in anticipation of a most joyous of culminating ceremonies, the wedding of Johrun Corvivios to Minka Soldevere, and hence the union of our two clans. These past few days have been the highlight of my long life, and I could wish to see them prolonged for an indefinite time. And, as matters eventuate, I am going to get my wish, to some small and not entirely amenable degree. Intensely vital business matters, arising out of the blue, demand the off-planet presence of our conjoined boards of directors, for just a few extra days. Perforce, the wedding must await our return.

Naturally, we cannot hold any of you here against your wishes, acknowledging that you all have equally pressing concerns of your own back home. But if continuing free accommodations and all the amusements that Danger Acres can provide are any inducement to remain, then I hope you will. And as additional small kumshaw to indicate our high regard for your attentions and to palliate any inconvenience, allow me to do this!"

One tap on Xul's vambrace summoned up an instant sonic response from two hundred other vambraces: a chorus of the universal sound icon for "funds received."

Johrun's own vambrace registered not funds, but a silent message from Xul: *10K chains apiece to each guest. Even to your foolishly liberated chimeric wetnurse!*

Two million chains dispersed without a quibble, in addition to all prior and future costs associated with the wedding. Johrun experienced a kind of mortified pride. Again, this family heritage was a weighty load.

The attendees erupted in massed applause and hoots that went on for minutes. The food preparers caused their cooking fires to roar skyward, the drinks flowed like floodwaters, and the sylphs launched into an ecstatic dervishing propelled by maenad music.

By the time the festivities were over, and Johrun conducted a weary Minka back to her room and bade her goodnight, he had almost forgotten the attack in the WC. But memory of it resurfaced with a jolt, and caused him to doublecheck any hiding places in his room, and to triple lock his door.

In the morning, after breakfast, the family members who were about to journey to Bodenshire to quell the machinations of the mysterious Redhook Combine assembled outside the lodge. Johrun and Minka joined them, but no grand show was made of their departure, and in fact any of the guests who might have been inquisitive had been subtly discouraged from tagging along as spectators. Lutramella, however, had shown up unbidden and was readily accepted into the party.

The ten humans and the splice marched solemnly down the path that led to the landing site where the Devilbuster ketch named *Against the Whelm*, the Corvivios family craft that had ferried them from Sweetmeats Pasturage, awaited.

Johrun experienced a nearly overwhelming storm of emotions: apprehension, pride, affirmation, eagerness, anxiety, love, disappointment, irritation, a longing for closure. He almost envied those who would be leaving Verano, despite any trials that faced them. How he would endure the wait without going round the bend was less than clear—especially with the lingering presence of some assassin to consider. He wondered if he should bring the capable figure of *Bona* Tipstaff into the affair as his confidante and helper.

At the ship, the family exchanged hugs, kisses, and reassurances that all would be well, and be soon mended. Johrun's elders trooped up the short ramp, each one turning at the portal to wave goodbye. Their faces looked at once utterly familiar and utterly foreign.

The ramp retracted, the hull assumed integrity, the ship lifted.

When it was only about a kilometer high, looking like a child's toy, *Against the Whelm* and all it contained, a fragile cargo of love and hope and history, was transformed without warning from a soaring confident craft into a massive wavefront of radiation.

When Johrun could see again, with eyes he wished were blind, nothing of the ship—or its beloved occupants—remained.

CHAPTER 8

Oz Queloz was provably not a man without sympathy. Molded of the common clay of all mankind, a superior grade in fact, he possessed a warm heart, a sharp and receptive intellect and a kindly disposition. On the other hand, he was by trade and nature a licensed Invigilator, the nearest thing to a professional interstellar lawman that the Quinary offered, and that meant that he was merciless in his quest for justice; decisive and perhaps even somewhat arbitrary in his conclusions and discriminations; and inclined to treat indisputable malefactors with a heavy stick minus any juicy carrot.

Affiliated with the military-grade security forces of the Motivators—the same bunch that had come to Verano just a few days ago to pack up the rustlers captured at Sweetmeats Pasturage—he had a remit wider than that force's standing directives, which were merely to suppress unsanctioned hostilities, corral prisoners, and enforce Quinary rulings. Often the only Quinary representative for lightyears around, he could legally function as jurist and hangman, overriding the wishes and protocols of local law enforcement.

Of course, in his current assignment—rationalizing the destruction of the Verano-registered braneship *Against the Whelm*—he had no planetary police with whom to interface. This was a situation both salutary and restrictive. No interference, no help.

All this Johrun Corvivios knew—or had learned or intuited—after three days of dealing with Queloz. The affable yet brusque fellow—a lanky yet solid bruiser with a chin like an alchemist's ancient stone mortar, save for its central dimple; a flyaway mop of wheat-colored hair; and an omnipresent sidearm which *Bona* Tipstaff had identified as the maximally lethal Hoffnung boson disruptor—had, with seemingly unlimited but perhaps deliberately distracting candor, revealed everything about himself in days of measured but relentless questioning and probing, ever since he had arrived some forty-eight hours after the destruction of all of Johrun's dreams and all his reasons for existing. Five days of mental torture, an intensity and a kind of pain unthinkable before the tragedy, but now seemingly inevitable and eternal. Any of the famous palliative effects of time passing, the conferring of cold but comforting wisdom, had not yet accumulated in this short span, and Johrun could not foresee how they ever would.

The first seconds, the first minutes after the cataclysmic evaporation of the airborne family ship had consisted of stunned immobility, succeeded by piercing, bestial cries and wailings, wrung from the belly, the soul, and the very fiber of Johrun's self. Minka had fallen to the ground insensible. Lutramella had loosed an endlessly protracted, uniquely chimeric sound that Johrun hoped never to hear again, for it evoked the cries of an infant being strangled while lying in a bed of hot coals.

Of course, dozens, scores, seemingly the whole establishment came running. Helpers flocked to uphold Johrun and pick Minka up off the ground. Some primitive noises resembling words were dredged from the pureed soup that now seemed to fill Johrun's skull. Apparently he made himself understood, limned the incredible situation with staccato phrases and helpless gestures.

Doctor Fraisine Zahkuala and her co-workers raced up. When she learned what had happened, she immediately insisted that every single individual on the premises undergo high-grade anti-radiation treatment. Whatever the exact nature of the explosion, the complete destruction of the vessel, even a kilometer high, argued for a huge sleeting release of energetic particles injurious to cells and tissues, organs, and prosthetics.

And so the first twenty-four hours had been devoted to medicining—and reassuring—all the guests and staff. Johrun had to make a hundred decisions, issue a hundred orders. Minka remained catatonic in her room. In taking care of others, he managed to put his private anguish on a shelf for that busy interval. At least until it came time to snatch a few hours of troubled sleep. Then the sheer titanic impossibility of events, the impassable wall they had erected between him and any happy future, reasserted their dominance in a parade of ghastly images, real and imaginary, mixed with more tender memories that burned implacably and with savage irony due to their very tenderness.

By the end of that first stretch of emergency prophylaxis, Doctor Zahkuala felt secure in deeming all her patients utterly saved, hale, and hearty. Furthermore, no residual radiation remained in the environment—a finding consistent with a catastrophic failure of the ship's strangelet reactor. So Johrun could erase one potential debt from his ledger of worries. At least Danger Acres had not killed everyone.

The next twenty-four hours consisted in arranging the mass evacuation of guests. Danger Acres could not, of course, go on as if it were business as usual. The majority of the well-off wedding guests had arrived in their own braneships, and so they had a ready means of departure. Socially interconnected as the guests were, an elite network of six degrees of separation or less, those who had ships handy arranged to carry those who did not. So in a mass exodus all the revelers left. Saying goodbye to two hundred folks, accepting their commiserations, left Johrun a limp sack of bitter woe.

The regular guests then had to be dealt with. Luckily, the capacious tourist liner christened *Girl of the Pleasaunce* was due to arrive at Verano in her regular circuit that very day. When she emerged from branespace, she was walloped by the news of the disaster. All those preparing to disembark on Verano got an instant change of plans. Goodbye vacation, hello circuitous return home. As a tribute to the compassionate spirit of the visitors, no one even complained of the inconvenience. The instant refunds and a stipend for extra expenses authorized by Johrun (in comatose Minka's name) might of course have elicited such fine feelings. Soon the liner was loaded with the current guests and underway to her next stop, the Harvester world of Venex Tertius, whose untethered continents floated in complex circuits around the globe, providing leisurely passage through a thousand different artificial climates. Meanwhile, all future bookings were cancelled via the Indranet.

That left the staff. No one wanted to leave. Nor did Johrun want them to go. Faint, almost impossible glimmerings of a day far in the future, when the business might resume, and the necessity for reassembling all the well-trained personnel, counseled Johrun to keep the workers close. He mandated an indefinite continuation of pay without duties, leaving the workers to entertain themselves in their dormitories and on the premises as best they could.

The response of *Bona* Jebb Tipstaff was typical of the employees. The safari guide hugged Johrun in an embrace of steel, then held him at arm's length. Tears coursed the guide's cheeks.

"Whatever you need, young pard, my arm or gun or guts, you've got it. The Soldevere and the Corvivios families—they are mine in all but name."

"Thank you, Jebb. That counts for everything."

Throughout these trials, there had been one pillar of support who upheld Johrun so intimately, so essentially, that he barely acknowledged her as a separate entity. She seemed instead some inner daimon, a stalwart bedrock fragment of his own psyche, whom he could rely on perpetually, night or day.

Lutramella brought him meals when he forgot to eat. She sat by his bed, stroking his brow, as he tried to find sleep. She anticipated tasks that needed doing and did them. She made him shower and change his clothes. She held him while he wept. Not many words were exchanged between them, but the important things could not be said, only witnessed or enacted.

Additionally, Lutramella kept Johrun informed of Minka's recovery. The splice could not get in to see the woman herself, however, because of a cordon of self-appointed caretakers who stressed the need for peace and no distractions.

The graduates of Saint Squared U—Braulio, Ox, Braheem, Trina, and Viana—had not departed with all the others. In fact, the *Bastard of Bungo* was the only non-family ship still on the grounds. Minka's friends had moved into her suite and set up a round-the-clock watch on her, with regular visits from Doctor Zahkuala. Lutramella conveyed bulletins that found Minka awake and mostly sensible, but weak and with wandering attention. She was subsisting mostly on broth and juices.

Johrun added his grief for her to the ocean of grief for their dead families, and found it hard to discern the increase.

Then, on the third day, arrived a one-man ship dubbed *The Wine of Astonishment.*

The craft, a Miran Hedgehopper, was hardened for travel in those faster-than-fast branes inimical to human life, the routes that the quick artilect drones took. Inside, Johrun later learned, was a lazarus tank to hold the passenger. The occupant of the ship would be scientifically killed prior to leaving the human universe, seeded with Smalls zeptocrobes, then revived once he or she successfully transited the death zone. The execution process was said to be excruciating, the revival more so. (And the process worked not at all in the case of everyday accidental deaths.) But such a craft could deliver its corpse at top speed wherever the revenant was needed.

Johrun had received notice of the ship's arrival in the Wayward's Spinel system, and so—Lutramella by his side—he was waiting outdoors for its descent and touchdown.

Port opened, ramp extruded. Down came the foreannounced Oz Queloz, frowning like a minor demigod frustrated in his pursuit of some mortal paramour. Smelling of some brisk peppery cologne, the Invigilator invaded Johrun's personal space, then demanded, "What cretinous jugheaded jackass sent all my goddamn suspects away?"

Instantly Johrun turned sick inside. He felt all the blood flow from his face and pool in his feet, which somehow nonetheless felt cold as ice. How indeed could he have been so stupid? If the destruction of *Against the Whelm* had been a deliberately engineered act—a terrible thought Johrun had been mostly successful in keeping at bay—then the culprit in all likelihood would have been one of the many guests, and Johrun had blithely dismissed them all from the scene of the crime, sending them scurrying to freedom. But he had only wanted to forget everything, to be alone and wallow in a black and wordless despair.

"But I— I just—" Lutramella let out a small growl, as if she were ready to attack Queloz.

Queloz's full-bodied laugh belled out, and he gripped Johrun's bicep and shook him like a rag doll. "Relax, relax! There was no way you could have enforced their stay. And every single one of your fled guests has already been met—or will be met—and plucked by my peers. This in addition to individual vitagraph workups of a density and depth and focus that simple citizens can never command. The ones we contacted were all deemed as innocent as baby chicks, and I suspect the rest will be proven clean as well."

Johrun relaxed a tad, and Lutramella emerged from her coiled state.

"To be honest, my gut informs me that the sad end of your family ship was a standard failure of the strangelet drive—rare but not unknown. Believe me, the Brickers don't publicize such things. Decillion to one odds. But then again, there are a billion flights made in the Quinary every day, so you do the math. You recall the incident of the *Hannu Mora*, out of Warsaw Seven, do you not? No? Two thousand souls lost just upon takeoff, much the same as in your case. Nevertheless, I had to see how you'd react to my indignant thrust, didn't I? Were you mastermind or dupe, heinous or holy? Or somewhat admixed? Such are the primitive but potent strategies of us Invigilators, rough tactics which have not changed since the days when our species was living in caves on Gaia!"

Johrun's limbs loosened all the way. He did not feel relieved or disburdened from recent horrors, but somehow the presence of Queloz had lifted some tiny portion of responsibility off his back. "I— I see. Well, where do we go from here?"

"No evidence left to parse, so it's all face-to-face work among the staff. And I understand that the Soldevere heir is still present, with some of her old classmates?"

"Yes, Minka and her friends are here."

"Perfect! Then we begin with you. I need to know of any suspicions or theories you might harbor, also any untoward incidents of the recent past. But first, I require food and drink! Being reborn always ramps up my appetites! Come, do you keep all your guests standing out forever under this unnervingly wholesome amethyst sun?"

There followed three days of intensive questioning, commencing with Johrun.

Johrun laid out everything that had preceded the deaths of the two families, including the assault on him in the loo. Queloz pondered the account for a long time in silence, then said, "How can we link these two disparate events? If you were the sole object of someone's hatred, then sabotaging the ship would not harm you directly, since everyone knew you would not be on it. Contrarily, if someone wanted to remove your elder family members from existence, then why attack you earlier, and not go straight for the real targets? No, I can't make a solid link at this point. Better to regard the attack on you as the work of some jealous or insane grudge-holder."

"But suppose someone just wanted to harm Danger Acres and Sweetmeats Pasturage in general?"

"Then why murder? A step too far and cumbersome. Wouldn't damaging your physical plant or hurting some guests or discrediting your reputation have been a better strategy? The twin corporations have not been ruined by this disaster. In fact, if you'll permit a brutal observation, the brushwood in the line of command has been pruned. You and Minka inherit streamlined enterprises, ready for a new era of increased profits distributed into fewer pockets."

Johrun saw crimson, and raised a fist toward Queloz. He was stopped by the wry look on the Invigilator's face, and calmed down.

"Another telling jab?"

"Precisely! Your new wisdom now qualifies you as my junior assistant in the rest of the proceedings!"

Queloz had every Danger Acres employee into his office for an interview, then had them all back again. His initial conclusions: no complicity anywhere. Finally there remained only Minka and her nursemaids.

As Johrun and Queloz approached Minka's apartments, Johrun said, "Why do you not use some kind of telltale gadget in these sessions?"

"That arms race has been won by the culprits, I fear. There is currently no machine extant that cannot be foiled by various undetectable stratagems."

"What of the inquestorial meshes?"

"The meshes only measure one's *âmago,* an unimpeachable but vague indicator of existential contingency, or core centrality — entanglement, so to speak, between actor and act. For instance, I ask you, under the meshes, 'Did you cause the Corvivios ship to explode?' You reply, 'No.' Your *âmago* waxes bright or wanes dim on the readouts. This indicates that you embrace my question as somehow fundamental to your life pattern or destiny. Or you flinch from it as if from a wrenching deracination, baffled and repelled. The disaster means something vital to you, or not. But what, exactly? Truth or falsity, guilt or innocence do not manifest."

Johrun considered this. "So on Bodenshire, my grandsire Xul would have been asked, 'Did Honko Drowne make over the deed to Verano to you?'"

"Precisely! And the brilliant shine of his *âmago* would have told the Bricker examiners all they needed to know."

Present for most of the other questionings, Lutramella had begged off from today's.

"Your fiancée disdains me, Joh. My presence would only hinder the search for truth."

Much as he hated to affirm this, Johrun had to admit Lutramella was correct. Reluctantly, he had left her behind.

Queloz and Johrun gained admittance to Minka's rooms after pinging her permission, and for the first time since that fateful day of the explosion Johrun saw his fiancée.

Sitting up in bed among a plethora of pillows, Minka looked ghostly and thin, hollow-eyed and gray-skinned. Her lustrous hair was drab. Her quarters had a sickly smell to them. Her friends sat in various chairs, close by and across the room. Their expressions ranged from bored—Anders Braulio—to empathetic—the women and Braheem. Ox's anomalous countenance revealed little.

Minka made no special greeting to Johrun, but just gave a feeble nod in his direction.

Queloz advanced to her bedside and took her hand. Another ploy, wondered Johrun, to gauge the reality of her condition, to surreptitiously measure a pulse or nervous clamminess of skin?

"*Mir* Soldevere, I cannot fully express my sorrow for your loss. But with your help, I might be able to lay to rest any doubts, quibbles or phantoms that still attend the tragedy, and provide you with some small measure of solid perspective that will lead to a timely resuscitation of your life."

Minka's voice matched her appearance. "Ask what you will. Nothing matters to me any longer."

Johrun's heart hurt at this response, although it mirrored his own condition. His petrified emotions began to show a few cracks, to shed a few flakes of self-pity and obstinate remorse. He resolved then that he had to start to pull himself out of the trough of despondence, so that he could be a pillar of strength for Minka, and an honor to the memory of those loved ones who had perished.

Queloz took Minka through the standard line of questioning that Johrun had heard during the other interviews. Despite general correspondences from session to session, there was always a uniquely personal slant to Queloz's probes. Finally he concluded by asking, "And how will you proceed from here, *Mir* Soldevere? Will you carry forward the legacy of your family, or cast it all down?"

"I can't say right now. The days ahead are lost in a fog of anguish."

Queloz turned his attention away from Minka and toward the others.

"If I may see each of you individually in the adjacent chamber, I believe we may be able to bring my researches to a conclusion right now."

One by one Minka's classmates went off for private interrogation, Ox volunteering to go first. Johrun regarded the mute and not particularly sorrowful-looking Anders Braulio askance. Had Braulio tried to kill him during the hunt? Had he been behind the ambush in the WC, even if his had not been the actual hand that had clamped on Johrun's throat?

A sudden memory, buried until now by the welter of events, jumped out at Johrun. Braulio's field of study had been strangelet engineering! Could he have somehow sabotaged the engines of *Against the Whelm*?

Johrun practically quivered in place until Queloz emerged from interviewing Ox.

"*Vir* Queloz, I need to see you outside for a moment."

The Invigilator lifted one eyebrow quizzically. "Indeed."

Out in the corridor, at some remove from Minka's chambers, Johrun quickly spilled his thoughts. Queloz listened impartially, then said, "This is a weighty tidbit already known to me from

Braulio's vitagraph. So of course, I immediately pulled up all the pre-flight telemetry from *Against the Whelm,* extending back to the moment that *Vir* Braulio and company arrived on Verano. Audiovisual feeds and instrument dumps in toto. There is, I am frustrated to report, nothing anomalous."

Crestfallen, Johrun said, "I suppose the obvious solution is never the correct one."

"Not so. But neither is the obvious solution *always* the correct one."

Back in Minka's suite, Queloz soon reached the end of questioning. He and Viana emerged from their privacy, and Queloz said, "I am ready to render my official report now. I stipulate that delivery of same does not stamp the case permanently solved or foreclosed. It means only that we have reached a certain plateau of knowledge. New developments or insights might cause a burst of activity at any time hence. *Mir* Soldevere, would you please send your friends away? You are free to share my report with anyone you wish, after I deliver it—formal copies will also post to your vambraces—but I do not desire to make a public spectacle of it now."

"Please, do as he asks," Minka said.

When the crowd had left the trio in privacy, Queloz launched into his précis.

"Here are the background occurrences relevant to the explosion onboard *Against the Whelm.* First, an unknown actor known as the Redhook Combine instigated a suit against the Corvivios and Soldevere families, contesting your ownership of Verano. This campaign was the direct cause of the launching and subsequent destruction of your ship. Had there been no need to travel to Bodenshire, the ship with all your relatives onboard would not have launched. But of course, the ship would have been used at some point in the near future, to return to

Sweetmeats Pasturage, at which point it might or might not have experienced an identical engine failure.

"Second, Johrun Corvivios was assaulted the night before the launch, by an unidentified person working either alone or in cahoots with others. I do not include in my list the dangers he experienced during the recent safari, since those do not constitute a provable attempted murder, but might well have been sheer happenstance.

"Now, can we decisively infer from these data that a plot is afoot to deprive your families of their holdings, by legal or illegal means, up to and including assassination? I fear the links cannot be forged, for lack of hard evidence. And in fact, certain factors militate against such a conclusion. The suit by Redhook must have some validity, or the Brickers would not have allowed it to be filed. Why would your opponents risk queering their judicial victory by attempting murder? And who were their agents on the planet, if all the guests, staff members, and principals have been cleared? Furthermore, if only the elder generations stood in the way, why bother attacking Johrun, the inconsequential scion? You'll pardon that impartial description, I hope, *Vir* Corvivios. And why was there no similar attempt to remove young Minka from the gameboard?

"But neither can the antithesis to this thesis be dismissed with total insouciance. In fact, your clans might very well be under attack by forces unknown, for reasons unknown. I cannot firmly endorse either interpretation of events, but only state that for the moment, I lean ever so slightly toward regarding the tragic demise of your extended families as an entropic failure of fallible Motivator technics—especially in light of similar past catastrophes. I would suggest that you pursue a suit against that arm of the Quinary, although I cannot offer sensible odds on your success."

Johrun digested this report. Minka seemed likewise contemplative. Johrun wished that Lutramella had been present to hear everything, and offer her advice and opinion. He would have to let her read the formal statement later.

Minka finally spoke, with world-weary lassitude. "Your conclusions are as acceptable as any paltry deeds which one could expect from a level-headed but basically dull civil servant. Please go now, and send my friends back in."

Johrun stepped forward with imploring gestures. "Minka—"

"No, you go too, Joh."

Johrun and Queloz left. Braulio made a point of roughly brushing his shoulder against Johrun as they traded places.

Down in the hauntingly empty lobby of the lodge, Queloz said, "I truly wish I could have provided greater closure, an enemy to lash out at, a face to smite in return for the blows you have suffered. But it was not within my powers. Yet you may rest assured, *Vir* Corvivios, that your affairs remain on my docket. I do not consider this case settled to my own satisfaction. And the itchy curiosity of an Invigilator is to be both feared by the malefactor and desired by the victim. The informational tentacles and remote effectuators of the Invigilator corps extend far and wide. If I learn of anything that will bring more certainty to your affairs, you and *Mir* Soldevere will hear from me at once! But now, I fear, I must die again, to be reborn where I am next needed."

Johrun shook Queloz's hand and thanked him sincerely. Despite such a tenuous and frustrating ending to the official inquiry, Johrun felt they had taken one step forward toward some dimly sensed return to normality, however shattered and glued-together such a life would inescapably be.

The two men walked together to *The Wine of Astonishment*. Queloz entered his ship in order to be killed and tanked for revival far away. The craft took off.

Irrationally half-fearing another explosion, Johrun watched *The Wine of Astonishment* ascend until it had dwindled to a dot. He began to turn away. But then motion in the skies caught his attention.

A small ship was dropping down to Verano. Had something made Queloz return? Johrun pinged the craft. It returned his query with its name: *Due Tidings Ninety-seven.*

The ship settled to Verano's sweet turf. In brief course it disgorged a lone occupant, a man. The unimposing fellow was short and fussy-looking, dressed with no style. He squinted against the mild light, as if he regarded all of nature as a crafty shyster.

Spotting Johrun, the visitor trotted over. He offered his limp hand perfunctorily.

"*Vir* Corvivios, yes? My name is Fidelio Fang-Blenny. I am a Bricker Steward of the Magenta Distinction, and I am here to impound your planet."

CHAPTER 9

As bureaucrats went, the gauche Fidelio Fang-Blenny was not the common type who cared to pad out his work routines with useless fluff and nonsense so as to exert himself minimally, impede progress, and torture his clients with delays and needless hinderances. Rather he was the type of punctilious vambrace-fusspot who trotted deliberately through every mandated clause and codicil of the regulations he was enforcing in the most stringent manner, brooking no requests for exceptional treatment or mercy. He invested no emotions in his tasks, neither glee nor remorse, pride of accomplishment or solidarity with his employers. It was as if he were a kind of soulless Turing machine whose invariable output could be precisely predicted based on the coded input.

For this reason, when Johrun stutteringly demanded what this intruder could possibly mean by his impossible statement—"impound the planet"—Fang-Blenny insisted that he would not be troubled to repeat himself, and since his message was intended equally for *Mir* Minka Soldevere, he must insist that she be fetched to hear it at the same time that Johrun did.

Johrun raced back to Minka's room and explained what had just happened. Her friends listened attentively as well, but without any particular sentiments discernible. Minka, however, was motivated to hastily throw back her covers and slide out of bed, wearing just black leggings and a white camisole. Barefoot, she hastened out of the room, attended by her cheering squad.

Johrun followed, detouring only to fetch Lutramella.

"Joh, what's the matter?"

"I don't really know, but I suspect the worst."

"Let's face it together then."

Outside, Johrun discovered Fang-Blenny still planted like a stolid goalpost exactly where Johrun had left him. Minka was haranguing the man for an explanation of his mission, but he stayed mum, awaiting Johrun. A few of the curious laid-off Danger Acres workers had assembled as well.

When Johrun and Lutramella arrived, the Steward of the Magenta Distinction snapped to life as if a switch had been flicked.

"*Vir* Soldevere, *Mir* Corvivios. You are aware of the suit against your families regarding the legal title to the planet known as Verano in the Wayward's Spinel system. You are also aware that the deadline for responding to this suit came and went two days ago."

Johrun interrupted. "We were not informed by our elders of the exact deadline. We knew only that it was imminent and pressing, and that they were promptly dealing with it."

"You have now been so informed. Thus any claim of ignorance is negated and becomes null and void as a legitimate objection to my mission."

Johrun protested. "But our clan elders fully intended to engage with the authorities in good faith before—before they died."

"All that matters is their null response. Causes for the dereliction are irrelevant. And thus, having failed to respond in a timely manner to the suit, your families have forfeited all defense and all preexisting claims to the planet. This is not to stipulate that the Redhook Combine automatically assumes ownership of Verano, but only that their patents may now be examined for validity. Consequently, at this point in time Verano exists in a kind of legal limbo or state of receivership, without permanent owners. As the original issuer of the planetary title, the Brickers become wardens, guardians and/or regents of Verano until such time as a new permanent owner is settled."

"What does all this mean in a practical sense?" Minka demanded.

"Only this. As the current heirs to the old and negated title —and please find attached an official statement of condolences on the deaths of your progenitors—you two are disbarred immediately from all further access to the planet, its holdings, assets, profits, savings, futures, bonds, chattels, intellectual properties, and Indranet representations, as well as, of course, all liens and encumbrances. Meanwhile, the planet shall be maintained at highest functionality, and all its enterprises conducted, under Bricker Stewardship, of which I am the ultimate plenipotentiary, invested with all condign dominions and magisterial powers."

Minka said, "You mean to say you are stepping into my family's shoes and taking over the planet, and kicking us out?"

"That is a non-technical statement of my brief, but essentially correct. Do you understand?"

"Of course I understand!" Minka yelled. "But I won't let you!"

"And you, *Vir* Corvivios? Do you understand?"

Johrun's mind was awhirl. First the tragic deaths of his folks, then this disinheritance. What more could possibly go wrong? "Yes, but—"

"In accordance with all outstanding Bricker user agreements, your statements of comprehension constitute the compliance and assent necessary to enact my orders."

Fang-Blenny triggered a script on his vambrace.

Instantly, from a loss of haptic syncing, Johrun knew his own vambrace was dead. He saw Minka regarding her own quiescent Indranet cuff with astonishment.

"You—you've deplatformed us!"

"This is a potentially libelous misapprehension. Deplatforming means to deprive a user of selected Quinary services based on some crime or infraction. You two have committed no crime or infraction, and therefore cannot be subject to deplatforming. I have merely put a lock on all your fiscal accounts, both personal and corporate. You both have zero assets now with which to fund such things as your Indranet connections. Any outstanding balances have been relegated to termination fees. This sequestering of funds is an entirely different state of affairs from deplatforming, as I think you will admit."

Minka fell to weeping against Braulio's shirtfront. Her classmates crowded around her, patting her back and making soothing sounds.

Johrun said, "How are we expected to survive? Without a single link or chain to our names, we cannot hire lodgings here. And you wanted us to leave Verano, I believe. How can we even buy a ticket on the next cruise ship?"

"We do not demand the impossible from you. Your tickets offplanet have already been purchased out of Bricker exigency funding. You will both depart on the next herple-meat freighter leaving Sweetmeats Pasturage, in approximately three days. There is ample rudimentary passenger space adjacent to the cargo area. The freighter will convey you to Bustard's Gully, where you will happily discover a number of employment opportunities at the meat refineries that require no prior experience, such as degristling assistant, haunch hanger, and sluice laver. Until then, you may accumulate room and board charges here at the lodge to the amount of no more than ten chains per diem. That is sufficient to provide a cot in the janitorial storeroom and three daily rations of mycoprotein shakes. Of course, you will be expected to reimburse all these outlays once you do undertake longterm employment."

Anders Braulio spoke up. The decorative silver mites in his hair now moved at an agitated pace in their drunkard's walk, as if to mirror his own upset.

"None of this will be necessary, you pompous functionary! And you may cancel all those anticipated charges for *Mir Soldevere*. Minka is leaving the planet with me, aboard my ship. I will take her to my family's home on Maradyth."

Minka responded by ceasing her sniffling and looking up worshipfully at Braulio's proud countenance.

Fang-Blenny responded with a bookkeeper's dispassion. "The Quinary appreciates your assumption of these costs. Now I must establish myself in the front office and begin to revive this enterprise. Anyone may find me there if I am legitimately needed."

The busy Steward of the Magenta Distinction set off for the lodge.

Poleaxed by the instant cratering of all his fortunes, all his visions, all his goals and roles in life, the implicit status, duties, and privileges that heretofore had been as much a natural part of his existence as breathing, Johrun could not imagine at first how to respond to this outcome. The universe seemed to have been inverted and reconstituted along absurd dimensions.

He took a few steps toward Minka, reached out imploringly. "Minka, don't go with him. Stay with me. We can face this side by side, retrieve our dreams, rebuild our life together. This nightmare will soon end, and we will be restored to our birthright. This I believe!"

Minka looked coldly and calculatingly at her quondam husband-to-be. "Can you guarantee this optimistic fairy tale? How will we keep body and soul together until that possibly faroff day of our redemption, wandering without a link to our names?"

"I can guarantee nothing but my undying love! And surely if we yoke our energies and resources and skills together, nothing can stand in our way."

Minka's face assumed a seemingly genuine look of disappointment and regret. "Joh, what we had—it's not dead, but it's—it's in abeyance. These dread circumstances have overruled our own desires. I need safety and support and stability, now more than ever. And you cannot offer me any of that, can you?"

Johrun's silence was tacit admission of the truth of her statement.

Braulio took a victor's magnanimous tone. "Don't make a big deal of this, Jay Cee. Just a small detour for you, I'm certain. A little change will perk up your life. We all get into a rut. Good to try the unexpected. Degristling assistant sounds like a career path with a fine future. And you needn't worry about your girl. Minka will be well cared for on Maradyth. She already knows my parents from another holiday, and they're crazy about her. In just an hour or so, we'll be on our way."

Johrun waited for Minka to contradict any of this insulting speech, but she said nothing. He turned and stalked blindly away in disgust.

After a dozen meters, a hand dropping upon his shoulder from behind stopped his impulsive flight. Johrun spun around, fists cocked, eager for a fight, whether it were Fang-Blenny or Braulio at his back.

The sight of Lutramella drained all the starch and bitterness out of him. Her sleek furry damp-nosed face, wearing a sad expression and constituting one of his oldest memories, instantly catapulted him back to childhood. He began to weep, this time not, as during the past few days, for his dead parents and grandparents, and Minka's dead relatives, but for his own downfall.

Lutramella did something she had not done in many, many years. She cupped his jaw and licked the tears from his cheeks with a raspy pink tongue. Then she wetted her own paws with her saliva and slicked back the stray hairs from her charge's temples.

Startled by this old devotion, Johrun regained control of his emotions. He drew the back of his forearm under his flowing nose.

"Oh, Lu, but what can we do in our bankrupt state? How can we ever win back our adored world?"

"I am glad to hear you say 'we,' Joh, because when you say 'we,' that means you'll accept what I bring to our quest."

"And what's that?"

"Have you forgotten your own generosity so soon? You settled forty thousand chains on me. And then your grandsire gave me another ten, when he made kumshaw to the wedding guests. Fifty thousand chains, Joh! That's a fortune. Maybe not by your old standards, but by our new ones it is." Lutramella held up her vambrace with a big smile. "And remember this? An account prepaid for ten years! You see, what you sowed upon the waters comes back to you!"

Johrun experienced a pang like a hot knife in his heart, both sweet and sharp. Nothing he had ever done in his life merited this unprecedented devotion and grace. He felt at once small as a bug and large as a galaxy.

"Lu, no, this is your personal stake, for your own dreams."

"My dreams are yours now, Joh, and yours mine. It always was so, and must continue to be so. Don't deny me this!"

"I— I can't—"

"Can I say something to you I never have said before?"

"Of course."

"Shut up!"

Startled at first, Johrun started laughing and could not stop, his first laughter in so many sad days. Lutramella joined in, a blended gurgle, squeak, chitter, and trill.

When they had wound down their spontaneous joy, Johrun immediately began to plan. "With these funds we can purchase passage to Bodenshire and approach the Brickers ourselves! Get on the Indranet, Lu, and see when the next liner is due here."

"May I suggest something, Joh?"

"Of course."

"Consider the cost of two tickets to Bodenshire. Maybe ten percent of our funds. Something tells me we could be embarked on a very long road home. Conservation of our money is imperative. Would it not be better to get there for free?"

"And how would we accomplish that?"

"Let us swallow our pride and ask Braulio for a lift."

Johrun bristled at this notion. "That contemptible jumped-up cocksman! I'd rather attempt to walk through the deadliest branes all the way to Bodenshire than beg a ride from him."

"Joh, this is allowing your hatred and jealousy to conquer your wisdom. I taught you better than that, didn't I? Think also that if you spend another day or two on his ship with Minka, you might get her to come around to your way of thinking."

Johrun pulled at his stubbled chin. He realized he hadn't shaved since the obliteration of his family. "There's much to your plan I hadn't considered. Do you really think he'll consent?"

"I believe he might relish to chance to lord it over you even more than he has. But we'll never know unless we ask him. And if he says no, we are not worse off."

The pair returned the short distance to where the *Bastard of Bungo* rested. Its ramp was down, and Ox was carrying a half-dozen pieces of luggage onboard. Seeing Johrun, he explained.

"Old Fungus Bunny allowed your lady pal to claim a few clothes, but he wouldn't let her take any other possessions. Says they all belong to whoever eventually gets this world."

"Where are Minka and Anders now?"

"Back at the lodge."

Johrun hurried to Minka's suite, Lutramella by his side. He found her stuffing one final bag under the watchful eye of Fang-Blenny, who annotated every item on his vambrace. Looking on impatiently, Braulio nodded to Johrun, giving him an opening to pitch his request.

"Anders, I know you think poorly of me, for whatever reasons, and I do not dispute your right to do so. Perhaps I appear to you as naive and unworldly, a cossetted farmboy. That may well be. The gods know I might not have ended up in my current plight if I had been more savvy about galactic affairs, more forthright and active on my own behalf. But be that as it may, I think and hope that out of your regard for Minka you might consent to do me a favor. Would you carry me and Lutramella to Bodenshire in your ship, before you return to Maradyth?"

Minka looked up from her packing with a suspicious glimmer in her eyes. "Exactly what are you intending?"

"I hope to reclaim Verano for our families, Minka, and Bodenshire is the obvious place to begin. It's where Xul and the others were headed, to meet with the Brickers. Maybe they will listen to me instead. And if you came along for an interview too—"

"Forget it! You recall what we were told by Xul. Only the testimony of one whose *âmago* is entangled with the original transmission of the deed can reestablish our rights. Your testimony and mine are useless."

"Nonetheless, I have to try!"

Braulio intervened, a smug smile on his face. "It pleasures me to aid such a quixotic folly. I call it 'greasing the skids.' Although I do hate to deprive the refineries of Bustard's Gully of a star sluice laver. Jay Cee, you and your slimy pet have your ride."

Johrun shook hands with his rival, too excited to feel insulted. "We'll be right down! Lu, go pack—quickly!"

Silently observant until now, Fang-Blenny said, "Once I lock up this suite, I will oversee your packing, *Vir* Corvivios."

In short order—Johrun had with him only a week's worth of clothing, and much of that too formal to be of use—Johrun met Lutramella down in the lobby. He grabbed her small single duffel from her and began to hurry toward the exit. But she interrupted their departure by addressing the Steward, who had tagged along with them and was now heading for his office.

"*Vir* Fang-Blenny, could you please open up the lodge's souvenir store and sell us some things?"

"Any potential legitimate profits under my regency cannot be declined."

In the store, Lutramella hastily assembled, for Johrun and herself, some practical outerwear emblazoned with the Danger Acres crest, as well as hiking boots more substantial than the summery shoes Johrun wore, and a pair for herself that were certainly supplemental to her own bare feet, although not a perfect fit, being designed for humans. Thick socks as well. Finally she advanced on the weapons department, where departing guests who were not professional hunters could avail themselves of deadly souvenir instruments whose backstory they could elaborate at will. ("Yes, I killed six kroke lizards in the swamps of Verano with this very gun!"). She studied the rack of pistols before selecting a compact model, a Kingslake glial jammer. To this she added a poignard of Smalls manufacture, composed of smart carbon picotube fibers that actively facilitated deadly cuts and lethal insertions. A sheath and belt were included for the price.

Lutramella sighted down the length of the blade admiringly. "I don't like guns. But I do like this. It is a very sharp tooth."

To Johrun's momentary embarrassment, the splice did the paying for them, vambrace to vambrace with Fang-Blenny, and she buckled the knife around her nearly waistless midsection as they left.

"I suggest you pocket your gun now, Joh, and keep it always with you."

Halfway to Braulio's ship, Johrun got a sudden urge.

"One quick detour."

He hastened with Lutramella to the monument commemorating the discovery of Verano: the plinth with the half-sized replica of the Jangalo one-person explorer named *Bumming Around*.

DROWNE'S LANDING
HERE HONKO DROWNE FIRST
TOUCHED THE LOVING SOIL OF
VERANO AND CLAIMED IT FOR HIS OWN—
ALTHOUGH HE WAS NOT TO HOLD IT FOR LONG
THANKS TO THE GOOD FORTUNE OF
THE SOLDEVERE AND CORVIVIOS CLANS

Johrun placed his hand over his heart. "Mother, father, Xul and Chirelle, and all the Soldeveres. I swear I will reclaim our world and honor the memory of your accomplishments. Nothing will stop me!"

Lutramella said, "Best to anticipate success, but prepare for disasters. Let us move sharply now, or we'll face the setback of losing our ride before we even begin!"

CHAPTER 10

The initial hour in space proved to be a soul-stirring experience for Johrun, bringing with it the flotsam and jetsam of a thousand unbidden thoughts, comforting and dismaying, and a flood of wordless heart twinges. Like the vaporized *Against the Whelm*, the smaller ship of Anders Braulio, the *Bastard of Bungo*, had the capacity to turn practically all of its interior surfaces into a massive contiguous omnidirectional viewing sphere. When activated, the feature caused the voyagers to feel as if they floated almost naked in the vacuum, observing the splendors of the cosmos with a godlike eye.

The first novel sight to impinge on Johrun's sensibilities was the totality of Verano. Never having been further out than a suborbital jump, he had never seen the full disc of his beloved planet. But in a few minutes after takeoff, there it hung, the mottled green-grey-blue-tawny beauty of his native world against the clamor of the myriad brilliant features of globular cluster M68. A few more minutes fast travel under conventional fifth-force drive shrank the planet to merely the largest object in a whole enormous field of dusty nebulae, throbbing pulsars, rich gemstone stars and a hundred other exotic cosmic species. Constellations such as Yattaw's Mermaid and the Seven Wolfheads carried a freight of legend. An empty tract dubbed the Pessoan Marches, with one blue star at its center, resembled a baleful eye. The purple light of Verano's nearby primary, Wayward's Spinel, had been stepped down with a protective software filter so that the star did not blind them.

Absorbed in the spectacle, Johrun took some time to notice that Lutramella was shivering with a kind of holy terror beside him on the divan. He put an arm around her shoulders and drew her close to comfort her.

Till that moment, his fellow passengers had ignored the two hitchhikers, busy making small talk among themselves and detailing unlikely and nonconventional constellations.

"There's the Bishop's Prick!"

"The Slatternly Fishwife has never looked sharper!"

But when they observed Johrun offering Lutramella some solace for her instinctive fears caused by the immensity and humbling grandeur of space, the classmates laughed and mocked, causing Johrun to seethe. Lutramella visibly composed herself, quelling her shakes at whatever cost, and turned her attention to her vambrace. She said in a dignified manner, "I will study up on our destination now, if you please, Joh."

Minka addressed Johrun after the gibes had subsided. "I hope you realize how ridiculous you look, Joh, babying that creature in such a manner. It's juvenile behavior at best, and quisling betrayal at worst. You're a human, and she's a splice—even if now she is free! Haven't you any sense of proportion? Your feelings toward this old drudge are humiliating, to you and her. Splices don't care for human affections. All they need and cherish is a warm doss and a full belly."

Johrun had to wait until the red scrim in front of his vision had faded before he could bring himself to speak calmly.

"I attribute your ignorance about what matters to a chimera, what their true capabilities are, to not being raised around them as I was. Even during those months you spent each year at the Pasturage I always noticed you avoided and slighted our nonhuman staff. But because you made no overt disparagements, I always told myself your attitude didn't really matter. But now I know better.

"At Danger Acres you were used to human workers who defined their relationships to the Soldeveres strictly in terms of money given for labor received. Their inner lives did not come into the equation. You did not have to cultivate their esteem. But when employing splices, more than mere commerce comes into play. They react like all sapients to good will and camaraderie, generosity, and caring. And their portions of human genes only amplify whatever animal heritage they possess. A playful and loving nature emerges for most. Savage and predatory for others, as the specs of the sartors compel. And with a longtime companion like Lutramella, who guarded my welfare for years, asking nothing in return but love and loyalty—well, there's no difference between her and, and—"

Minka said coldly, "Her and me."

Johrun jumped up and fervently took Minka's hands. "Don't be mean-spirited and vindictive, Minka! You know that's not the comparison I was seeking to express."

Minka withdrew her hands and turned toward the others. "I don't know about you all, but I could use a meal. With my fellow humans."

Braulio said, "Let me just make the transition to branespace first, and then we can relax."

He toggled off—and locked down against accidental triggering—the viewing augmentation, returning the interior surfaces of the craft to their true appearance. There was nothing to be gained—and much to be lost—by displaying the non-Euclidean

topography of branespace. Many a human, in the early explor-
atory days of such travel, had emerged with their nervous
systems deracinated and lateralized. Nowadays, the onboard
artilects would easily handle the reiterated fractal mappings that
would bring them to Bodenshire. With that precaution taken, a
simple command string sliced open the multiverse and inserted
their ship into shortcut otherness.

Unconcerned with any holistic *âmago,* the six ex-students
were quite happy to conjure up their favorite dishes from the
ship's fabricators. Soon various delicious odors filled the small
central salon of the ship.

After everyone else had been supplied with their orders,
Johrun had to ask Braulio, "Would you engineer a simple meal
for Lutramella and me? My vambrace is dead, you know."

Braulio said with a nasty smile, "I don't recall meals being
included as part of your tourist package. Only transportation.
But it's only two days to Bodenshire. I'm sure you can survive
until then. Water, of course, is readily obtainable from the basin
spigot in the loo."

Johrun turned away and joined Lutramella. She shared a
commiserating look with him, then unseamed her duffel and
reached inside, to retrieve two generic splice nutribars.

"This is my favorite flavor. Carrots and sourpango."

Johrun accepted a bar with an overblown genteel gesture.
"As the Lonely Bard of Farundel said, 'A goldflake cocktail in a
goblet of Transrekian crystal among one's enemies is less to be
cherished than a drop of dew shared with a friend.'"

Minka and her crew snorted.

"Don't you care for poetry?" Johrun asked coldly.

"Yes, of course," said Braheem. "But we dissected the lyrics
of the Homely Bard of Farting Dell in first-year post-transcrip-
tives, and determined them to be utterly without merit."

Unable to make a response, Johrun unwrapped his bar and bit off a chunk. It tasted more like the unknown sourpango than the familiar carrots.

During the next several hours, while the university graduates played cards, Johrun and Lutramella quietly familiarized themselves with Bodenshire and the local outlets of the five Quinary omniafirms.

The Smalls, the Indrans, the Pollys, the Motivators, the Brickers—those consortiums that welded galactic civilization together—had no central headquarters. No single planet was devoted to a command nexus; there was no unique concentration of forces and resources and executive corps. The omniafirms existed as distributed nodes across the Milky Way, a network of branch offices, so to speak. Not every system hosted representatives of all five consortiums. But Bodenshire happened to be home to an office for each arm of the Quinary. The Bricker node was located at a place called Nesiotium Neomeniarum.

With no exterior time cues, the passengers aboard the *Bastard of Bungo* had to rely on their body clocks for bedtime. And Johrun's physiology was telling him that he had run a marathon across a desert with lead shoes while being pelted with stones.

The Corvivios family craft had afforded twelve cabins. Johrun thought to identify four on Braulio's ship. How would the sleepers be divided up? Would Minka favor him with an invitation to hers? But what then of Lutramella? Could she sleep on this short divan?

Johrun's speculations were put to an end by the disintegration of the card-playing crowd.

Ox stood up and swept giggling Viana and Trina into his large embrace. Those three headed to one cabin.

To Johrun's immense surprise, the next pairing was Braulio and Braheem!

Minka then quickly claimed cabin three, without so much as a backwards glance at Johrun.

Inside the fourth cabin, Johrun sagged down with bone-tiredness and fully clothed onto the bed. It took him almost ten seconds to fall asleep, but that was long enough to register Lutramella's warmer-than-human backside pressed up against his.

Baggage in hand and paw, Johrun and Lutramella stood at the foot of the ramp of Braulio's ship, Minka above him, framed in the portal. Seeing her beautiful indifference wrenched at Johrun's heart. Although he knew what her answer would be, he could not restrain himself from making one last plea.

"Minka, won't you cast your lot with mine? Come help me regain our world."

"I don't chase mirages, Joh. Verano is gone from our hands. I've faced this reality, and you should too. This is goodbye, until you come to your senses. Find me on Maradyth. Farewell."

Ramp retracted, hull again seamless, ship slowly levitating. Accelerating to swift invisibility. Gone.

Johrun sagged a bit. Not favored by his fiancée with so much as a "Good luck and travel safely!" This truly seemed a milestone moment in his life, but not one to celebrate. Exiled from his homeworld, pauperized save for the slim resources of his companion, chasing an impossible dream. What other burdens could an iron fate and he himself pile onto his own shoulders?

Lutramella spoke. "We need to get out of this rain, Joh. And find transportation to Nesiotium Neomeniarum."

After two days jackrabbiting through branespace and another half day, post-egress, advancing through basalspace to reach Bodenshire—a period of high and low insults from Braulio and company—Johrun had suffered the final indignity. Braulio had insisted on depositing him far from his ultimate destination.

"You've made me detour wide enough of my home. The delay proved really insufferable. I'm not carrying you like a prince to the doorstep of your palace."

"But it will only take you about an hour longer on this inbound approach!"

"True. But if I land directly at the main port in Bodenshire's Quadrant Ninety-five Hundred, I can visit the tourist entrepôt and purchase a case of Kreuger's Posset, which is absolutely my favorite liquor and sold nowhere else! Thus will this boorish side trip justify itself."

Disinclined to argue, Johrun rationalized that any delay would be trivial and inexpensive, even if frustrating. And so here he stood, for the first time on another world, though not precisely at his goal.

Lutramella's comment on the weather suddenly brought his foreign surroundings into sharper reality. The sky above was a leaden shade Johrun had never experienced before. In just the past few minutes, a slow but persistent drizzle had wetted down his hair and dampened his new jacket.

"Why is the air so damn cold? Is this what they call winter?"

Lutramella consulted her vambrace. "It is only ten degrees below Verano's median temperature."

"It's horrible. I feel as if someone had dumped an icy drink on my head. Do people actually consent to live in such a place?"

"This is considered mild weather here, Joh, as it would be on many other worlds as well. The natives think nothing of it."

"They are plainly all brain-damaged, their cortexes frozen into premature senility. We need to ensure that we can return to Verano as its rightful owners before we too succumb."

"I see what appears to be a refectory over there. We could get something to eat while we plan our passage to Nesiotium Neomeniarum."

"I'd appreciate anything that does not taste of sourpango."

"I'm sorry you did not enjoy those bars."

Johrun instantly regretted his thoughtless words. "Those bars were literally lifesaving, Lu. Your foresight in packing them is rivalled only by the time you suggested to me that climbing atop a herple and goading it with an electro-prod would not be a wise move."

"But did you listen to me then?"

"No, of course not. And I suffered the busted head and limbs I deserved. But this doesn't mean I can't appreciate your wisdom in retrospect."

After crossing the glistening green geopolymer tarmac, they reached the canteen and escaped the rain. The class of odors inside unmistakably somehow denoted breakfast, and Johrun got some sense of local time after days of travel limbo. The noisy place was thronged and colorful, with most of the patrons looking like port workers, cheek by jowl with the occasional offplanet visitor of unfastidious tastes.

Seated gratefully at a table, Johrun and Lutramella soon did justice to a spread consisting of rashers of sea pig, buttermilk scones, wine pudding, and two pots of hot whey-thread cider. The meal considerably improved Johrun's disposition, and Lutramella seemed to derive a boost from the food as well.

Finishing the last scone crumbs, Johrun said, "I could wish the Bricker enclave were closer by. But I suppose we owe its whimsical location to Lubero Varadkar's personal sense of style."

Each of the five omniafirms sported a figurehead prime representative, more mascot than chief operating officer, whose role was not so much to issue ukases and plot fiscal conquests from on high—the enterprises were actually guided by a blend of emergent consensual decision-making among the stockholders and vizier-level artilect heuristics—but rather to embody the unique spirit and esthetic of each firm in the eyes of the public.

As head of the Brickers, Varadkar projected the image, factitious or true, of a sedate landed collector and architect, a fancier of arcadian prospects.

Saudia Thrace, helming the Smalls, favored the aspect of a meditative ascetic.

Sterk Zazum, emblematic of the Indrans, assumed the role of madcap adventurer and daredevil, explorer of new realms.

Felicia Obst, in the forefront of the Pollys, had seemingly devoted her glossy life to high fashion and the nightlife.

And Derek Balash of the Motivators played the sportsman, with a particular fondness for elegant and dangerous race cars.

Here on Bodenshire, each firm had established its outpost in a signature fashion.

The Motivators shared space with a lush country club whose wicket-ball courts were famous across the Quinary.

The Pollys maintained offices in the Designers' Barrio of Port Calash.

The Indrans could be found in a huge lighter-than-air ship that roamed the globe.

An innocuous and humble corner of the Monastery of the Blind Shepherd served well enough for the Smalls.

And the Brickers were housed in a beautiful mansion at Nesiotium Neomeniarum.

Lutramella's deft researches had selected the cheapest transportation to this outpost from the port in Quadrant Ninety-five Hundred where Braulio had dumped them.

"First we ride a local ship to Whetstone, the ninth moon of Bodenshire. Unfortunately, our ride makes intervening stops at moons one through eight first. But upon arrival, it's just a short hop to Bisko, the moon of Whetstone."

"The moon has a moon?"

Lutramella sighed. "That's quite common. Did you ever really pay attentions to any of your lessons?"

"Only enough to pass your quizzes, after which I promptly forgot most of it. Not much seemed relevant to my life on Verano. And that I knew in my very meat and bones."

"Let us hope we do not ever have cause to regret your scholarly slackness. In any case, once we land on Bisko, we simply fly overland a short ways. We have a scheduled appointment for you to go under the inquestorial meshes tomorrow at three in the afternoon. Our ship departs in four hours."

With his activities for the next twenty-four hours all delineated and their path clear, at least for the very near future, Johrun experienced a sudden sense of excitement and freedom. Despite all his grief and travails and the uncertainty of success, he knew himself as still a young man, sound of limb and mind, unencumbered by mundane obligations, and standing on an alien world. An irrepressible vitality coursed through him. The allure of the new beckoned like an enchantress.

"Could we see a little of this world in the next three hours perhaps?"

"Very little. Bodenshire is a superplanet, seventy thousand kilometers in circumference. This continent we are on, just one of a dozen, constitutes an area greater than all the land masses of Verano combined. There are approximately fifty billion inhabitants scattered across thirty thousand significant metropoles. The dominant language changes approximately every thousand kilometers."

The numbers daunted Johrun, who had considered the crowd of two hundred assembled for his wedding to be almost intolerable.

"Suppose we order another pot of cider and just wait here?"

"My notion exactly. But we might also use the next few hours to avail ourselves of one of the port's hamams. I believe I'm beginning to smell like my non-sartorized ancestors. And you as well!"

The fifth-force rental flyer from the shipyard on Bisko took Johrun and Lutramella over a verdant, unstained landscape. Manicured copses of purple-fringed trees. Herds of galloping big-horned ungulates. It seemed that at least part of Bisko was a nature preserve.

All the moons and all the moonmoons of the Bodenshire system featured conditions harmonious for human living unmediated by any suits or masks. The concealed Harvester engines and infrastructures maintained proper gravities and atmospheres and ecosystems flawlessly, as they had for eons, just as they maintained Verano at its mellow tropicality. Without them the satellites would be lifeless hellholes of solid gases and razored, cratered terrain. The inhabitants took this for granted. Daily familiarity even with the work of gods incurred indifference and ingratitude.

Piloting the skysled with long-established competence, Johrun guided them successfully to Lake Akinmusire. From the shoreline first encountered, no other shore could be seen, so broad were the pearlescent waters. The craft sped out over the mild waves. Soon it reached an expansive island: Faybo. In the middle of Faybo occurred another lake: Villet. And in that lake was the island known as Nesiotium Neomeniarum.

"On an island in a lake on an island in a lake on a moon of a moon. A songwriter could have a field day with this situation!"

Lutramella brought up a shaped-light enactment of a singer serenading an audience. Her lyrics chronicled this very scenario.

"Lina Lool, performing 'My Heart is an Island with a Lake on the Lake of Your Island Heart.'"

The Bricker mansion occupied the center of a large land-scaped clearing. The structure exhibited a fashionable minimal-ism, consisting of severe aluminum and glass boxes cantilevered out from a central mass that appeared to be a tumbled mass of unpolished boulders, but which resolved itself into a series of grottoes.

Johrun set the skysled down on an appointed pad. Unsure of where they would be heading from here, they had taken their luggage with them. Johrun now activated the sled's security to protect their meager possessions.

A human receptionist awaited, an elderly man with a seamed face and an enormous rick of white hair. Johrun had seldom seen anyone displaying such obvious traits of aging, and the look seemed something of an affectation to him, a flouting of conven-tion. The man was busy with some sort of construction toy of blocks and rods and connectors, but put it aside to help them.

"Yes, yes, you're to see Calleia Suttles. I've sent the path-marks to your vambrace."

Johrun waited until they were around a turn and out of ear-shot to comment. "Obviously a form of charity employment. Give the decrepit codger a simple job to make him feel useful."

"That was Lubero Varadkar himself, or one of his clones. He maintains an army of thirty thousand, so the chances of encoun-tering him personally wherever you go in the Quinary are not as astronomical as you might imagine. Especially if you visit a Bricker facility."

Past abstract artworks and glossy plants in large ceramic pots. The high-up room housing the inquestorial mesh system proved to be bare of anything but a chair and the probe device, the latter seemingly nothing more than a simple opaque homeostatic tank with a hinged lid.

Calleia Suttles loomed over the visitors at two-point-five meters tall, but certainly weighed less than Johrun. In a loose smock and leggings, patterned in orange splotches on a black background, the willowy, wide-eyed, pale-faced technician resembled one of the serpentine creatures said to lurk right here in Lake Villet.

"Please take your seat, *Vir* Corvivios."

Johrun was strapped down in the chair, arms and legs and torso. The technician's slim, very long fingers applied grey paste from a canister to Johrun's hair and the back of his neck. The concoction smelled not unpleasantly of exotic spices and unidentifiable organic essences. Without further ado, Suttles raised the lid of the tank. From it surged a wet gelatinous black hairy mass, all curling tendrils and no body, like some ensorcelled wig. It swarmed up Johrun's back like a gecko up a wall and enwrapped all its fibrous self around his head and face. Johrun managed to strain against his bonds and give out a muffled "*Glimph!*" before he sagged back and went quiet. His chest seemed to register no breaths.

Lutramella moved to go to Johrun's rescue, but yielded to calm restraint from Suttles.

"There is no danger. The engineering of the Pollys is impeccable. From a creature related to the ultra-dangerous phagoplasms of Irion, they have crafted a simple 'eater' of *âmago*. The mesh resonates psychically with the subject's numinous qualities, and transmits the results to my vambrace. Now, let me see what question I am to ask . . . Ah, yes. 'Johrun Corvivios, were you a participant and witness of the deed transfer of the planet Verano from

Honko Drowne to the Soldevere and the Corvivios clans?' We should see the telemetry in just a moment . . . Yes, all done!"

Suttles took a generous dollop of paste from her can and dumped it as a reward and lure in the tank. The creature quickly retracted all its parts into a compact nucleus and scampered back to its habitat. Suttles closed and locked the lid. She freed Johrun from his straps.

Johrun looked dazed but unharmed. "That was . . . That was uncanny. I seemed to travel up and down the timestream in search of lost knowledge. However long that took, it seemed an eternity."

"You may clean up in the room right next door. I will process the raw results into my official report and send it to your vambrace. There is no need to return here. Goodbye, and good luck."

His face and hair and neck freshly washed and dried, Johrun exited the lavatory. The expression on Lutramella's face told all, but she let him read the report.

"Subject disseminates no *âmago* traces consistent with primary credibility regarding the formal topic, although strong secondary echoes of affiliation to those with primary knowledge do register. His testimony thus fails to resolve the central dispute . . ."

Neither Johrun nor Lutramella said anything until they were back in the skysled and returning to the Bisko spaceport. Johrun spoke first.

"Where does this leave us, Lu? I can see no fresh avenue."

"No? I do. Our only hope."

"And that is?"

"We need to find Honko Drowne."

CHAPTER 11

The various lodgings clustered around the spaceport in Quadrant Ninety-five Hundred on Bodenshire ranged the gamut from luxurious to louche. Gauging their funds, the estimated length of their stay, and their tolerance for noisy midnight altercations or drinking parties in adjacent rooms, Johrun settled on an establishment called Botofogo's Chambers of Amenities. The hostel's motto—"The most gracious and pampering accommodations for their price in the entire Laniakea Supercluster"—made an extravagant claim of which the actual rooms fell rather short. But *Vir* Raymonde Botofogo himself, a heavily muscled and outrageously mustachioed fellow with the air of an ex-brawler, proved to be an honest innkeeper who could maintain peace and quiet and get fresh towels not much later than two hours after they were requested. He also ran the small seedy estaminet next door, where Johrun and Lutramella could take their meals at a discount, given their tenure at the Chambers. (Although after two weeks, the specialties of the place, including capercaillie pie with a side of mashed macaoca, began to pall.)

But since dry, safe, cheap quarters with a mattress of sufficient thickness to shield backbone from the bed's armatures
was all Johrun wanted while engaged in his quest, he was quite
content with his choice.

Johrun and Lutramella had returned from the Brickers'
outpost on the moonmoon to their original point of entry on
Bodenshire for three simple reasons: lodgings on the exclusive
satellite Bisko would have been too expensive; any location was
as good as any other for their purposes; and they had a glancing
acquaintance with the spot where Braulio had deposited them,
a chance familiarity that seemed to lend the place an irrational
tinge of home, especially in comparison to any other unknown
spot on the enormous planet. (And at the back of his mind,
Johrun always harbored a dim hope that maybe Minka would
have a change of heart and return for him, and where else would
she look but here?)

And so from Whetstone the ninth moon they had wended
their slow way with other commuters and tourists and voya-
geurs and couriers and business types past all the partnered
eight moons until they had set foot again on Bodenshire. But
they had used the tedious journey to best effect, as they began to
study up on Honko Drowne.

At the start of their investigations, en route to Bodenshire
and then once settled there, Johrun experienced a queer new
feeling of being a stranger to his own family history. The name
of Honko Drowne had been a byword among the Corvivios and
Soldevere clans for Johrun's entire life. Wasn't there even a monument to the man? And the one anecdote about how Xul and
Brayall had wrested ownership of Verano away from Drowne
was well-polished from many tellings. A simple game of chance
where Drowne had gambled his planet and lost. But all the rest
of that man's history—both contemporaneous with the youths

of Xul and Brayall and afterwards—had been a locked closet to Johrun, a repository of knowledge in which he had never thought to rummage. Now he marvelled at his old incuriosity, and felt somewhat ashamed. He said as much to Lutramella.

"It's never too late to mend our ways and improve ourselves, Joh."

"That's easy for you to say. You always know the right thing to do."

Lutramella chitter-hissed her denial. "Not so! It's only that the life of an indentured splice is simpler than that of a free sapient—as I'm just beginning to learn. And so with fewer choices possible, the correct action is often more clearly displayed and selected."

"I'd like to attain that simplicity."

"And I'd like to attain a sense of the human multitude of pathways."

"Then we'll teach each other."

"As we always have!"

In the matter of Honko Drowne's vitagraph, their learning moved in parallel. And it brought unwelcome, and even life-upsetting revelations.

Over one hundred and fifty years ago, three bold lads who had grown up together on the world of Hodak—Honko Drowne, Xul Corvivios, Brayall Soldevere—had formed a surveying and prospecting concern: Green Hills Unlimited. Their massed savings had been just enough to purchase and outfit three small patched-up second-hand braneships. The *Bumming Around* (Drowne), the *Cast a Wide Net* (Corvivios) and the *Be Prepared!* (Soldevere). Off they had flashed from Hodak to three scattered points of the galactic compass, with a vow to rendezvous back on Hodak in a year's time and pool their finds and cash out their conquests in life-changing riches.

Thanks to long-ago Harvester interventions, so thick with fine lovely worlds was the galaxy that despite millennia of human exploration and colonization there remained many untapped planets—although nowadays one had to go farther and farther afield to find the best. And by common practice, all it took to claim an entire uninhabited world for one's own was to land on it and register its coordinates with the Brickers.

Honko Drowne's daring resolution to probe the tricky crowded stellar neighborhoods of the M68 globular cluster paid off well.

Back on Hodak, the three foragers disclosed their finds.

Xul Corvivios had discovered an abandoned congeries of Lagrange-point habitats in the Corsino system. They were leaking atmosphere and their vegetation had run wild.

Brayall Soldevere returned with title to a very small ringworld at whose center hung a strange artificial star. But the orbit of the ringworld was decaying, irreparable by current technics, and it was fit only for quick salvage.

And Honko Drowne, of course, had come upon Verano.

Exulting, the trio calculated that the three properties combined and sold would give each of them a nice payout, with Drowne's input constituting the richest part. But such inequality of contributions meant nothing among good friends. To celebrate, they paid a visit to the pleasure world known as Nil Sequelae.

The next thing Honko Drowne knew, he was awakening on Soldevere's doomed ringworld. He managed to escape on the *Bumming Around* just before the construct grazed its primary and began to violently disintegrate.

Once his Indranet connection was reestablished upon his return to civilization, he discovered two things.

He had apparently deeded over Verano to his partners exclusively, renouncing all his shares in the world, although he had no memory of doing so.

And he was a wanted criminal, accused of a campaign of murder, theft, and moral turpitude on Nil Sequelae. Journalistic accounts, already eagerly viewed across the Quinary by billions, painted a vivid portrait of his mad depredations, complete with recorded scenes of vault-breaking, kidnapping, wild skysled chases that endangered innocent bystanders, and the unprovoked abuse of harmless splices.

Even as he learned of his new infamy, Honko's ship began to register pings from a variety of law enforcement vessels eager to have a word with him. Realizing he could never defend himself against such an elaborately contrived misrepresentation and frameup, he fled. His mind and soul wrenched by this betrayal, Honko Drowne vowed to become what he had been libeled as. He embarked on a life of interplanetary crime, soon aided by a crew of allied malcontents.

At this point in their researches, which had amassed and collated many facts from both primary and secondary sources which had never heretofore been assimilated into a gestalt, Johrun looked up from Lu's vambrace and into the splice's sympathetic eyes with an ocean of sick feeling in his gut.

"Grandpa Xul, Grandpa Brayall—is it possible they cheated Drowne of his earned wealth? Is all our family history built on this horrific crime? Did they steal our summer world from its rightful owner?"

Lutramella's sober voice and expression confirmed Johrun's own worst fears. "Although these ancient accounts never make such a claim, we can read between the lines. It does appear as if your ancestor and Minka's finagled the deed away from a man temporarily not in possession of his right mind, due to drugs or other impositions, and then placed him in such a fix that he could never protest."

Johrun began softly to weep. He could only picture the shining, noble faces of his family as they climbed aboard the *Against the Whelm* on that day when his life came crashing to pieces. How to reconcile his lifelong love and admiration of his people with these new horrors? Did there remain anything to his legacy that wasn't tainted?

Eventually Johrun regained his equilibrium.

"Forgive my weakness, Lu. It's just—"

"You need not explain. I understand completely."

Johrun realized that only by speaking aloud his new sad determination would it register as reality. "The only correct course of action is to return Verano to Drowne. Abandon all our stake in the planet. Let him assert his claim against the mysterious Redhook Combine, without interference from us."

"That might not be possible. He is still an object of fraught pursuit in the Quinary. The man responsible for the Starvation Blockade of Scharpling, the Harrowing of Bergen V, the Great Swampworld Scam of Fifteen-ought-nine, and the Impossible Museum Vanishment of Hailstone City might not be well received in the placid examination room at Nesiotium Neomeniarum."

"But surely a readout of Drowne's *âmago* would clarify everything."

"Yes. But getting him to cooperate and bringing him here is a dicey enterprise, even if the promised outcome is to his benefit. Title to a wonderful planet would mean nothing to someone imprisoned in the Smalls' Hell Matrix. And he is apparently quite content in his retirement."

In his most recent years, as he had aged out of high-risk and high-energy plundering, Honko Drowne had taken his booty and established himself on the faraway world of Itaska, becoming the "Red Lion of the Spires" and the chief of the local natives surrounding the Spires, who were known as the Arnapkapfaaluk. With such a sedentary, well-advertised lifestyle, it might have seemed an easy matter for the Quinary authorities to roust out

Drowne and return him to justice. But one fact intervened. Drowne had chosen his hideout wisely.

Itaska was a Supressor World.

The long-gone Harvesters had embedded engines and nano-mites in the planet's very bones which rendered all higher technics useless. Subject to realtime quantum interventions by omnipres-ent smart agents, all the vaunted tools and weapons of modern civilization and warfare, from gunpowder on up, simply refused to function on Itaska. With one exception. There was an invisi-ble high-technology zone, basically a kilometer-wide column of atmosphere from the ground to orbit, in which a braneship might continue to function, landing and taking off at will. That single zone existed over one thousand kilometers away from the Spires.

Taking Drowne by force from his redoubt would have involved waging an overland campaign of imported cavalry or footsoldiers armed with edged weapons against fierce and basi-cally innocent tribesmen who regarded Drowne as their hetman. This was not a bloody excursion the Quinary could justify. Thus, so long as Drowne restricted himself to Itaska, they would leave him alone.

Johrun acknowledged Lutramella's logic. "Drowne is happy where he is. Dragging him away by coercion seems impossible. Nonetheless, it's now my moral duty to follow through. I feel that if I could only talk to him and convey my shame and sorrow at how my family cheated him, he might consent to make at least a flying visit here to Bodenshire to resolve the matter. Perhaps he could get in and out fast, before his presence was known to the authorities. He must have methods of dissimulation. And then, with Verano officially registered in his name, maybe—well, maybe I could return as a kind of caretaker. It seems the best possible outcome." Johrun paused for a moment, with a new hope suddenly gleaming in his eyes. "Although perhaps under

the meshes, Drowne might reveal that the original deed trans-
action was legitimate! Maybe Verano really does belong to the
Corvivios and Soldevere clans . . ."

Lutramella rolled her eyes. "And there's a slim chance I am
the Lost Princess of Golden Perdolomo. Still, if you desire to
carry this scheme to a conclusion, despite knowing what you do,
and if you admit to yourself that all the future you once assumed
will probably be cast aside by your actions, then I am with you."

Johrun hugged the wiry splice. "Wonderful! Truth be told, I
never would have wanted to go on without you, Lu! Now, since
we can't communicate with Drowne through the Indranet, we'll
have to voyage there and present ourselves humbly and hope
for the best. We haven't money enough to buy a ship, so we'll
have to seek some enterprising hireling to ferry us there— and
possibly back, if Drowne declines our offer to return. Even such
a limited contract will take most of our remaining cash. But if
we can find someone daring and adventurous enough—a kind of
freebooter or corsair for whom bragging rights about such a trip
would matter—then we could do it."

Lutramella's fingers commenced to fly over her vambrace. "I
am composing our solicitation right now."

The next three weeks were a mix of anxious waiting, intense
boredom, and a few fleeting moments of forgetful pleasure
during which the weighty affair of Verano's fate could be shuffled out of mind. When not hanging around the hostel or the
port anticipating a response to their advertisement, Johrun and
Lutramella availed themselves of the cheapest daytrips to local
attractions—defined as those no further than ten thousand kilometers distant. The outings all originated from the Quadrant
Ninety-five Hundred port.

They visited the Moresby Firefalls, where they amused themselves by flash-roasting over the fiery spume the raw goat kebabs

purchased from vendors. They went swimming in the lumines-
cent waters at Biondine Beach, where Lutramella cavorted like
a pup. And they made a trip to see the Isolato, a living mountain
that occasionally answered the questions of visitors in an oracular
fashion. Out of a mossy cleft in hillside issued a reply to Johrun's
query.

"Shall I ever return to my beloved home world and call it
mine again?"

"Call any world home, and the answer becomes yes."

The frustration occasioned by this opaque truism was the
only time Johrun actually felt even momentarily downcast
during the three weeks. Mostly he discovered that he appreciated this expansion of his life and sensibilities, even though it
had been forced upon him at great cost. The influx of youthful
vitality that he had felt immersed in—before his disappointment
with the results of the mesh interrogation—returned in full
force, imbuing him with a sourceless and perhaps indefensible
optimism. Lutramella seemed to share in his good mood.

And on the twenty-fourth day since placing their solicitation, when they had begun to doubt anyone would express interest, they received their first response.

The invitation to meet and explore terms came from an individual who provided the digichop of "Celestro." His ship, the
Mummer's Grin, had just arrived from Gwethalyn, and was now
docked at the port.

Hastily arranging a meeting time for later that very day,
Johrun and Lutramella raced through a quick meal next door
to the hostel as usual, then hopped on the port's free fifth-force
trolley, which traversed a neverending circuit of all berths on
the expansive concourse. Ships small and large came and went
silently overhead, weaving the bonds of commerce, knowledge
and desire that held the Quinary together.

"I've just worked up a quick vitagraph of this Celestro," Lutramella said. "He appears to be an entertainer of some sort, peripatetic by nature. Most recently, he spent a month on Gewthalyn, and before that he was on Bangsund, Tappenzee, and Gamma Corvi III for similar periods."

"What is the exact nature of his act?"

"It's hard to say. He bills himself as a "Cognoscente of Cosmic Clairsentience and Comic Conducement.""

The *Mummer's Grin* was a not unrespectable craft, a Stonefish Class boita whose stardust-pitted exterior reflected at least fifty years of hard travel, but also betokened regular upkeep. Since its ramp was down with no barrier to entry, Johrun and Lutramella stepped onboard.

A central salon was decked out with a profusion of overstuffed hand-quilted pillows, colorful throws and carpets, and an elaborate water-pipe from which diffused the remnant heavy perfumes of its combustible contents.

Johrun called out a greeting. An inner door opened, and Celestro emerged.

A middle-aged man of average height and build, with skin the bold shade of saffron, Celestro had chosen either not to remedy a genetic disposition to partial baldness, or to engineer such a look. In either case, his mostly bare cranium was partially circled, for an inch above his ears, with a border of silver hair, a strip that made a striking contrast to his complexion. His features were rather large and coarse, but his yellow-pupil'd gaze was piercing. His attire utilized about three times the amount of gaudy blue and orange fabric necessary for mere coverage, with a ballooning of tight-cuffed sleeves and pants legs. His shoes turned up at the toes.

Celestro's booming voice conjured up associations with deep canyons and a strong wind surging through brushy treetops.

"Might I assume that I stand in the presence of my potential clients, *Vir* Johrun Corvivios and *Mir* Lutramella von Creche Eight Thousand Forty-nine Backslash Rippington Dash Fifteen Ought Eighty-seven?"

Johrun was impressed that Celestro bothered to confer an honorific on Lutramella and cite her Indranet-accessible birth code that served as surname. That small nod to her individuality conveyed a sense of dignity and caring to the man's otherwise somewhat pompous presentation.

"Yes, this is correct. And you are Celestro?"

"None other. Please, take a seat, and I shall summon up some refreshments before we begin our discussion."

Johrun fully expected the man to pull viands and drinks out of thin air, but instead Celestro caused them to be fetched in an utterly conventional but unanticipated manner.

"Taryn! Your service is required."

From the same door through which Celestro had come, a young woman emerged.

Her looks and demeanor could not have presented a greater contrast to Celestro's. Perhaps a year or three younger than Johrun, she carried herself with a natural grace and dignity that was nonetheless overlaid with a weary air of subjection and compromise and lack of any future prospects. Her clothing consisted of a utilitarian mouse-grey coverall and black work boots akin to those of the braneship mechanics who roved the yards. The shapeless coverall hinted at what might be a fine figure. Her short sandy hair, blue eyes, a smattering of freckles across her cheeks, pert nose, and demure lips added up to an over-the-backyard-fence attractiveness dimmed by early lines of sorrow and fatigue.

"*Mir* and *Vir*, this is Taryn Endelwode. She is a restavek from Anilda. No parents, no kin. I have taken her into my service as general dogsbody, companion, and assistant in my performances. Her virtues are several, her only vice a foolish and impossible longing for fields beyond the ken of man, and certainly above her status. Taryn, these are the people I told you about who want to rent our ship."

Taryn gave a polite but sincere and wistful smile which struck Johrun directly in his core. Hearing her status as orphan—a plight that matched his—he was instantly disposed to sympathize. And the woman's gentle bearing further stirred his compassion.

"I'm very pleased to know you both."

"Taryn, bring us those anise cookies and the decanter of plum brandy."

While Taryn was in the galley, Celestro immediately and forthrightly addressed the reason for their gathering.

"You wish to hire my ship to take you to Itaska. I assume you intend to confront the legendary Honko Drowne for some nontrivial purpose."

"Precisely so."

Celestro clapped his hands together. "Perfect! This consorts with my own desires. If you have entrée to Drowne's company, then I will certainly be able to perform for him. Once accounts of my performance are disseminated across the Quinary, immense luster and an outlaw panache will accrue to my reputation, and I will afterwards be able to command much greater sums for my act."

Johrun chose not to disclose the tenuous nature of his actual connection with Drowne, and the uncertainty regarding access to the pirate. "It seems as if our desires lie along precisely the same vector then. What, by the way, does your act involve?"

"I create amusing astonishments by a variety of methods, distracting my grateful audiences from their mundane cares and existential doubts. I pluck personal and mildly embarrassing secrets from the air, esoteric knowledge from the cosmic substrate. Moreover, by my skills of psychic conducement I am able to instill in my subjects uncanny temporary abilities, desires, and visions. In short, I manifest the wonders of creation which all of us in our grim diurnal trudging need to be reminded of."

To illustrate, Celestro snatched up one of the pillows at his elbow. "*Mir* Lutramella, if I may borrow your knife for a moment . . ."

Lutramella handed over her poignard. Celestro split open the pillow with it. He shoved his hand inside and emerged with a gun.

"I believe this is yours, *Vir* Corvivios."

Johrun took the Kingslake glial jammer in his hand, and the gun came alive in response to Johrun's genetic signature.

"Remarkable!"

Celestro waved aside the compliment. "Mere frippery. Now, as to price. I would need thirty thousand chains to cover the investment of my time and ship."

Johrun looked to Lutramella. They both knew that after three weeks no other offers seemed ever likely to materialize. The splice nodded.

"We agree."

"Excellent! Now we have a real reason to toast, other than mere proximity as thirsty strangers!"

Taryn returned bearing a tray with the refreshments. Celestro poured the drinks, including one for Taryn.

"To the success of our mutual endeavors!"

Johrun took passing notice of Taryn's slight hesitation in raising her own drink to her lips, her failure to engage his glance, but never thought more of it until many, many days later.

CHAPTER 12

The ineluctable transit time from Bodenshire to Itaska across the infinite topological complexities of branespace occupied six days. A few additional hours on either end of the journey, moving through basalspace against the inhumanly resplendent background glories of the stars and planets in each system, made the trip last approximately a week. During that time, Johrun had plenty of empty hours in which to contemplate his untroubled youth and his dubious future; to plan his exact angle of attack upon Honko Drowne's uncertain sympathies; and to get to know both Celestro and Taryn better.

The former proved to be, paradoxically, at once transparent and impenetrable. He was extremely voluble and forthcoming about his performing career, providing a steady stream of often quite entertaining anecdotes. "That night on Tullia, entertaining the Conclave of Majordomos, I excelled myself. With one elegant whisk of my hand, I caused the Serenissima's skirt to vanish!" He also liked to lecture on the theories behind his art. "The Pensativists believe that the implicate order of the multiverse is merely the obverse of the human racial consciousness. Thus they maintain that access to the entire range of the powers of creation are inherent in all individuals, but must be brought out with a course of controlled sensory derangement." And he was far from shy about sharing even intimate moments of his biography. "The Diabolerinas of Overland Gap boast that no man can withstand their persuasions for more than ninety seconds without attaining complete and utter ecstasy. But they sheepishly confess that alone among their conquests, I, the Omnipotent Celestro, held out until three full minutes had elapsed!"

All these accounts naturally contributed to the positive side of the Celestro ledger. Johrun felt confirmed in his choice of hire.

On the other hand, when questioned about his deep past or his ultimate goals for his career—what was his native world; how had he come into this line of work; did he foresee an end to his peregrinations and a cozy retirement?—he managed artfully to divert the conversation to other topics. Johrun could claim no solid sense of the arc of the man's life, or his ethical principles. He seemed as wayward and irresponsible as a cloud.

Celestro's behavior consorted with his speech: flamboyant and amusing, inconsequential and whimsical as a butterfly's path through the skies. He continued to spring upon his passengers the occasional seemingly impossible feat, reveling in the honest applause from Johrun and Lutramella. (When alone with Lu, Johrun wondered aloud, "Is the man truly endowed with paranormal abilities or not?" Lutramella said, "After all these millennia, science has yet to decisively affirm or deny such wild talents, and much can be simulated with technics. We will see if he can pull off such stunts on Itaska, with its Supressor fields.") At regular intervals outside of sleep hours, Celestro mysteriously retreated to his room alone. "Please excuse my momentary unsociability, but I must regather my forces by meditating beneath the Shroud of Nubilio until all my metachakras are realigned."

As for Taryn Endelwode, she commenced the journey almost as a taciturn appliance, politely refusing all conversational gambits while responding to commands and requests with deference and a minimum of speech. But by the third day, she had let down her guard so entirely as to become nearly chatty—especially during those hours when Celestro was sequestered beneath the Shroud.

For this transformation, Johrun could take little enough credit. The catalyst for Taryn's opening-up was Lutramella.

From the first, the young woman had appeared fascinated with the splice, standing closer to her when serving food than to others; asking if Lutramella needed special nutrition; offering to bring her extra blankets and pillows if desired; asking timidly to stroke her fur. It was obvious that Taryn longed to converse at length with Lutramella, but was unsure how to proceed. Then, early on the morning of the third day, Johrun awoke to discover that Lutramella was not in their private room with him. He stepped out quietly a pace or two into the darkened salon, then halted. Lutramella and Taryn were sitting side by side, heads lowered and almost touching, whispering together. The splice held one of Taryn's hands in both of her own.

Johrun backed into the bedroom and closed the door.

That morning at breakfast, Taryn hummed a lightfooted melody while she served. Celestro looked somewhat annoyed at the unwonted sprightliness of his servant girl, but refrained from direct criticism.

That afternoon, during Celestro's recuperative retreat, Taryn dropped down on the couch next to Johrun as, deprived of his own vambrace, he was holding an old-fashioned slate and reading about their destination, Itaska.

"*Vir* Corvivios, please tell me about your planet. Lu says it's paradise."

The prospect of conveying the wonders of lost Verano was a bittersweet one, but Johrun could hardly refuse.

"I'll do so on two conditions. First, you must call me Johrun. And second, when I'm done you must tell me about your past on Anilda, and what brought you here."

Taryn mused on the stipulations as if she were being asked to sign a peace treaty to end a hundred years of war. "I can do that—Johrun. Now, is it true that your family raises snails as big as this ship?"

The afternoon passed all too swiftly. Johrun found Taryn to be an appreciative, sharp-witted listener. Her own limited experience caused her to ask for many clarifications, but Johrun didn't mind.

Celestro's gruff reemergence put an end to their conversation that day, but over the next few days Johrun gathered a substantial outline of Taryn's history.

The island continent on Anilda on which she had been born was a mix of vast interior deserts and seaside lushness. One trading town, Remy's Post, hosted a Quinary-level culture, but elsewhere the scattered isolated inhabitants lived simply, outside modernity. Alongside subsistence fishing, her native village, Vevaliah, relied exclusively on its extensive orchards of nut palms for sustenance and outside income. The citizens of Vevaliah were all toddy-tappers. From earliest childhood they learned to climb the palms and harvest the big nuts for their meat and juice and weavable shell fibers. Taryn had been the only child of Cleuza and Shen. Life had been rewarding and pleasant, albeit not eventful, until four years ago, when Taryn was fifteen. A plague had arrived that killed all the nut trees. Desperate, the villagers had thought to migrate, but soon learned that conditions were the same everywhere on the continent.

It was at that point that Cleuza and Shen sold their daughter into restavek servitude.

Johrun was horrified. "But surely there was some alternative that could have kept you all together as a family?"

Taryn registered no lingering debilitating shock or regret, but only a mild sense of an inevitable loss mellowed by time. "No, none. No help was available from local sources. Everyone was in the same fix."

"But what about an appeal to the Quinary and their vast resources?"

"I knew nothing about the Quinary back then. But from what I have learned since, the omniafirms take no interest in extending charity to non-customers. And often not even to those who do inhabit their mutual economic sphere. Only profits and losses and market share apply."

Johrun had to admit that Taryn's barefaced but neutral assessment of the Quinary's self-interests was accurate. He had simply never been put in circumstances that would force him to acknowledge the same.

"But for your parents to send you into near-slavery . . ."

"Oh, they were so kind! I honor their sacrifice every night before I go to sleep, with a prayer to Apma Tagaro. They knew it was the only way I would live. Both of them died of starvation when the fish went extinct, along with everyone else left in Vevaliah."

Johrun found his heart going out to this young woman who had suffered losses equal to his. For had she not felt, on some instinctive level, that she owned her planet as much as he owned Verano, only to lose it as well? And had her whole family not gone down into dust just as his had, if less dramatically?

Serving with her new family in Remy's Post ("They gave me fine quarters, right above the kennels."), Taryn had attended, on her one monthly free day, a show put on by a visiting entertainer: the Omnipotent Celestro. Awed and curious about this stranger and his magical ways, Taryn had sought him out back-stage after the performance. Flattered by her attentions and in need of an assistant, Celestro had bought her from her current owners the very next day.

"All this happened a little over a year ago. Since then, my life has been as you have seen. Except that you haven't witnessed how I help in the act."

"What do you do exactly?"

Taryn lit up. "I wear shocking finery! I sing, I dance, I distract. It's all a lot of fun. Listen, I'll sing a little now, just for you."

Taryn launched into a haunting, lilting lament in her native language. Johrun found himself riveted. When she stopped, he took a moment to gather himself together before saying, "That was beautiful. But your life is not all song and caperings. Between times, there is only drudgery."

Taryn shrugged. "It's not as hard a life as being a toddy-tapper. Although I could go back to that pursuit in an instant! See how flexible my toes still remain!"

Taryn kicked off her slippers and pivoted on her rear end upon the divan to swing her legs up to a side table. She plucked a long green fruit from a bowl with her toes and, before Johrun could react, had peeled it down to its naked creamy flesh.

"Here, have it," she said as she lifted it effortlessly under his nose with her feet.

Johrun accepted the prize but forbore from consuming it immediately.

He wanted to ask if Taryn's duties included having sex, willingly or otherwise, with her owner. But he hesitated out of delicacy and a certain shyness. As if reading his mind—a trick learned from her master?—Taryn volunteered, "There is one troubling thing in my life. I have gaps in my memory."

"How so?"

"Whenever Celestro summons me into his quarters, I remain aware of everything until the door closes. Then comes a period of blankness. Then I regain my senses back on the far side of a closing door."

Was she being coy? Johrun looked into her sincere face and decided she was not. He fumed at this revelation, but replied mildly. "I am sure it is only a harmless fugue brought on by overwork."

Taryn nodded agreeably, but Johrun was not sure she fully bought his lame explanation any more than he did.

The remaining days of the voyage further deepened the connections among the three people forced to orbit around Celestro, until Johrun felt he had known Taryn for a good part of his life, and Lutramella had adopted her.

When the *Mummer's Grin* transited back into the familiar universe, Johrun and Lutramella felt compelled to give their equipment one final going over. Purchased on Bodenshire before takeoff, the outfits had depleted their small remaining funds even further. If this mission came to naught, they would be on the verge of utter poverty.

"Do you regret spending your manumission endowment on this mad chase, Lu?"

"I would have spent ten times as much gratefully, if I had had it."

"When we are on top of the world again, Lu, I will pay you back that tenfold amount."

"Just make a place for me by your side always, and I will be happy."

Their rigs consisted of extremely heavy outerwear and boots; snowshoes; a primitive medical kit devoid of Polly or Smalls technics, all powders, creams and plastic bandages; sharp-tipped walking sticks; goggles and mittens; condensed

nutriments; backpacks to hold everything with built-in canteens and sipping hoses; sleeping bags and blankets. Because
Johrun's gun would not function on Itaska, he now owned a poignard like Lu's.

Celestro had insisted on being provided with identical
accoutrements for himself and Taryn. "If we are to accompany
you to Drowne's demesne, we must be properly equipped."

"But you're going there for your own benefit, not mine."

"Nonetheless, as leader of this wild-eyed expedition, you
must provide."

Rather than argue, Johrun had negotiated a slight discount
with the outfitter for his bulk purchase and caved in.

Regarding all this stuff, Johrun said, "I still have no real
conception of the conditions on a heimal world. Will it be as cold
as those wet and gloomy days on Bodenshire? That was horrid."

Lutramella snorted. "Bodenshire is to Itaska as Verano is to
Bodenshire. Times ten."

"Perhaps I should just hurl myself out into the vacuum and
be done with life now."

"You might have done so before you spent all my chains. But
now that you are in my debt, you must stay alive for eventual
repayment."

"What a cruel taskmaster you are! Ever since you made me
clean up all the mess resulting from my bedroom dissection
of a spratling herple. How was I to know their stomachs were
pressurized?"

Lutramella's chimeric laughter filled their room.

The artilect guiding the *Mummer's Grin* found the hole in the
atmosphere that permitted a safe descent. Had they entered at
any other spot, their engines would have instantly died, causing
them to plummet helplessly to the ground. Indeed, from space
they had detected with their instruments several such wrecks.

Once settled down on the planet's icy surface, they geared up inside the ship before opening the door. Johrun felt like a mummy excavated from the famous tombs on Sandhill.

"One never keeps an audience waiting," declaimed Celestro. "Let us make our entrance anon!"

The sky overhead resembled thin dirty cotton batting, with the sun a mere irregular swathed lozenge of relative brightness. The clouds seemed pregnant with snow that they might deliver at any moment. The brutal air smote Johrun in the face like a cruel assailant. A strange phenomenon: he could see his exhalations! If he had imagined that he knew the essence of chilliness on Bodenshire, he had been insane. This frigidity was beyond all his imagination. Even inside mittens and boots, his extremities tingled as if ice crystals were forming inside them. Probably not true. He hoped. For a person who had spent all his life to date on a world of perpetual summer, this environment was some kind of calculated insult toward, and rebuttal of, all he held dear.

For three-hundred-and-sixty degrees around the cradled ship, the landscape was the same: a wrinkled savannah of ice and snow. In one direction the minor anomaly of distant jagged hills broke up the horizon.

After half-expecting to be greeted, the four humans saw no welcoming committee. Wouldn't the inhabitants naturally keep watch over the single landing area where unwelcome visitors might arrive? Based on heat sources and other telltales, they had pinpointed the location of Drowne's hideout, the Spires, from orbit, and had had the foresight to bring magnetic compasses with them with which to navigate. But would they really have to walk a thousand kilometers to reach Drowne? Johrun had vaguely counted on a ride of some sort. Not for the first nor last time, he thought how ill-considered and insane this expedition was. Not only did they have to reach Drowne, they had to convince him to help them, and then sneak him into and out of the Quinary's ekumen. Unlikelihoods piled upon impossibilities. And even if they succeeded, Johrun would never win back Verano for himself and Minka.

Thoughts of Minka drew his mind briefly to his unwedded bride. He pictured her cavorting on a nice warm beach with Anders Braulio and the others, uncaring for the plight of her ex-lover. Someday, perhaps, she would thrill to his exploits, all pursued for the betterment of their joint life, the restitution of their heritage and honor, and acknowledge his courage and dedication. But for now, he would have to persist without that support.

Lutramella walked about one hundred meters from the ship, then called out, "This is the edge of the technics zone. My vambrace just stopped working." She returned to her companions.

Taryn stooped and gathered up a double handful of snow. She fashioned it into a ball and heaved it at the ship.

"I've read of such things! Who wants to have a fight?"

Celestro waved an admonishing hand. "Quiet, girl! I sense something!"

Now Johrun could feel and hear a disturbance underfoot. A subtle juddering of the ice, along with a sound like warehouse's worth of glassware being crushed in a compactor.

The icy plain suddenly spewed a tremendous geyser of particles and shards as something enormous jabbed up through the surface.

The creature was all tubular scaled body and an enormous flanged maw, the whole of its flesh colored a glassy translucent blue like the pane in a stained-glass window. However much of it remained buried, the part aboveground swayed some ten meters high.

The visitors stared in helpless fascination at the creature, which made no further approach. Nothing to call it, Johrun fleetingly thought, but an ice worm.

Suddenly, from either side of the worm, two small segments detached and dropped down. Once Johrun's mind and eye adjusted to the unexpected, the detached parts were seen to be humans who had been plastered to the creature's side, even during its underground passage.

The two natives approached.

Here then were members of the Arnapkapfaaluk people, Honko Drowne's minions.

Essentially of Gaian regularity, the natives nonetheless exhibited distinctive features. They were utterly naked, except for something like a thick pelt of spiky black fur that began just under their navels, wrapped around hips and rear, and extended down and between their thighs for a few centimeters. The fur appeared a bodily outgrowth, not a garment, and reasserted itself atop their heads in profusion, forming a kind of puffy protective cowl. Its blackness contrasted with the radical color of their skin, which was a pure milky white that disclosed veins of indigo blood. Their noses were mere slits under flaps, their eyes protected by an extra membrane, and their lips thin.

Johrun had his hand on his knife before he realized what he was doing. But as the natives came closer and seemed unthreatening, he took his hand away. Little good his toothpick would do against their mount anyway.

Face to face, the humans and natives considered each other for a few moments. To Johrun's eyes, the men were identical. Then one of the Itaskans spoke.

"I am Ulik. This is Oolik. What do you have to say before we bid you depart?"

Johrun found his tongue in a dry mouth. "My name is Johrun Corvivios. I am known to your hetman, Honko Drowne. We wish to visit him."

Ulik and Oolik conversed quietly in their own language, then turned to regard the visitors. "We can convey this message. But a response will arrive only after some time. We would ask that you wait outside your ship during that interval, in our presence, so that we may more easily kill you if the hetman so commands."

Johrun gulped. "Agreed."

Ulik—or Oolik—made a gesture at the swaying ice worm. The beast surged up entirely out of its tunnel, like a rogue subway car, revealing a rear that tapered to a point. Johrun had an instant vision of being impaled on that terminus. Then the creature swung about and stuck its head back in the tunnel. Oolik—or Ulik—walked to its side and began palpitating its scales in a complex pattern, like someone issuing commands on a vambrace.

The ice worm emitted a shrilly booming sequence of sounds muffled by the ice. It paused, then commenced to repeat its message over and over.

The Itaskans returned close by the ship. They dropped down to sit comfortably on the ice.

Celestro said, "Given the rate of sound transmission in ice, I estimate the message, oft-boosted by worms intervening between us and Drowne, will take approximately an hour to reach the Spires, and as long to return. I suggest we make ourselves comfortable. Taryn, go inside and fetch some stools and my hookah."

Taryn's move towards the ship provoked some quivering alertness in the Itaskans, but when she returned with the innocent gear, they relaxed.

Johrun found the waiting interminable, especially in the intense cold. Unfortunately, the *Mummer's Grin* did not carry any such thing as a portable heating unit, the need for which had seemed nonexistent until now. Nor did it offer any combustibles for an old-fashioned fire. He alternated sitting with stamping about to goose his circulation. Celestro calmly enjoyed his perfumed smoke. Taryn and Lutramella played noughts and crosses by scratching the ice with their knives.

The ice worm that had brought the men eventually ceased broadcasting. It reversed itself again, sticking its tail back in the hole.

Two hours and some minutes passed, slow as a well-fed herple in search of a place to doze. Then the ice worm quivered and belled forth the coded transmission it had just received from the underground sonic relay.

The Itaskans arose and approached the alert visitors. Although apparently unarmed, they might still be formidable foes, toughened by their harsh environment and especially backed up by their titanic steed. Johrun again gripped the pommel of his blade, intent on not going down without a fight.

"Hetman Drowne consents to see you. You will leave in a brief time."

Johrun felt the tension drain from his body. Although many challenges remained, they had survived this first critical encounter.

He said, "Are we going to have to walk all the way? Or even worse, ride beneath the ice on that monster?"

For the first time the Itaskans displayed emotion, laughing in sharp barks. "You could never master the implacable protocols for fraternal worm communion. Even among us, worm riders are an elite. No, in just a short time your transportation will arrive."

Another hour crept by before figures appeared on the horizon. When they resolved, the new contingent proved to be two Itaskans, two worms, and two sleighs. The surface worms were a quarter the size of the subglacial one. Harnessed to the sleighs by a complicated rig buffered by springs and pistons, they slithered across the ice with a curious combination of humping and undulating, producing a jouncy ride.

Ulik—or Oolik—announced, "The journey will take five days. I put you in charge of Cupuni."

The female Itaskan thus singled out exhibited a generic likeness to the men, save for naked breasts of moderate dimensions.

Celestro chuckled. "The proverbial witch's tits against which all degrees of coldness are measured. Life eventually affords the reification of all cliches."

Cupuni remained stolid, not deigning to acknowledge Celestro's remarks, even if she grasped their meaning. "You may board the *qamutikla*, two individuals per conveyance. Do not trail any appendages over the sides, or you risk losing them should we cross a razor ridge clumsily."

Celestro and Taryn climbed aboard one sleigh, Lutramella and Johrun aboard the second. They took their seats gingerly, since the "benches" were more like hammocks, skins stretched taut with cords secured to the bone framework. There was a bar to offer a handhold.

Cupuni jumped atop one worm, straddling it, and her companion did likewise.

Without any verbal preamble the worms surged into motion, the *qamutikla* jolted forward before settling to a relatively smooth flow, and the journey to an unknown fate had commenced.

CHAPTER 13

The first several hours of the ride, Johrun found invigorating and exciting. Lightweight yet effective insulated blankets from their packs kept him and Lutramella as near to warm as possible. In fact, Johrun found he could almost pretend that the wind coursing past his hood was a summery Verano breeze. The worms appeared to be travelling at roughly twenty kilometers an hour, consistent with the promised five-day journey of one thousand kilometers, allowing for periods of rest, meals, and sleep. The frigid alien landscape showed a certain harsh beauty, especially when the sun emerged from the clouds and struck colors and sparkles from various ice formations. Donning his goggles allowed easy viewing. Johrun assumed the membranous eye coverings which the Itaskans enjoyed gave similar protection.

But the next several hours of the trip became merely tolerable. Due to its invariance, the countryside ceased to enchant. One had to hold to the safety bar continuously, bracing oneself against unpredictable jolts, some so severe as to threaten to dislodge the riders from the sleigh. Johrun's muscles soon became strained.

By the second half of that first day's travel, Johrun felt himself trapped in some kind of interminable hellscape. The boredom, the unease, the helplessness—all conduced to a state of apathy. Conversation with Lutramella was nigh impossible, due to the wind of their passage and the frozen quality of Johrun's face.

Stopping for lunch did provide some relief. (Water they could have at any time, thanks to the accessibility of the built-in canteens.) The concentrated nutriments they carried were packed with energy boosters. But the halt had also involved watching the Itaskans eat.

Cupuni and her companion, a fellow named Inuk, each went to their respective worms. They made a small ritual obeisance, then lifted up a scale and made a short incision in the revealed worm skin with a sharp fingernail. Purple worm blood began to flow. The Itaskans pressed their lips to the wound and drank till sated.

Turning away from her meal with stained lips, Cupuni saw Johrun watching. "I fail as a proper host. Would you care to join me? There is more than enough. It is only coarse hunter's sustenance, not what you will enjoy at the court of Hetman Drowne, but it is still very good."

Johrun could only shake his head as he repressed his gagging.

By the time night arrived and they made camp, Johrun felt, while motionless, as if he were still moving. He had a headache which he partially alleviated by analgesics from the medical kit. Even an auroral display failed to delight.

Cupuni and Inuk caused the worms to lie down head to tail so as to form a circle around the sleighs.

"They will protect us from roving *orqoi* and *lupalik*. I myself do not fear the claws of the *orqoi* so much, but the fangs of the *lupalik* are poisoned."

Taking vague mental pictures of these beasts to bed with him, Johrun curled up with Lutramella in their conjoined sleeping bags, while Celestro and Taryn did the same. The Itaskans scuffled together a heap of snow and burrowed inside.

The second day was much the same, a tedious test of endurance.

But by midafternoon of the third day Johrun began to feel seriously ill. He found mental concentration impossible. His joints ached. His skin was hot. His eyes felt as if someone had removed them and rubbed them first in lemon juice and then in grit before rough reinsertion.

Johrun decided he would ignore all these symptoms and tough things out. After all, they were more than halfway to the Spires, where he could rest and recuperate. Fulfilling their mission was paramount.

But Lutramella sensed something amiss in his condition—possibly when his head dropped forward involuntarily and his brow impacted the safety bar, eliciting only a pained grunt.

"Stop! Stop the sleigh!"

Johrun tried to protest. "No, don't . . . Feel fine . . ." But the splice gave no heed to his words. Lutramella wrestled him upright.

Johrun found himself somehow stretched out on a blanket on the snow. Blurry faces peered down at him in a ring from above. Was that Minka? He tried to lift a hand to caress her cheek, but his arm flopped down after rising only a few centimeters. He knew there were pressing matters of great importance which he must be attending to. Didn't his father want him to check that the herples had not all flown away into space on their gossamer wings? How would Sweetmeats Pasturage survive?

And then darkness and unconsciousness came down.

Johrun awoke to a familiar chimeric paw on his forehead, much as when he had been sick as a child, and the words, "His skin feels normal now."

He opened his eyes. Lutramella and Taryn Endelwode were beside him, one on each side of a raised pallet. They had divested themselves of their heavy outerwear.

Johrun knew himself to be naked, lying atop and under furs. The walls and ceiling and floor of his room were fashioned from ice of indeterminate thickness. Daylight came through cutout windows in opposite walls, covered with tightly pinned hides scraped to translucency. A small spherical bone brazier on legs radiated a paltry warmth from some glowing moss visible behind its slotted facade.

"Where am I? What happened?"

Lutramella said, "We are at the Spires. You remained unconscious for the last two days of travel, and for another day here."

Johrun tried to sit up but failed. Taryn said, "He's still weak. He needs food. Something hot." She got up and left.

"What was the matter with me?"

"Celestro has a theory. He feels that your Veranonal nanomites came into conflict with the Itaskan Suppressor nanomites. They were at war with each other."

"Why weren't you affected?"

"As a splice, my physiology includes sartorized workarounds to accommodate frequent displacements to other owners on other planets. And whatever species of internal mites Celestro and Taryn harbor did not provoke such an attack."

Taryn returned, bearing a steaming bowl of what proved to be fish soup. Celestro followed right behind her. Johrun managed to sit up, propped against a heap of furs. He took the bowl and gratefully downed half the broth in one gulp.

"Who healed me? Lu, was it you? Celestro? Taryn? Does Honko Drowne have a doctor in residence?"

Taryn began to giggle. Lutramella looked away. Celestro coughed into the crook of his elbow.

Lutramella finally answered. "It was Cupuni."

"Cupuni? But how?"

"She recognized your symptoms and knew just what to do, possibly from seeing other victims. She shared her Itaskan internal biome with you, endowing you with her immunity and effecting a new equilibrium."

"How so?"

Taryn laughed. "She fucked the living daylights out of you! That's how she passed the gut bugs. What a show! I've never seen such tongue work, even during the sharing days of Apma Tagaro back home! She was all over you like stink on swamp orchid! Even though you were mostly insensible, you cooperated like a puppet. A very enthusiastic puppet. Wow!"

Celestro sought to drape a dignified mantle about the event. "Really, *Vir* Corvivios, your dignity remains intact. We all averted our gaze."

"I certainly didn't!" Taryn countered.

Johrun felt utterly mortified. Also, the image of Cupuni's bloody lips resurfaced. But when he considered that death was the probable alternative to having been the subject of such a lubricious public display, his chagrin began to dissipate.

As if to bolster Johrun's shifting sentiments, Celestro said, "There was no other option. None of our archaic drugs did a thing."

"Well, I hope someone thanked her properly."

"Oh, we were saving that job for you!" Taryn said.

Johrun developed a sudden preoccupation with the rest of his soup. When he had finished, he said, "If I might have some privacy, I'd like to get up and get dressed. I assume Drowne knows why we're here."

"Not in detail. That diplomatic conversation falls also to you."

"I'm ready."

Celestro and Taryn obligingly left the room. Johrun threw back the furs and got to his feet. A bit unsteady, he improved as he moved about. Lutramella helped him dress, including his underjacket. Away from the little brazier, the room of ice maintained its chill. Johrun was careful to strap on his poignard, for whatever good it might do him. He noticed that Lu wore hers.

"This chamber—are we in a house of some sort?"

"Best you see the arrangement for yourself. Follow me."

The single doorway led to a kind of pantry and kitchen, with naturally refrigerated larder and fire-moss stove; this middle room also exhibited windows on each side. The subsequent doorway gave onto a parlor of sorts, chairs of bone and hide, and more windows in, say, what might be either the east and west or north and south walls. The exit from that room led directly to a curving staircase flush against the far exterior wall: steps carved into the ice, winding up and down.

"Honko Drowne awaits us below. But we can spare a minute to go to the rooftop."

The climb was only another storey or two. The egress was straight up through a hatch in the roof as the stairs came to an end.

Johrun shivered as he stepped into the open air. But with a lack of wind and full sun, the temperature could be tolerated without heavy coats for a short while.

He and Lutramella stood upon the flat top of a polyhedral tower of ice, some twenty storeys high, no balustrade or parapet for protection. Scattered irregularly about within the radius typical of a large sports stadium were a dozen other such towers, shafts of pure ice rearing to the heavens.

"I have learned that they are a natural formation, a type of ice spike that grows upward from the ground over the millennia. Itaska has unique conditions allowing them to reach this incredible height. The Arnapkapfaaluk people never bothered with them, preferring to live on the ground with their worms. But under Drowne's leadership, using imported hand tools, the spikes have been turned into habitations. Thus, the Spires."

"So Drowne maintains some minimal contact with the Quinary ekumen, to secure such things as tools?"

"Apparently so. There are always providers of goods who are willing to overlook a criminal's status to reap their profits. He likes to import both luxuries and necessities for himself and his wife."

"His wife?"

"You'll meet her in a moment. I will warn you, she's a problem. I don't like her, and I don't think you will either. But let us go down now, and you can make your own judgments."

"Will Celestro and Taryn accompany us?"

"I thought it best to have them hang back, until we solidify our own position with our host."

"Very sensible, Lu."

The descent down twenty storeys left Johrun's weakened legs all aquiver. But once at ground level, while still in the stairwell, he summoned up all his courage and determination, massaged his sore calves, thrust back his shoulders, and entered Drowne's quarters.

The ice walls and ceiling and floor were ameliorated by a profusion of carpets and hanging tapestries. A fire-moss chimenea cast a comfortable warmth—comfortable by Itaskan standards. On Verano, the temperature would have been considered incapacitating. Several Itaskans stood or lounged about like courtiers or functionaries. And on two large chairs, almost thrones, sat Honko Drowne and his wife.

It was obvious how the substantial, barrel-chested Drowne had earned his nickname of "Red Lion of the Spires." His wild hair, shot through with some threads of grey, was nonetheless a fiery corona. An untamed beard of the same bold auburn shade completed the effect of an encircling lion's mane. His rough-hewn countenance evoked a bust by some primitivist artist.

Drowne's wife was a native Itaskan. But unlike every other member of that race whom Johrun had seen, she was enormous. A tall woman to begin with, she dominated her personal sphere with a bulk as large as her husband's. Her fleshy face manifested a kind of avarice and willfulness. Unlike her comrades, she was clothed, in a robe of yellow and silver horizontal stripes, although her feet remained bare. An additional gesture of differentiation was the close cropping of her black hair.

Drowne's narrow eyes of frosty pewter drilled into Johrun. The Red Lion of the Spires shot abruptly and impulsively to his feet, pointed at Johrun with arm outthrust, and bellowed, "Tell me why I should not have you killed where you stand, for the sins of your family!"

Had Johrun not recently been subjected to a similar confrontational greeting from Quinary Invigilator Oz Queloz; had he not lost the entirety of his patrimony, and all his loved ones save for Lutramella and Minka; had his marriage to his childhood sweetheart not been dissolved before it was even formalized; and had he not recently faced exile on Bodenshire, the harrowings of a wintry pilgrimage, and death through nanomite cascade—well, then perhaps Drowne's accusatory shout might have seemed scary or life-threatening. But as matters stood, Johrun found—to his relief, surprise, satisfaction, and even pride—that the Red Lion's verbal assault provoked not fear but laughter.

As Johrun's hearty chortles crescendoed, Drowne gradually lowered his arm, perhaps realizing he looked foolish when his interlocutor would not play his assigned part.

"Are you mad?" asked the Red Lion. "Has your illness unbalanced your mind?"

Johrun wiped tears from his cheeks. "Far from it, *Vir* Drowne! I am coming into a kind of sanity, I think, for the first time in my life. And my freshborn clarified mentality reveals your question to be hollow, a sham. Why won't you kill me on the spot? Because you haven't! You could have let me die already, or cut my throat as I slept. But the fact that I am now standing here means you have no intention of taking my life—at least for the moment—and also that you might in fact welcome my presence, if only out of mere curiosity, or because you think that I might benefit you somehow."

Drowne tried to glower for a moment, but gave it up for a bad job. Instead he climbed off his chair and came right up to Johrun. He clapped big hands on the younger man's shoulders and regarded his face intently, before finally saying, "Yes, goddamn it, you are young Xul all over! Not so much in the face, but with his same spirit and powers of intellect! How I am carried back down the river of the years! I recall once when we were boys together on Hodak how that sly bastard got me to admit by syllogisms that I did not deserve my own girlfriend, just because he wanted her more."

Here Drowne lapsed into a solemn frown again, discontinuing his friendly grip on Johrun's shoulders. "And that incident, as well as others, should have warned me of the vile larceny he and Brayall Soldevere would perpetrate on me. The theft of my newly discovered world and the subsequent impugning of my character became a wrenching millstone around my neck that sent me down the hard path I still tread today. Reiver, plunderer, a wolf among sheep! A sad fate for a fellow who once dreamed only of a quiet cottage and a passel of brats. As one who shares my betrayer's bloodline, Johrun Corvivios, you have much to atone for."

Johrun ventured to take one of Drowne's hands in both of his, an impulsive gesture of sincerity. "That ancient but still vivid crime is precisely why I'm here. Having learned of it only over the past few weeks, I have made it my mission to undo it, insofar as I can, and to save the world we both cherish."

Drowne looked at once suspicious and hopeful. "What do you mean?"

"Let us sit down, and I will explain. It's a long story."

Drowne waved at his minions and chairs were brought for both Johrun and Lutramella.

Throughout this fraught introduction, Drowne's wife had registered everything with a concentrated focus but without participating. Now Drowne made a substantial nod toward her and said, "This is my wife, Akna. Her wise counsel forms fully half of my resources. So if she asks you to expand or clarify, do so with all alacrity!"

Akna spoke. "I would know the status of this odd creature who accompanies you. I mislike her looks. Is she your consort?"

"No, *Mir* Drowne. She is my lifelong advisor and friend. Without her, I would be lost."

"She reminds me of one of those fierce martens of the *nunatak* crags, who can filch a bit of meat right out of the jaws of a *lupalik.*"

"I assure you, *Mir* Drowne, her ethics are impeccable."

Content to let Johrun make her defense, Lutramella said nothing, but merely showed many teeth in a grin.

Akna appeared to accept this reassurance for the moment.

Johrun composed his mind and began to tell his tale.

The account stretched on for much longer than he had intended. But Drowne paid close attention throughout.

After he had finished, Drowne said, "You seek my help to clarify the status of Verano, to preserve it from unknown interlopers. You think I might come into my rightful ownership of the world at last, and perhaps save you a small place there. I accept your formulations and requests as honest. And I do offer my genuine sympathies for the deaths of your family members. Much as I came to hate the names of Corvivios and Soldevere over the rueful decades, such a treacherous ending against which no man could fight was ignoble. Although it *was* swift and painless, and thus more lenient than what I often envisioned for them!"

Johrun said, "I appreciate your commiserations, *Vir* Drowne, and take them in the spirit in which they are given."

"Enough with honorifics! After all, in some sense I am almost your infamous bad uncle, am I not? Call me Honko."

"With pleasure."

Drowne dragged fingers thoughtfully through his rufous beard. "Back to your request. To do as you ask would involve exposing myself to the dogs of the Quinary who want my hide. I'd risk losing all I have here, for an uncertain future. I'm basically content and happy now, in my exile and retirement. The scope of my ambitions has dwindled, the itch for plunder and revenge has been quelled. The theft of Verano happened a long, long time ago. No, the risk is too great."

Akna Drowne smiled hugely, plainly pleased by Johrun's obvious discomfiture and the denial of his plea.

Johrun sensed all his goals rapidly slipping out of reach. "If only I could assume some of the risk for you, I would do so in an instant!"

Akna Drowne leapt into the opening provided by Johrun's hasty proclamation.

"Husband, why not gauge how reliable a partner this boy would be by assigning him a test? Let him risk something big, although he cannot share in your specific dangers, as a measure of his courage. You have tested your lieutenants similarly in the past to good effect."

Johrun had an instant fancy of being compelled to wrestle an ice worm, or make love to Cupuni again. "What would convince you of my willingness to share all our mutual hazards?"

Challenged, Honko Drowne did not make an immediate proposal, allowing Akna to lean over and whisper in his ear. Drowne's face brightened.

"I have just the test. Tomorrow at dawn, you will climb one of the Spires. Hand over hand, up the outside walls. If you reach the top, I will reconsider my participation in your quest."

Before he could quail or equivocate, Johrun forced himself slowly to rise and said, "I accept!"

"Excellent! At least you show spirit. We will see tomorrow if your decisiveness and physical prowess correspond. And if you survive, we will have a big celebration! A banquet! I understand your traveling companion—Sinestro? Cilantro?—is some kind of entertainer. He will do his act for us. We are not exactly on the main circuit for performers here."

Johrun said, "I'd like to rest for the remainder of the day, if I might."

"Certainly. But let me show you just one of my treasures. It has relevance, should you decide to try to make an early departure without meeting your obligations."

Drowne conducted Johrun and Lutramella outside. Akna and some of the other Itaskans accompanied them.

The cold hit Johrun like a shovel across the face. Although also underdressed for outside temperatures, Drowne seemed not to mind it so much, having no doubt adapted over the years of his tenancy here. But Lutramella too was shivering.

The Red Lion led the party to an open space some distance away from the Spires.

"Summon Tizheruk!" he commanded.

One of the Itaskans started to dance. His intricate heavy steps involved lots of exaggerated patterned thumping on the resonant ice.

In a short while Johrun heard the by-now-familiar crunching, grinding, splintering sound of the underground passage of a worm.

The eruption of the arriving worm was even more spectacular than that which had greeted the visitors back at the brane-ship, a veritable fountaining of flinders, powder, and hail, for this worm, colored like a piece of green driftglass, was easily twice the size of that other creature, or eight times the size of the sleigh worms.

Drowne moved to proudly pet the flanks of the glossy half-erect giant. "My darling! She can cover five hundred miles in a day, and track down any quarry. I have a special carriage which she hauls at top speeds. But no such guidance is needed when she mercilessly hunts down any off-planet visitors who unwisely decide to depart by night before I bid them farewell!"

CHAPTER 14

Lutramella had always recommended the value of learning handicrafts. They taught dexterity and concentration. In his youth, Johrun had been introduced to fiber arts and pottery making, wood carving, and bead stringing. In his cluttered bedroom back at Sweetmeats Pasturage hung a lopsided blanket he had woven. He had enjoyed these hobby pursuits to varying degrees, without any of them becoming a passion. But certainly he had never imagined that knowing how to sew might someday save his life.

Lutramella finished cutting up one of the tough blankets they had brought with them from the ship. The strong light-weight insulating fabric had yielded reluctantly to the edge of her poignard, and Johrun found that pushing a needle through it required using the underside of a bone saucer rather than his sore thumb. But despite these impediments, they were making good progress on turning Johrun's shell jacket and outermost snow pants into what might, with luck, serve as a makeshift wingsuit. Accordion'd pie slices of fabric under the arms and between the legs had to be fashioned so as to still allow for a free range of climbing movements, and the improvisational tailors had had to take apart and redo the design a couple of times. Now the evening was growing late, and they hurried so as allow for some much-needed rest.

The illumination in their chilly room in the Spires came from lighted wicks floating in bowls of some kind of organic oil, casting wavery shadows, and Johrun had a fleeting hallucination of being sent back in time to some antique era of Gaia's long history.

At last they finished, as best they could, and just at the moment when their comrades arrived. Celestro and Taryn, lodged one floor below in the ice tower, brought their own contributions to the anticipated success in the morning of Johrun's dangerous ascent of one of the natural ice spikes.

"Here you go," said Taryn, handing over the gloves she had modified as partially fingerless. "With luck, your hands will stay warm, and yet you can find your holds."

"What of the shoes?" asked Lutramella.

"Oh, yes, of course. Here they are."

Lutramella had donated her special footwear purchased on Bodenshire. Lacking a rigid sole, the splice's flexible shoes would afford Johrun's feet more responsive purchase on the climb. But gussets had had to be inserted to allow for Johrun's wider foot. Needles and tough surgical thread from their medical kit had been invaluable in this hasty retrofitting.

Johrun laid out his gear and studied the pieces. "I suppose this is good as it gets with what we've got. And if I had not often climbed the Salazar Escarpment and other rock faces on Verano before, no amount of gear would help me."

Celestro stepped forward with a handful of nutriment bars. "I've selected the comestibles from our stock that should provide the largest metabolic boost and aid your glycogen processing. Consume them at least an hour before dawn."

"Thank you."

"And then there is this."

Celestro removed from an inner pocket of his billowy blouse a small flat leather case. He flipped open the case to reveal a rank of one-shot injectables. He selected a certain unit from its cradle.

"Luckily, Suppressor nanomites have no grudge against mere chemicals and biologics, even while they deny the more sophisticated products of the Smalls and Pollys. This is a very affable stimulant which should provide you with increased mental acuity, heightened proprioception, and an abundance of energy. The payback when it wears off is somewhat onerous. But I think you'll foot the bill gladly. The effects are almost instantaneous, so administer at will."

Johrun took the drug. "This might make all the difference, Celestro. I am in your debt."

"Tut tut, lad. We can discuss that later. And now, we'd best all be off to sleep."

Celestro shook hands with Johrun and the splice. Taryn hugged and kissed both. Her lips met Johrun's in a more than sisterly fashion. My god, he wondered, was she still thinking of his involuntary interlude with Cupuni? But before he could think how best to respond, she was gone.

Inside the conjoined sleeping bags, Johrun wrapped his arms around Lutramella from behind, for both warmth and comfort. She nestled closer, smelling like river water and earthen dens. He expected sleep to come laggardly if at all. But he was out before he could formulate a single worry.

A rough jostling dragged him into consciousness. An Itaskan stood beside the bed. Wan daylight leaked through the hide-covered windows.

"Hetman Drowne and his wife await."

Johrun first scarfed down his food bars. He used the primitive water closet—a seat, a hole, and a chute—then dressed. Lifting his arms and widening his stance, he tested the batlike folds of cloth. He felt unconstrained by the excess material. And if he fell off the tower, the modifications might at least slow his plummet. Making sure he had the drug injector in one pocket, he descended the stairs with some care. With no melting, the ice never grew extra slippery—but it was still ice. Lutramella came right after him.

They picked up Celestro and Taryn one flight down. Realizing there was nothing more to be said at this point, the pair merely nodded solemnly and followed.

Outside their particular Spire, Honko Drowne looked fussy and misassembled, as if he were more used to sleeping in of a morning, rather than rising with the sun to judge the squirrel-like merits of a potential business partner who happened to be the descendant of his mortal enemy. Heavyset Anka seemed more alert, sizing up Johrun and his weird outfit quizzically, but registering no objections.

Johrun attempted to make the all-too-human figure of the Red Lion jibe with the sanitized family legend memorialized in the statue at Danger Acres, and also with the unholy bogeyman bandit who had reaved life and wealth from so many victims across the galaxy. Drowne had attempted to humanize and endear himself yesterday as a "bad uncle," but Johrun was under no delusions that the man would hesitate to slit Johrun's throat if he stood in the way of the Red Lion's desires, or if doing so would turn a profit.

"At last!" Drowne exclaimed when he saw Johrun. "We can proceed with this festive carnival now. Breakfast awaits whether you succeed or smash! You didn't happen to bring any mocambo with you, did you? Our supplier is late with ours, and I'd kill for a cup!"

"Unfortunately, no, Honko. But I can offer you all the ice water you might want."

Drowne laughed and slapped Johrun's back. "Save that ice water for your own veins, boy. Now, let's pick your opponent."

Following Johrun's lead, the party moved slowly among the scattered titanic residential spikes, acquiring tagalong spectators. Johrun soon found what he was looking for: a tower whose walls featured the largest proportion of useful irregularities on the side that was catching the sunlight. The small warmth and increased clarity offered by the sunlight might prove consequential.

Johrun cast his gaze upward. Wispy clouds ambled across the aquamarine sky. Twenty stories, only fifty meters or so. He had climbed much higher in the past. But never on ice, and never after just emerging from a sickness. Still, he felt good, and counted on resting at each window opening. And on Celestro's drug. Which he must somehow now secretly administer.

Johrun caught Celestro's eye, and his co-conspirator took his meaning.

"*Vir* Drowne! You are a gambling man, I assume. Might I make a wager with you on the success of my comrade? Look at the quality of this ring of mine. Genuine toadstone from the Smudgepot system. Certainly you would match at least a thousand chains against it? A bagatelle for a man of your standing. And wouldn't the ring shine fine on *Mir* Drowne's dainty finger? *Mir* Drowne, come have a look."

While the Drownes were busy, Johrun hastily infused the drug. He felt its enhancements immediately. How long they would last, he could not say.

"I'm ready now, if you don't mind."

The Drownes turned their attention back to Johrun. He limbered his fingers, then began to climb.

The icy protuberances and clefts soon rendered his fingers numb. He found he had to rely on vision to gauge the almost invisible handholds rather than touch, jamming his insensitive digits into cracks and wrapping them around lumps of ice as if they were mechanisms rather than intimate parts of his body. His feet fared better, protected by Lutramella's slippers. But his exposed face, and even his chest and thighs beneath the clothing began to absorb the chill. How very far away any kind of summer seemed!

Pausing to rest on one window ledge and to blow hot breath on his fingers, Johrun dared to look down. Halfway. Best to move quickly, lest the drug fade or muscles stiffen.

He noted gratefully that the tower seemed to taper slightly from bottom to top, so that rather than facing a strictly vertical surface, he could imagine he was inching up a slope, however steep. Such mental deceits sometimes made all the difference.

Finally, impossibly, he reached the ultimate storey. Standing on the last window ledge, he found his eyes almost level with the rooftop, just slightly below. There was no easy way to make the final surge, so he just did it before he could think about it. In one essential sequence, he braced his palms on the unseen roof, leaped upward and converted his arms to levers that would push the rest of him higher. He flopped forward at the waist onto the roof, then dragged and crabbed himself forward until he was entirely atop the Spire. He lay exhausted for a few moments, then began to draw a knee forward and push up, so as to stand.

Feet and legs entered his vision from across the width of the roof. He looked up.

Akna Drowne stood where the stairs debouched, out of sight of those on the ground. With her were two more Itaskans. Without a word, she gestured to her henchman. They trotted forward, picked Johrun up by ankles and wrists and slung him into space.

In mid-air Johrun tried to spin around like a cat to face the earth. He whipped out his arms and spread his legs. He could feel the wind catch in the extra folds of cloth. Stitches tugged, then held. He seemed to be dropping more slowly. Familiar instincts from his low-mass gliding pursuits back home took over. He banked and curved down, moving much faster than desirable, but not, he hoped, at bone-breaking speed. He caught a glimpse of the people below racing to position themselves to intercept his landing. A patch of ground seemed more snow than ice, and he aimed for it.

Just before impact he curled himself up as best he could. No way he could land on his feet without shattering both legs . . .

The patch was indeed mostly snow. But there was plenty of hard ice as well that dug and clawed.

The breath was knocked out of him. He half skidded, half rolled, half plowed, yet held on to consciousness.

By the time the crowd reached him, he was actually able to get upright under his own power. But one wrist felt useless, and every other part ached.

Lutramella and Taryn moved to help support him. They gave him water and a bar.

Drowne glared for a whole minute at Johrun, during which time Akna made her uncommented-on return. Finally the Red Lion said, "You achieved the top. That met the test, and was indeed a feat. Well done. But then you failed somehow, with victory so close, and nearly ensured your doom. Not good. Shows a sloppiness that could ruin any scheme. Do you have an explanation?"

Drowne looked at Akna, who returned his gaze with an ultimate sangfroid.

"No. Your assessment is substantially correct."

"And you also revealed a certain level of chicanery, a coward's precautions. What were you really risking, given that you could always fall back on that sneaky contraption?"

"Don't you prefer your partners to anticipate all contingencies and be nimble?"

"Bah! That is the mincing logic of a scholiast, not the bold attitude of someone who could guard my back when I exposed myself to the Quinary. No, I think this test, however amusing, proves I would be unwise to place my fate in your hands. And besides, in the end, why should I help anyone who bears the hated name of Corvivios? Our dealings are at an end. You may stay the night here, and then be gone. We will see in the morning if I choose to provide a ride back to your ship. Or perhaps I will decide to keep you all here for a while, in order to examine your imperfections more closely."

Drowne turned away. He placed an arm around his wife and said, "Your notion to test this fellow was most wise, pet. We learned that the rot in the Corvivios line is still extant." They walked off together.

Johrun felt on the verge of collapse. All this effort, risking death, for nothing.

Celestro sought to buck him up. "I know just how you feel, lad. Utterly shattered. Me too. There's no chance I can claim my winnings of a thousand chains from that peevish rascal now."

Honko Drowne was a stickler for ceremony and for carrying out his hostly duties. Or perhaps he merely relished any excuse to indulge his appetites with a banquet. Or perhaps he was simply hungry for company. Johrun could not imagine that he received too many visitors. All his old comrades from his corsair days were dead or imprisoned or on the run. And while the Itaskans, like any nation, had their own rich culture, its dimensions fell more along the lines of composing epic poems about soggy maritime hunts than debating the acting talents of the latest Pondicherry dream queens. Or perhaps Drowne simply enjoyed lording it over people, exhibiting his superiority.

Or perhaps his sadism was immeasurable.

After crushing Johrun's hopes, Drowne had pretended that their visit was still an ongoing pleasant affair, and insisted on treating them like tourists. Johrun—once his wrist and ribs were taped up, and primitive pain pills ingested—had been forced to accompany his friends on a tour of the Spires conducted by Drowne himself. They visited native workshops and child nurseries, kitchens, and butchers, a boatmaker's yard, full of small skin-sheathed kayaks. Celestro took a seemingly unfeigned interest in the sights, commenting that he was surprised that the Itaskans enjoyed access to tools forged of metal and not just bone.

"All my doing," said Drowne. "Every bit of worked metal is imported. But I don't begrudge spending a few chains here and there on my people if it makes their lives easier. My treasury is sufficiently large not to notice such trivial disbursements."

"Might we be privileged to see this repository of the, ah, levies you formerly made upon the citizens of the Quinary?"

"Ha! You'd love to rummage among my valuables, wouldn't you! But no, I fear that stop is off the itinerary. However, I will show you my pride and joy."

A large, anomalously modern outbuilding alongside one of the towers, a prefab geodesic dome of plastic panels, held what Drowne laughing called "my chariot."

The vehicle consisted of a single enormous wheel of deft engineering, plainly an import as well. Its inner rim or track supported a passenger sphere—with door and windows—riding on its own wheeled undercarriage. From two opposite points on the sphere's equator, fittings supported a worm harness.

"You understand the concept of a monowheel, I hope. The outer wheel, the part that actually traverses the ground, is propelled by the motion of the inner wheel—or sphere in this case—as it attempts to climb the inner rim, forcing the outer wheel to turn. Something like a toy ball with a rodent inside, a simple fulfillment of gravity. Generally, the inner device is motorized. But that can't be on Itaska. And so I simply hitch this to my monstrous Tizheruk, and off I go, monarch of all the lands I crisscross!"

"Fabulous! Such a feeling of freedom. You are indeed a lucky ruler."

This excruciating forced march occupied most of the day, leaving Johrun utterly debilitated by the time they were allowed to return to their quarters, in the late afternoon.

"You may rest for approximately three hours. And then I command your presence in my quarters for our feast. And I shall expect the promised entertainment from our conjurer."

Johrun fell like a sack of bricks onto the pile of furs. Without being asked, Lutramella commenced a massage. Soon he drifted off to sleep.

When he awoke, he felt a little better, and was actually somewhat hungry.

"It's time to go down," said Lutramella.

"I hardly care what happens downstairs, so long as we are fed first."

"I would not presume to guess at our fate, Joh. But it might not be what at first seems most likely."

At the landing of Celestro's quarters, they encountered Taryn and her owner, ready to descend. From his pack, Celestro had selected a costume of surpassing gaudiness, all colored silks and scintillant spangles.

Johrun was not inclined to applaud Celestro's panache. "You resemble one of those gimcrack mechanisms used to scare away mist weevils from the millet fields on Legato Prime."

"Appearances can be deceiving, as the bacillus said to the emperor."

"Why is your assistant not garbed likewise?"

"I thought it best not parade her opulent charms before Queen Akna."

"Yes, a smart move. The Queen is a jealous and vengeful sort. Well, let's go have our last meal."

"Remain sanguine, my friend! You have the Omnipotent Celestro at your side."

The room where Johrun and Lutramella had been first received by the Drownes was laid out with a fine array of foods and drink. Familiar imported viands from many worlds of the Quinary found local rivals, such as braised pinniped snouts, dewhiskered, and stuffed albatross. A plethora of candles contributed both heat and light.

From his perch, Honko Drowne welcomed them heartily. "Fill your plates, lounge at ease! The evening is just beginning."

From the cohort of attendant Itaskans emerged a trio of musicians. Their instruments were fashioned of baleen and strung with dried fish guts, and rendered a shrill cocophany, presumably by intention.

Johrun ate with abandon and drank numerous goblets of some kind of pink alcoholic fizz. By the time Celestro was summoned to perform, Johrun was feeling pleasantly apathetic. Let his foolish quest expire in a fug of grease and alcohol.

The entertainer recapitulated many of the tricks he had done onboard the *Mummer's Grin* en route to Itaska: things turned into other things, and either manifested where they should not be, or disappeared from where they should be.

Then, with Drowne roaring with laughter, and even Akna looking amused, Celestro embarked on a new routine.

"Now, *Vir* Drowne, with your kind permission, I shall attempt to becloud your senses and impose a new and foreign mindset on you. Are you willing to proceed?"

"The robust persona of Honko Drowne is invincible! Try your best to overwhelm it!"

Celestro brought his face into proximity with Drowne's and locked eyes with him. "Feel my ineffable soul effusions as they seep into yours!" Celestro slowly raised both hands and dropped them upon Drowne's bulky shoulders. The Red Lion gave a start, as if pricked. A sudden lassitude swamped his being.

"Your will is now an extension of mine. You must do as I command! Dance a tarantella for us."

Drowne got up from his chair and performed a clumsy jig.

"Enough! I think this small demonstration affirms my mystical powers. It is not necessary for me to make any other arbitrary demands, such as 'Come to my room just before dawn.' No indeed, 'Come to my room, Honko Drowne, just before dawn' is something I utter merely as a lark. And with this, our little game is finished! Honko Drowne, when I snap my fingers, you are again your own man!"

Celestro made the clicking sound, and Honko Drowne emerged instantly from his abstracted state.

"What did I tell you? Invincible, was I not?"

No one contradicted the Red Lion.

"Quite so." Celestro confessed. "I am humbled."

The strained festivities ran their course for another few hours. Then Drowne signalled an end to the evening.

"Sleep well, my guests, for tomorrow is a new day, with new demands and duties."

Trailing behind the rest of his party, Johrun climbed the staircase of ice with leaden feet and empty mind and heart.

At the entrance to Celestro's apartments, the conjuror halted. "*Vir* Corvivios, I find myself lonely tonight, even with my restavek for company. Would you and your splice care to fetch your packs and spend the next few hours until dawn with me?"

"What foolish whim is this, Celestro?"

Celestro showed his right palm. In it rested one of the injectables from his kit, drained.

"Whim yes, foolish no, think you not?"

Fully dressed for the planet's frigid clime, their packs shouldered, having not slept a wink, the four visitors to Itaska waited by the exit to Celestro's rooms, saying nothing. Johrun hardly dared to believe what might be about to transpire.

As the faintest light begin to seep around the edges of the parchment shades, a dim sound of shuffling footsteps coming up the stairs reached them.

Honko Drowne entered the apartment, a sleepwalker's demeanor evident in every movement. He was wearing a thick flannel gown, tasselled nightcap, and fur slippers.

Instantly Celestro slapped a second injectable against his neck. The Red Lion's frame juddered.

Celestro spoke sotto voce. "Honko Drowne, you hear my voice of command. Lead the way outside."

Johrun and the others slinked along behind the Red Lion.

At ground level they were just about to file outside, past the thick curtain of hides that shielded the entrance to the tower, when a voice accosted them.

"Halt! What goes on here!"

Akna Drowne, clad in like manner to her husband, stood at the portal to their apartments. With a quickness of perception, she assessed all the meaning in the frozen guilty tableau. Anger flooded her face, and she opened her mouth wide to shout.

But no words emerged, only a hearty freshet of bright indigo blood.

Lutramella pulled her begored poignard out of Akna's ribs before the woman could even fall.

"So fat was the meaty bitch, I had to shove it in all the way to the guard!"

"Swiftly!" Celestro urged. "Conceal her inside!"

Taryn and Johrun hefted the weighty corpse and carried her into the apartments. They deposited her between bed and wall, then hastened to join the others, already outside.

If Drowne were cognizant of his wife's murder, he was unable to react, exhibiting a mute dispassion. Celestro gave him more orders.

"Fetch the worm dancer to summon Tizheruk. Have your chariot brought here. Then rejoin us. Speedily now!"

Drowne moved off at a brisk clip, as if fully in charge of himself.

"Dare we trust him unsupervised?" Johrun said.

"The manacles of the drug are unbreakable. Have no doubts."

Drowne soon returned with the sleep-fuddled worm dancer. Not far behind, four Itaskans pulled the monowheel by its traces.

The next events happened almost faster than Johrun's dizzied brain could comprehend. Within the space of a quarter hour, the titanic ice worm dubbed Tizheruk had arrived and been yoked to the monowheel. The opened door to the passenger sphere revealed a compartment with a circular cushioned couch just able to seat five people if they all coordinated their in and out breaths. There was no room for luggage.

Johrun said, "Stuff your pockets with food bars. We'll have to drink melted ice. It's only two days back, if Drowne did not exaggerate the speed of this beast."

Celestro said, "Wait! We need a worm rider."

Johrun said, "Let's get Cupuni. She knows the way, and was somewhat sympathetic to us."

Taryn said, "That's a new description for the services she rendered."

Celestro whispered in Drowne's ear, Drowne repeated his words to his minions, and in short form Cupuni showed up. She received her orders directly from Drowne with no evidence of suspicion.

The five riders bundled into the sphere. Johrun leaned out the open door and said to Cupuni, "Take off!"

He barely got the door latched before the monowheel jumped into motion. Outside the windows, the Spires rapidly shrank to a cluster of nubbins on the horizon.

The next two days passed in a quasi-hallucinatory fugue of boredom, anxiety, awkwardness, discomfort, and anticipation. Conversation soon lost its charms. (But before talk petered out, Johrun did manage to express his gratitude to Lutramella for her decisive act of savagery. She only smiled and said, "Better I assume the burden than you, Joh. Splices have no consciences for blood to stain. Or so humans always say.") They never stopped save for sanitary reasons or to collect ice to melt by body heat alone, lacking as they did all other heat sources. They were never cold in the cabin, thanks to that same body heat, but sleep was difficult, not only due to elbows-rubbing proximity but also to the swaying, sometimes bouncing, sometimes convulsive motion of the monowheel.

After the first twenty-four hours of incessant motion had passed, Johrun thought, during a stop, to ask Cupuni how she was faring under the demands for speed.

"I drink Tizheruk's juices while I ride, and sleep atop him as well. It is not a routine I would endure forever, but two days is easy."

Drowne gave no trouble and undertook no independent actions. But he did begin to seem twitchy after a day and a half, and Celestro administered another injectable of compulsion drug.

"My last dose. We could of course simply tie him up at this juncture, but it's easier to have him docile."

Finally, after a seeming eternity of stagnant, chafing travel, their braneship came into sight. Johrun thought he had never seen anything so beautiful.

Cupuni received orders from Drowne to halt the worm a little distance from the ship. Johrun feared that Tizheruk might inadvertently harm their craft, and strand them.

Everyone emerged from the capsule. Johrun's legs felt stiff as wood. The wrist he had injured throbbed. Onboard the ship there would be high-tech solace.

Johrun turned to Cupuni. "All my thanks for your unstinting service, Cupuni."

The Itaskan smile, seldom seen, revealed its kinship to all human benevolence elsewhere.

"You take some of me to the stars. Don't forget."

They began to march awkwardly forward. Lutramella kept checking her vambrace for signs they had left the Supressor zone behind.

The signature barrage of sounds made by a subterranean worm burst upon them. One of the behemoths erupted into the air. It shed a dozen Itaskans who had been clamped to its torso. They began to run toward Johrun and company.

"Our plot is revealed," Celestro said. "A force closer than the Spires must have been dispatched to stop us! Run!"

Lutramella was already in the lead. She suddenly stopped.

"My vambrace lives. Here is civilization! Johrun, take this!"

Johrun came abreast of Lutramella and snatched his Kingslake glial jammer from her hand. He turned and fanned the Itaskans with its invisible beam. Down they tumbled, like skittles, not permanently hurt. Outside the gun's range, the two worms, without human guidance, dropped peacefully to the ice.

The modest interior of the ship resembled heaven. It took but a few words to the artilect to initiate its climb to orbit.

Johrun and Taryn and Lutramella fell upon each other, laughing, crying, and exclaiming. Without orders, Honko Drowne, still in his soiled sleepwear, remained standing like a moribund puppet.

When their spontaneous relief had ceased to flow, Johrun said, "At last we bring Honko Drowne to Bodenshire and justice."

Celestro's voice was firm yet placid. "I think not."

Johrun turned to see Celestro pointing a large pistol at him and the others.

"My plans," the man said, "take precedence."

CHAPTER 15

First, many decades ago, Xul Corvivios and Brayall Soldevere had stolen Verano, the summer world, from Honko Drowne. Then, just weeks ago, the enigmatic Redhook Combine had managed to steal the planet—temporarily, if not yet decisively—from those two families. And now the Omnipotent Celestro appeared to have succeeded in stealing the arcadian world once more. For in assuming control over Drowne, the one man who could settle all disputations regarding the legal title to Verano, and declaring that he had no intention of allowing Drowne to testify on Bodenshire, Celestro had ripped from Johrun's hands the brief certainty of nailing down his beloved planet's ownership.

For Johrun's whole life, Verano had been something he could carry in his hip pocket like a lucky pebble, secure in his favored possession. Now it seemed a slippery illusion, a fungible commodity jumping from hand to hand. But his love for his home planet remained inviolable and non-transferable.

Staring into the barrel of Celestro's gun—Johrun recognized it as an Isher Brothers protein liquescer, an antipersonnel weapon much like his glial jammer, very safe to employ in fragile environments such as a braneship—Johrun had to force himself to instantly recalibrate all his earlier assumptions about Celestro's motives, nature, and actions. But the mental flipflop was surprisingly easy to make. Many of Celestro's past behaviors and deeds fell easily into the new alignment.

"This is something you've intended from the very first, isn't it? It's not a spontaneous thing at all."

"Quite correct. I am happy—indeed eager—to discuss all the finer points of my scheme with you, just as soon as you discard your gun and dagger. The same goes for you, *Mir* Furball. I have been impressed by your skill with that blade."

Lutramella and Johrun both complied, tossing their weapons onto the divan.

"Taryn, please take up those dangerous things and sequester them in the forelocker."

The mention of Taryn's name shocked Johrun. Faced with this betrayal by Celestro, he had for a moment utterly forgotten the very existence of the woman he had just been hugging and celebrating with. Now he turned to regard her with an imploring look. Surely she must resist these heinous acts, so alien to her easygoing and loving nature. Could she not deploy whatever sway she had over Celestro to stop him?

Taryn's face registered utter dismay and a deep sorrow. She returned Johrun's look in equal measure before asking Celestro, "Must I really? Is this the wisest course? Can't we all reach some kind of compromise, where everyone comes out okay?"

"No, dear, I am afraid not. Now, do as you are told. Or must I remind you of your bonds?"

Taryn picked up the three weapons, and, plainly heartsick, tried to explain to Johrun and Lu.

"When my parents sold me to that first family, the contract was witnessed by the bonzes of Apma Tagaro, and endorsed in the god's name. And when that family sold me to Celestro, the same bonds were transmitted unbroken. Such is our way on Anilda. If I break the strictures placed upon me, the ghosts of my parents would tumble into the lowest realms, where all is wailing and stones in the belly. This is the life of a restavek. As a child of Apma Tagaro, I am compelled to do whatever my owner commands. Even if he were to ask me to kill myself, I would."

"That won't be necessary, dear—at least for the moment. But please stash those weapons safely out of reach, so I may revel in my wonted peace of mind. Now, if you two will sit down, we can discuss your role in my plans, which actually requires nothing from you but devout inaction and obedience. Oh, yes, Drowne, you sit too."

Johrun sat between Drowne and Lutramella. His leg against the splice's, he could sense the tension in Lutramella's sinews, as if she were prepared to jump at Celestro, to take the deadly brunt of the first blast from his gun to allow Johrun a chance to subdue the man. He laid one hand on her thigh and squeezed in a way he hoped she would interpret as denial of her sacrifice. He sensed her muscles relax with reluctant compliance.

Celestro rested one hip on a table, but kept his gun nicely centered on his listeners, as if he too saw the splice's intentions. Again Johrun wondered if the man really could read minds.

Taryn returned from stowing their weapons and took a seat beside her master at the table. Content that all the actors were in their places, Celestro began his peroration.

"When I first saw your solicitation for transport to Itaska, and your promise that you could obtain an audience with its most infamous inhabitant, a rogue who would accept no strangers into his presence, I could not believe my luck. The person of Honko Drowne, a wanted fugitive on many worlds and in the eyes of the Quinary, had long attracted my interests. Capturing him and remanding him to a select authority could be very profitable indeed."

Johrun interrupted. "Then bring him back to Bodenshire! Take your reward from the Brickers!"

Celestro laughed. "The Brickers offer a handshake, a certificate of merit, and some coupons redeemable for their services. Not my preferred reward, especially weighed against what I am about to reveal. But in any case, let me continue. The timing of your naive appeal was exquisite. I was beginning to get very concerned about my tenure as a gadabout mountebank. Many planets, formerly lush picking grounds, were now *terra prohibitos*, so to speak—for unfair reasons we shall not delve into. So this opportunity to set myself up for a golden retirement was very much appreciated. I resolved not to lose it.

"Immediately I began contacting various parties whom Drowne had wronged, seeking to establish if their offers for his capture were still in force. I settled finally on the bounty offered by the Eternalists of Aevum Seven. Perhaps you recall that particular little escapade perpetrated by your bad uncle?"

Under the strain of being quizzed at gunpoint, Johrun had to ransack the memories of his researches into Drowne before he could come up with the reference.

"Not the Ravishment of the Ten Thousand Virgins!"

"Yes, the very same. Onto the sacred soil of Aevum Seven, just outside the nunnery of Saint Chriselma, your friend descended with a fleet of fifty cargo carriers helmed by various reliable ruffians of his circle. Onto each of the ships they herded two hundred nuns, offering them very undignified and insalubrious accommodations. Then, away to the fleshpots of New Thelema! True, the Eternalists later generously ransomed most of the captives—except for those who had become enamored of their new occupations. But their utility as nuns was at an end.

"All of this left the Eternalists with an understandable grudge against *Vir* Drowne. They believe that his *borxha*, his karma, is entangled with theirs, a permanent stain that must be removed. And they value my help with the removal of this stain at exactly ten million chains. A mere thousand chains per sisterly hymen, which I think is rather meager. But who am I to perform such numinous accounting?"

Johrun said, "So we're on our way to Aevum Seven, to turn Drowne over to the Eternalists."

"In an admirably compact nutshell."

Snatching at a straw, Johrun said, "Perhaps they would let the Brickers put him to the inquestorial meshes once they imprison him."

Celestro laughed uproariously. "Imprison! They have the most extreme and convoluted program of bodily and mental retribution laid out for Drowne that you could ever imagine! Since the Eternalist theology maintains that the greater the suffering, the higher into the Perfumed Plenum one is reborn, even if you are a sinner, they have no compunctions about conferring such a blessing on Drowne. It's all rather paradoxical, but I have never made any pretense at comprehending the religious mind. No, quite soon after I hand him over, Drowne will barely be able to recite the alphabet, never mind display his shattered *âmago* for your benefit."

Johrun slumped down. Here was the inescapable end of all his efforts.

Lutramella spoke with the practical outlook of her kind. "What do you intend to do with us?"

"Now you pierce straight to the heart of your fate, *Mir* Fishercat, with the poignard of your intellect, just as you tickled the heart of Queen Akna. Of course, I could have marooned you on Itaska, had I a mind to, or slain you anytime in the past half hour. The fact that I have not done so should convey the extent of my mercy and charity. I have always refrained from murder whenever possible. Who after all can affirm that god-botherers like the Eternalists and their ilk are incorrect? I might indeed face dire afterlife consequences for what the censorious worlds and their wives choose to regard as sins. So for the nonce, after I conclude my business I think I shall just strand you two someplace where you can't report my actions to anyone until I am safely settled out of general reach of busybodies. That is, I will extend this favor if you do not cause me any trouble in the meantime. Which I do not think you can accomplish if you remain locked in your cabin until we reach Aevum Seven. So please stand, and move to that very room. But first, *Mir* Mink, hand over your vambrace."

Lutramella unseamed her vambrace and passed it over. The swatch of her pelt formerly beneath the device showed as glossy as elsewhere, thanks to the quasi-living caretaker interface of the vambrace.

Inside their cabin, Johrun turned to face Celestro through the open door for one final plea.

"You know I own Verano. The planet is rich beyond my needs. Just one month's sale of herple meat brings in five million chains. I can pay you ten times what the Eternalists will pay for Drowne."

"Ah, but do you indeed own Verano? This Redhook Combine seems to have blocked you from the planet's wealth. No, I don't care to gamble away a certainty, even for potentially ten times the reward. But I appreciate your hypothetical generosity with other people's money."

Celestro closed and locked the door. His next words, addressed elsewhere, filtered through.

"Honko Drowne, enter this cabin, recline at your leisure and remain quiet."

The sounds of a second door closing and locking followed.

Johrun sagged to the bed. "I should have been more suspicious. I should have set up safeguards of some sort."

Lutramella placed a consolatory paw on Johrun's head. "None of us suspected anything. We simply invested unrequited faith in the goodness of our fellows. But I can never think of this stance as a weakness. Would you want to live as a black-hearted cynic? Death is preferable. Let us instead consider the miracles we have achieved. Returning with Honko Drowne was an accomplishment without peer, won with ingenuity and boldness. Perhaps the future yet holds more such victories for us."

"Your spirit puts me to shame, Lu. I'll try to match it."

Without the vambrace, the captives could not keep accurate track of the time. But growing hunger, hardly consoled by plentiful drinking water from the lavatory's faucets, indicated that surely half a day must have passed. Hearing a fumbling at the door, Johrun and Lu retreated to the far end of the cabin, not wishing to seem a threat and so suffer deliquescing.

Indeed Celestro stood with gun at the ready. But Taryn was also there, carrying a tray of food. She entered and set it down, before raising her wretched gaze to meet Johrun's.

"I'm so sorry, Johrun, believe me—"

"Touching sentiments that do you honor, dear, but a wink is as good as a nod, so you may cease prattling and come back out."

As Taryn left, Johrun said, "We don't blame you, Taryn. We know you only do what your conscience demands."

The meal was more than adequate. Celestro seemed determined not to be a harsh jailer.

Casting about, Johrun unearthed the simple slate he had used for his reading on the trip out. There was of course no Indranet access between the stars, but its large offline library was still accessible. He brought up *The Consolations of Beadle Egmont* and began to read the melancholy philosophical text.

The extravagant sufferings of the Beadle put Johrun's own troubles in perspective. Lutramella meanwhile plunged into a deep sleep. It hardly seemed credible, but their long and exhausting two-day dash across the icy wastes of Itaska had ended only a dozen hours ago. After several chapters of aphorisms, Johrun joined her in bed.

And so passed the next several days, a monotonous desert of meals, black funks, the formulation of plans without substance, reminiscences, and speculation—all seasoned with the maxims of Beadle Egmont, who never missed a chance to counsel acceptance and self-abnegation.

This stretch of time, Johrun soon realized, was the longest he had ever spent exclusively in Lutramella's company as an adult. Certainly their conversations were deeper and more wide-ranging than ever before. Her distinctive cachinnations always roused a matching laughter and cheer in his breast. He was impressed more than ever with the chimera's good sense that verged on genuine wisdom. Her indomitable hearty attitude towards life, despite what almost every human interlocutor would have deemed the scant opportunity and privilege given to splices, humbled Johrun. He, who had literally had a world at his feet, could hardly match her zest and joy. He resolved to embody her wordless lessons in living from this moment forth.

If Celestro truly intended to allow them to live.

The one moment of excitement came in the second day of their captivity, when the drugs given to Honko finally wore off. The Red Lion began to bellow and bang on the walls of his cabin.

"Let me out of here, you worm fucker, or I'll have your balls on a necklace! This is the Red Lion of the Spires you're messing with, not some pissant sneak thief!"

Celestro's contemptuous voice urged restraint. "Quiet, you hairy buffoonish jackanapes! I have to deliver you to your doom in sentient, undoped condition, to satisfy the esoteric criteria of the Eternalists. Them and their damnable *borxha!* But that does not preclude me from slapping a Barberini jelly muzzle across your face!"

Drowne ceased his caterwauling. The prospect of wearing a wet living adhesive ball gag for the rest of the trip did not appeal. He made no further outbursts, although from time to time, at all hours, Johrun could hear muffled curses and incessant pacing from the far side of their common wall. He did not envy Drowne's mental condition.

Finally, on what Johrun judged to be the sixth day of their journey, the *Mummer's Grin* made the transition back into basalspace. The subliminal sensations associated with this reentry to the home dimension were unmistakable. Several more hours crept by as they presumably traveled within the Aevum system. And now—was this the subtle, fifth-force-cushioned landing upon Aevum Seven itself? Hard to be sure.

The door to Johrun's cabin came open. No one was framed directly in the portal. He and Lutramella cautiously stepped out.

Across the salon, near the ship's still-sealed exterior door, stood the trio of Taryn, Celestro, and Honko Drowne. The latter had been permitted a new nondescript suit of clothes to replace his nightwear. He looked beaten, shrunken, lost. Johrun almost experienced a moment of pity for the fellow, who had toppled from absolute monarch to helpless slave. But then he reconsidered the man's long record of infamy—admittedly a response to base treachery, but a chosen path nonetheless—and reserved his feelings for the Red Lion's innumerable victims.

Drowne's slave-like status was further reinforced by the obedience collar he wore. Johrun had last seen the device used on the herple poachers when they were collected from Verano. The remotely responsive ring around the neck did not administer any kind of stab or jolt, but merely constricted by degrees upon command, ultimately capable of extinguishing the life of the wearer.

Not trusting the collar alone, Celestro held his Isher Brothers pistol at the ready. Taryn stood helplessly by. Red-eyed, she appeared to have been weeping.

"Come, you two," said Celestro. "I desire witnesses to my triumph."

Johrun and Lutramella walked toward the exit door as Celestro moved to one side to keep them covered. Johrun braced for a flood of invective from Drowne, but the man seemed to be reserving his hatred for Celestro, glaring at him like a basilisk.

"Open the door, Taryn."

The hull was broached.

"Down the ramp now."

Drowne suddenly stiffened and lunged toward Celestro. But a quick jab by Celestro at his vambrace and the Red Lion was down on the floor, hands at his cinched neck, his face purpling.

Another poke at the controls unclamped Drowne's windpipe. He got slowly to his feet, all the fight drained from him, and shuffled out the door. Johrun, Lutramella, and Taryn followed, Celestro bringing up the armed and monitory rear.

The ship had landed upon a large field of mustard-yellow grass. But little of the turf itself could be seen, for it hosted thousands of people. The rear ranks of the assemblage, stretching as far as Johrun's eye could encompass, seemed composed of ordinary citizens. But closest to the ship eagerly waited all the officials and dignitaries, the Eternalist priests, nuns, acolytes, deacons, monks, dob-dobs, rinpoches, herbads, pandits, tlatoques, and sadhus, each dressed more fantastically than their rainbow'd neighbors. They carried flags, prayer wheels, croziers, swords, spears, maces, wands, and giant leather-bound, gilt-spined tomes. A chorus of men droned basso mantras, while a chorus of women intoned a wordless melody that soared and dipped like the song of a drunken nightingale. Away in the distance reared the buttresses and lacy arches of a rose-colored cathedral.

The incredible variety of people, the noise, the radiance of the alien sun, the spice-scented breeze, the sudden freedom from the four walls of their cabin, the recognition that he had reached the end of his long trail—all these factors conspired to render Johrun somewhat dizzy. He strove to focus his wits.

A member of the reception committee stepped forward. He was a tall skinny fellow whose dark skin was blotched with pale patches. He wore a lofty feathered headdress, a robe woven of wide strips of tan barkcloth like a fruit basket, and calf-high boots of mauve lizard skin. He singled out Celestro and said, "I am Presbyter Khalfani. We have talked before. I see you have succeeded in bringing us the Repugnant One. It was brave of you to mingle your *borxha* with his. The contamination of your afflatus cannot be symbolically expunged until the Repugnant One's own excruciations are complete. For the safety of your inner genius, I recommend that you remain here in a state of privation and devotion until such a conclusion is reached. That should be only six months or so, depending on the Repugnant One's stamina."

Celestro chuckled. "A lovely offer. But I disdain living on salt crackers and barley water while clad in only a hairshirt. So please transfer my fee, and I'll be gone."

"But your soiled *borxha*—"

"My ten million chains, if you please."

Shaking his head ruefully, the Presbyter pushed up the sleeve of his gown and worked his own vambrace.

"It is done."

"Splendid! Now, I make you a further present. These two individuals with me have expressed a keen desire to labor for a few years in your incense mines, for the glory of the Eternalist church. Their lungs are strong, which I understand is a prerequisite. Please accept them into your service with all my good wishes."

Johrun stepped forward to protest. Celestro angled the gun warningly at him.

Lutramella leaped, as if out of a pool! Yet she aimed herself not for the weapon, but for Celestro's vambrace. She had her paws upon it, dragging Celestro off-balance. He awkwardly fired a capsule full of nanozymes that impacted her leg below the knee. Her flesh began to melt, a line of instant cellular disintegration advancing both up and down from the impact site.

An adjacent noise like a wet slab of liver hitting a floor composed of tiles and bubblewrap wrenched Johrun's attention briefly away.

Drowne's fuzzy and bearded head flew through the air, the obedience collar having instantly constricted his neck to the diameter of his wrist and launched his head high.

A gaggle of priests surged forward to restrain Celestro from further wild assaults.

Johrun flew to the nearest holy man bearing an edged weapon. He snatched the heavy blade away from the gawping cleric.

Lutramella lay on the grass, writhing. She saw Johrun approaching and forced herself into a taut quivering immobility. The line of death was inching ever upward, having eaten past her knee.

"Forgive me, Lu!"

Johrun brought down the blade with all his might.

The amputation was complete. The remnant chunk of Lutramella's flesh burbled away to slime. Johrun cast aside the

blade and ripped off his shirt. He dropped to his knees and tour-
niquet'd her upper thigh. Lutramella was insensible.

Members of the clergy stepped forward now, picked
Lutramella up and hastened her away. Johrun took a step to follow, then realized there was nothing he could do to help. His
bare chest bloodied, he gave his attention now to Celestro.

The mountebank's arms were pinioned by several holy men.
He looked stunned at this sudden undesirable outcome of his
schemes. Then he visibly drew strength and determination from
some vigorous inner well.

"Release me, you insufferable dunderheads! You can't
restrain me for merely harming a splice. Our dealings are at an
end, and I must go!"

Presbyter Khalfani regarded Celestro gravely, and with some
pity. "Our dealings are just beginning, I fear. I warned you that
your *borxha* was commingled with that of the Repugnant One.
He is now beyond our attentions, due to your mishandling of the
delivery, for which you were paid. Therefore you must take his
place. Only thus can celestial accounts be set right."

Celestro vented one long wordless ululation before he was
frogmarched away to a jaunty hymn played upon sackbut, lyre
and theorbo.

CHAPTER 16

Anilda was not Verano.

The climate of Taryn Endelwode's natal world—at least the littoral climate of her home continent—was considerably warmer than the equable, temperate, Harvester-mandated conditions of Johrun's home. The tropical heat and humidity and frequent drenching downpours followed by extravagant rainbows were certainly preferable to the polar winds of Itaska, but nonetheless came in second to Verano's perfection. This adopted world demanded adjustments from Johrun. As the first few weeks of his tenancy passed, he found himself shedding both clothes and worries. Next went initiative. And now, months into his stay, he found himself clad only in brightly patterned swim trunks, sitting on the veranda of Taryn's new home at Vevaliah with a tall frosty glass of Citrine Drizzle, doing nothing but contemplating the motion of the palm leaves in the breeze. From all about came the sounds of well-fed, busy, happy villagers, children and adults alike.

These pleasant circumstances suddenly struck Johrun as highly improbable, given his uncomfortable status of just a short while back, and he let his mind roam over that recent past.

Once Celestro had been hustled out of sight, bound for his involuntary surrogate expiation, Johrun's only thoughts were for Lutramella. He discovered Taryn to be likewise preoccupied concerning the splice they both loved.

"Presbyter Khalfani, please take us to our friend."

Unflustered by the recent violence and maintaining a serene manner that did credit to whatever precepts the Eternalists professed, the tall priest said, "You need not worry about her, I am sure. Your quick action saved her life, and our medical facilities are very much sufficient to repair her wound. But I understand your urgency. I will be with you just as soon as I install our substitute for the Repugnant One in his new, albeit temporary education-container."

Johrun and Taryn waited as patiently as they could, while Presbyter Khalfani absented himself. Workers came to clean up the bipartite corpse of Honko Drowne, as well as to splash deactivating agents on the pool of nanozymes that had eaten Lutramella's leg. The huge crowd gradually dispersed, until only a few stragglers were left. The three musicians who had provided the capital punishment ditty were the last to depart, having stayed to enjoy a hearty drink in repayment for their efforts.

Taryn rubbed a hand across her weary face. "I'm all at sea. Should I go to be by Celestro's side? I am still his restavek."

"Please don't go. You can't possibly help him, nor should you wish to see him under the awful ministrations of the church. You don't want to have that image be your enduring memory of the man. He was a scoundrel, and would have gladly sent us all to an early grave. But he did have flair and panache and bravery. Better to recall those good qualities than his bad. And besides, Lutramella and I require your company more than he does."

Taryn touched Johrun's bare chest. "Do you really, Johrun?"

Her freckled blue-eyed face, its attractive lines overlaid by what would, ideally, be transient marks of recent grief, showed a yearning to be needed and consoled that plucked at Johrun's heart. He realized that her presence over the last few demanding weeks had always conferred a subliminal lightness to even the most fraught moments.

Taking her hand in his, Johrun said, "Yes, Taryn, Lu and I need you close by."

The Presbyter returned at that moment. "Accompany me to our hospital now."

The basement of the huge brooding immemorial cathedral hosted a surprisingly modern suite of offices and the medical facilities for the staff. In a private room Johrun and Taryn encountered Lutramella, asleep. To her traumatized leg was affixed a standard morphogenesis apparatus of joint Smalls-Polly manufacture that would build new structural components, tissues, bones, nerves, and blood vessels, from the face of the wound down, using the patient's own genomic template.

The attending doctor was a short, round woman clad in buff-colored utilitarian pants and tunic, but wearing the full-face mask of a Gleeful Hierophant.

"We have the patient in a medically induced coma while the rebuild is underway. We've found that the results are better if the patient is totally immobile during the process. They tend to fuss at the itching involved."

"And how long will the rebuild take?"

"Since this is not a time-critical rebuild, we have set a moderate cellular assembly rate. Three days should see it to the end."

Johrun looked down at his unconscious lifelong companion. She seemed peaceful, and he felt a weight leave his soul.

"Would it do any good for us to stand by here?"

"None whatsoever. There will be no crisis. You could not help if there were one. And she can't appreciate your company. You might as well stay in your ship."

Johrun made effusive thanks, and then left with Taryn for the *Mummer's Grin*.

When they entered the ship, the artilect—a mid-range Proconsul model—instantly spoke up.

"Captain Endelwode, welcome back. What are your orders?"

Taryn looked with puzzlement at Johrun. "What does it mean?"

"*Mummer's Grin*, please explain your choice of honorific for Taryn Endelwode."

"The latest Indranet update drone has just arrived in the Aevum system. It disseminated a change in my ownership. My registered owner is now Taryn Endelwode. Therefore I address her properly as 'Captain.'"

Taryn plopped down in a chair. "How can this be?"

A few further inquiries laid bare the rudiments of the matter.

By Quinary insistence, the bonds between restavek and owner were not unidirectional. Should the owner predecease the restavek, the indentured person was entitled to a fair independence-launching settlement determined by length of service. However, in the case of an owner dying without any other heirs, the entirety of the estate devolved upon the restavek.

"But Celestro's not dead yet! That god-man said it would take six months."

"My former owner is legally dead," the artilect explained. "Once the Eternalists registered his initiation into the *borxha* cleansing, he was deemed officially expired by the Quinary."

"Ship," asked Johrun, "what does Taryn inherit beside yourself?"

"All other appurtenances, chattels, funds, and tangible properties belonging to Celestro."

"And what is the monetary figure in Celestro's personal accounts?"

"Ten million, thirty-three thousand, and sixty-five chains."

Wide-eyed, open-mouthed, Taryn could find no words. Johrun could not resist teasing her.

"Captain Endelwode, I believe that thirty thousand of those chains is the amount Lutramella and I paid for the use of this ship. Seeing as how we received prejudicial treatment that endangered our wellbeing, I would like to ask the new owner for a refund."

Taryn burst into tears that soon segued to wild laughter. She jumped up, threw her arms about Johrun, and waltzed him crazily around the cabin. Then they were kissing. Then they were tumbled into bed.

With a serious look, Johrun paused in disrobing himself and the woman. "I would not want you to think I was utterly mercenary in my ardor."

"Oh, you damn fool! The money came from Drowne's capture. It's as much yours as mine!"

"Not so. I—"

Taryn stopped his silly prattle with more kisses.

Lutramella, released, returned to the ship unannounced on the evening of the third day, before they could even go to meet her. The fur on her regrown leg showed a juvenile texture and color. But other than that, she manifested no repercussions, no limp or obvious fragility.

Johrun squeezed the lean-bodied chimera so tight she had to finally wriggle out his embrace. Then Taryn followed suit. When she had squirmed free again, Lutramella said, "What fine friends, to let me walk back nearly half a kilometer!"

"We wanted you to get into shape for some serious swimming."

"What do you mean?"

Johrun explained the sudden turn in Taryn's fortune—"Our fortune," she insisted—and their immediate plans.

"We have in mind to use some of the money to restore her village of Vevaliah and its sister communities that were decimated by the palm tree plague. We've already contacted the Pollys, and they have a line of fast-growth, disease-resistant trees for sale that will be just perfect. The toddy-tapper economy will be up and running again. And we have the Brickers ready to rebuild decayed housing stock and new units too. But we'll have to stay on Anilda for a time to supervise everything."

Lutramella said, "This is all more wonderful than a fairy tale. I'm so happy. But Joh, I must ask one thing. Have you given up your hopes of regaining Verano?"

Johrun paused before answering, making an internal survey of his deepest feelings. "Yes—yes, I think I have. Once Drowne died, our last avenue to reestablish our rights to the planet reached a dead end. I think about our old home often, but more with melancholy pleasure than real sorrow. After all, without my family and the Soldeveres alive to share Verano, what does the world hold for me?"

"And what of Minka?"

Taryn averted her gaze, as if not to influence Johrun's response.

Hearing the name of his former beloved did not fire quite as sharp a flaming arrow into his guts as he had anticipated. "I could try to win her back, I suppose. Even without the planet as my bridal price. But why? She expressed no interest in sharing my life of trials. Has she sought to contact me in all these months? The Indranet works in both directions, you know. No, I can't pretend my feelings for her are gone. But neither are they so intense as they were. It's probably better for both of us not to meet again."

Taryn looked up at Johrun, reached out, and squeezed his hand.

Johrun found he had something to ask Lutramella.

"Tell me, Lu, why did you choose to hasten the end of Drowne's life as you did?"

"I felt it was a more merciful fate than what the Church intended. He ended up here only due to our intervention. And he was doomed from the instant we landed here. There was no way, once the Eternalists got their hands on him, that we could bring his testimony to Bodenshire. So I removed him from the game board. And I knew that by doing so, I would free us from Celestro's grip."

"How so?"

"While you were maundering on and on with Beadle Egmont's whiney advice, I was studying the laws of *borxha* as promulgated by the Church. So I knew that once Drowne died, Celestro would inherit his sins, and be removed from interfering with us. But I had no idea that all his money would go to Taryn. If I had, I would have secured a finder's fee!"

Taryn hugged the splice again and said, "A third of it is yours, Lu."

"Ridiculous! Who ever heard of a rich splice? Although I might borrow a little for some rejuve treatments. I can't go through life with one limb young and the rest of me old!"

The authorities on Anilda in the town of Remy's Post were thrilled when they learned of the private rebuilding initiative that Taryn intended to launch, especially since it meant that the makeshift and overburdened camps full of seaside refugees could soon be dispersed. And within half a year the camps were emptied, with the returned villagers living easily on Taryn's dole until the rapidly growing trees and the restocked fisheries reached maturity.

Johrun took a long hearty slug from his Citrine Drizzle. He saw Lutramella playing on the beach with the gaggle of children that always surrounded her. He heard Taryn singing in the house as she prepared their noonday meal. Life was good.

Johrun stepped off the veranda to stretch his legs before eating. Motion in the sky snagged his vision.

A one-man braneship was settling down on the verdant open lawn. Johrun strode over with idle curiosity. He pinged the craft with his vambrace.

It was *The Wine of Astonishment*.

The ramp extruded. Down it boldly tromped Quinary Invigilator Oz Queloz, dead man come alive once again.

"*Vir* Corvivios, all your attention, please! The matter of Verano's disputed ownership is newly to hand!"

In the parlor of their Anilidan house, Johrun watched for the third time the shaped-light recording which Queloz displayed from his vambrace. And at last the accompanying speech from the Invigilator began to penetrate Johrun's shock and make some sense. The comforting presence of Taryn and Lutramella by his side aided his gradual acceptance of the unsettling information.

"Is the universe not full of impossible wonders?" Queloz said. "To think of a species able to reconfigure common memory crystals in realtime on a quantum level, and all while embodied in a human host. It gives one pause. Already the boffins among the Smalls are rethinking entire categories of knowledge. I do blame the Quinary's laissez-faire policies for allowing such dangerous ignorance to persist as long as it did, however. No one save the sartors of the inquestorial meshes really understood the powers of these creatures. If we were a more proactive polity, anything like a real old-fashioned government, we would establish galaxy-wide researches into all the odd corners of every planet. But as things stand, we are content merely to hawk our wares, soothe the marketplace, and tally our profits, until a crisis strikes."

Queloz's words were perhaps meant to provide some emotional distance from the scene that Johrun was watching. The video had been recorded with orbital cameras that could not be spoofed like the ground-level ones had been. Consequently, the angle of viewing was aslant. But the extreme high-resolution still allowed for positive identification of everyone involved.

"So here we are on Irion," continued Queloz, "at the famous Glass Grotto, which the Blue Doyens had wisely placed off-limits due to the phagoplasm plague. Now here come your irreverent bride and her friends."

Johrun watched as the daytrippers Minka, Anders Braulio, Trina Mirid, Viana Salp, Braheem Porter, and Ox Nixon traipsed capriciously from stone to stone above the pellucid waters. Suddenly, whiplike tendrils shot out of the Grotto and snared the foolish students. The unbreakable attachment of the tendrils allowed each amorphous phagoplasm creature to haul up its bulk and infiltrate the orifices of the victims. Like inhaled strings the parasites vanished up the noses, down the gullets and into the ears.

Johrun was reminded of his own experience under the inquestorial meshes.

The subjugated humans flopped down, half on stones, half in the water. They were quiescent for a time, then arose, brushed themselves off, and departed as if nothing had happened.

"The phagoplasm does not eradicate the consciousness or the personality of the victim. We are unsure if the host even knows he or she is possessed. Rather, the internal rider disinhibits the host, and counsels madcap adventures and irresponsible actions, all in the pursuit of an experiential richness which, being essentially a kind of sapient nudibranch or medusozoa, the phagoplasms cannot themselves otherwise obtain. And the urges from the riders grow more explicit and perverse over time. Experts are uncertain whether a host can be made to perform acts contrary to their innate ethos or not, but recorded incidents of such possessions often involve affronts ranging from misdemeanors to the highest crimes. And this case, I am sorry to say, involves the latter."

The next recording from an orbital camera showed a very familiar scene: the landing field at Danger Acres, the ship *Against the Whelm*, and the secret visit in the night by strangelet expert Anders Braulio to sabotage the ship's engines.

Queloz ceased the show. "The cameras onboard your parents' doomed ship showed nothing amiss, as we know. But only because of the quantum tampering."

Johrun felt his eyes begin to flood, and his breath to catch at the back of his throat. "Then their deaths are to be laid at Minka's feet."

"Not so, *Vir* Corvivios! Established legal precedents absolve the victims of phagoplasm infection of all crimes committed while being ridden. It is the same as invoking mental illness as a defense. Minka Soldevere and her friends were not *compos mentis* in the eyes of the law. However, they can and will be prosecuted for trespassing at the Glass Grotto and opening themselves up to infection. I believe the sentence for that is ten years of virtual incarceration."

"The horror of this is beyond belief. And yet you tell me there's more . . ."

"I fear so. You see, Minka and her associates are also the Redhook Combine. There are no other claimants to your planet. That was a deliberate mirage. We were able to obtain an injunction to get past the lawsuit's privacy strictures, once we knew of her contamination. Her claim to the planet would take hold only when she emerged as the last family member alive. And after killing all the rest of your clan, she needed only proof of your death. Those assaults against you on Verano—her doing. And then she had great hopes for you never returning from confronting Honko Drowne, your obvious recourse once you failed on Bodenshire."

"But why did she want to steal Verano? She would inherit it anyway!"

"She—or the phagoplasms—wanted to turn your summer world into a kind of refuge for their species, where they could conduct any and all outrageous behaviors. A wild frontier world of licentiousness and hedonism, beyond even such regulated places of carnal indulgence as New Thelema. She knew neither you nor your elders would ever consent to such a development. So she had to rid herself of you all."

Johrun heaved a mighty sigh that seemed to emerge from a vast hollow where all his organs had been, as if he too had been cored of meaning. "Where are Minka and her crew now?"

"Back on Verano, just awaiting their victory. They know nothing of your survival and current estate. You made no great show of your good fortune, and have sequestered yourselves on this backwater world. Please excuse my candor regarding your charming but trivial planet, *Mir* Endelwode! The infected sextet have established themselves at your family ranch, where Steward of the Magenta Distinction Fang-Blenny never ventures. He relies on Indranet reports, which have all been spoofed. He shall certainly receive an upbraiding for this, have no fear, perhaps being downgraded to Puce Distinction! Having discovered all this, I am tasked with nullifying the ridden vandals and bringing them to court. We have an effective technic for dispossessing the phagoplasms by injection of an antagonistic agent. I thought perhaps that you might derive some satisfaction and closure by assisting me."

Johrun stood up as if laboring under the gravity of a much larger planet. "Taryn, Lu—I have to go. You understand, don't you?"

"I'll be here when you return, Joh," said Taryn.

"And I as well," said Lu.

The one-man death-and-revival ship of Oz Queloz was left behind on Anilda as unsuitable, and they used the *Mummer's Grin*. Queloz maintained an elated air during the short hop from Anilda to Verano. "So, this is what normal space travel feels like! Luxurious and almost sybaritic! I might have to resign my post after this, and take up gallivanting for sheer pleasure."

Johrun knew that the man was merely trying to distract him from the grim revelations the Invigilator had delivered, and from the task ahead. He was grateful for the courtesy, though he could not fully participate in the sham.

This latest attempted theft of Verano, involving the death of his and Minka's families— Was it really all down to an irresponsible foray into readily avoidable danger by his flibbertigibbet bride? How could he live with this callous irony, this waste, this anger, this grief? How could Minka?

When their ship entered Verano's atmosphere, Johrun imagined he could feel any residual Veranonal nanomites, the ones not overlain by Cupuni's contributions, stirring to life within him, eager to be home. The ultra-familiar landscape displayed as the ship descended seemed like imagery out of some intimate dream. The world he had yearned to return to, the world he had yearned to replace in his back pocket, seemed now like a realm out of some old legend encountered as a child.

Queloz came in low, from over the horizon, and put the ship down behind a butte, out of sight of the ranch. Johrun and the Invigilator trekked by foot for an hour. The unique smells and violet radiance of Verano infused Johrun with hard-edged nostalgia.

At the perimeter of the household, Queloz whispered, "We will track them down one by one by vambrace. I have the ability to ping covertly without alerting them. Then we must function as a team. You distract, and I pounce and deliver the antidote. You understand?"

Johrun nodded. "Let's go."

Luckily the six perpetrators were not in each other's company. Perhaps each phagoplasm rider preferred to derive its fun jealously by itself.

Braheem Porter was found in a herple nursery, crushing spratlings with a hammer. Johrun snuck up behind the preoccupied fellow and tapped him on the shoulder. As soon as the man twirled around, Queloz was on him with the injectable.

Porter collapsed, unconscious, and slimy foulness poured from his orifices, leaving the temporarily insensate victim on the road to recovery. Queloz deliquesced the parasite instantly.

Trina and Viana were found in separate rooms of the splice quarters, having their erotic way with the subservient workers. They too quickly disgorged their riders, and were left where they lay, insensible for a while.

Ox Nixon occupied the kitchen. He had gorged himself with at least ten kilos of herple meat and could barely rise up from the table. In an instant he too was saved from his internal guest.

Anders Braulio saw Johrun approaching when he looked up from pulling the entrails from a dead splice splayed out on the lawn. Johrun recognized the faithful Arbona, one of the boss chimerae left in charge of the ranch on the eve of the wedding.

A red rage filled Johrun's mind and he charged at Braulio, who smiled and stepped forward.

They grappled furiously, battering at each other. Braulio's greater strength, weight, and reach were rendered less effective by a kind of awkward sluggishness, as if the man had surrendered too much control to the less-than-capable phagoplasm inside him. Still, the battle was hard fought. The larger man seemed on the verge of gaining dominance, and Johrun redoubled his assault. Finally, on the edge of surrender himself, trying for one last decisive punch, Johrun laid Braulio flat with an uppercut to what must have been a glass jaw of which the phagoplasm was unaware. With heaving breath and with sweat and blood pouring into his eyes, Johrun saw Queloz standing idly by and watching with a grin.

"I fancied this was a task you might wish to accomplish on your own," said Queloz. "Although I did have your back."

"Yes, yes . . . I thank you."

Queloz made Braulio safe from his parasite, and then they headed for the last of the invaders.

Minka had taken up residence in Johrun's own bedroom, which was a shambles. Empty liquor bottles of every variety carpeted the floor. His childhood lover moaned and writhed on the bed in some kind of delirium tremens. She stank of booze and sweat. Her loveliness was fled.

There was no need for distraction with such an opponent, and so Queloz simply administered the antagonist dosage, and Minka was freed of her alien alter ego.

"I go now to collect the others and confine them onboard the ship. You may stay here a while if you wish. Do not let her beguile you if she awakens."

Johrun nodded. "Resistance will be easy."

He sat by Minka for some time, until she came half alert.

"Oh, Joh, is that you? How—? I mean, where—? I feel—I feel as if some long nightmare is just ending."

Johrun stroked her greasy hair and contemplated all the childhood detritus of his past life. "For me, yes, it's finally over. But for you, dear Minka, I am not sure it will ever end."

ABOUT THE AUTHOR

Paul Di Filippo sold his first story at the tender age of twenty-three. Since then, he's sold over 200 more, afterwards collected, along with his many novels, into nearly fifty books. He lives in Providence, Rhode Island, in the shadow of H. P. Lovecraft, with his partner, Deborah Newton, and a cocker spaniel named Moxie. He hopes to explore the worlds of the Quinary in more detail in future novels.